Joyce ~

I hope you enjoy reading Peril in Paradise as much as I enjoyed writing the story....

Happy Reading!

Kimberfaw

W9-AUM-756

DEDICATION

To my mother, Rita Greb, for her love and support while I navigated the highs and lows of being a writer. And to all my family and friends who stepped in after her passing, continuing to cheer me on as I finished this novel.

ACKNOWLEDGEMENTS

This novel would have forever stayed in the land of creativity if not for the excellent input of my editors, and friends, Jeanne Silaski, Samantha Waltz and Shellie Hurrle. Ladies, thank you for your invaluable contributions to PERIL IN PARADISE. I'd also like to thank the many Beta Readers who bolstered my confidence by taking on the challenge of reading an unknown author. Thanks to Colleen Sell for her initial confidence in me as a writer and for her continued support, specifically how to write a perfect elevator pitch. And a big thank you to Paty Norman Jager, Author, for answering all my pesky publishing questions.

COVER

A thank you as wide as the Pacific Ocean to Deirdre Thompson who created PERIL IN PARADISE'S beautiful cover.

DISCLOSURES

This is a work of fiction. Names, characters, places, and incidences either are the product of the authors imagination or are used fictitiously, and any resemblance to actual persons, living or dead, businesses, companies, events, or locales is entirely coincidental.

Also my team of editors and readers, including myself, made every effort to insure this novel is error free. Of course, we are human so please accept our apologies for any missteps you might find.

COPYRIGHT @ KIMILA KAY
2008

PERIL IN PARADISE

KIMILA KAY

CHAPTER ONE

Damian Garza dragged the barrel of his gun across the tops of the hangers holding her clothes. A chink in the metal snagged a red silk blouse and he smiled at the blemish on the soft fabric. Desire washed over him as he imagined the marks he planned to carve into her flesh—a branding he'd perfected on several women over the past year.

He wandered to her dresser where the faint scent of her perfume lingered in the air. Rays from the midday sun bled through the sheer curtains, bathing the bedroom in a warm glow. Damian caressed her various baubles, hooking the chain of a silver star pendant with his little finger, admiring the encrusted diamonds as they glimmered in the sunlight. Smiling, he eased the necklace into his pants pocket.

Glancing at family pictures lining the wall, he meandered down the staircase toward the family room where a bottle of Patron beckoned him. Damian poured a splash into a crystal tumbler and took a sip. The familiar smoky taste filled his mouth as he savored the tequila. Glass halfway to his mouth again, his attention shifted to the sound of the front door opening and closing.

Good, she's early. Blood coursed through his loins in anticipation of his sweet release as he finally taught her a long overdue lesson.

He tossed back his drink, choking on the fiery liquid as Ally Marsh appeared in the doorway of the family room.

"What are you doing here?" Damian growled at his step-daughter.

"Duh, I live here."

Her impertinence shot a bolt of anger through him. Damian stormed across the room and his lips curved into a sneer as Ally's brown eyes grew round with fear, his massive hand encircling her frail neck, silencing the shriek blossoming on her lips.

CHAPTER TWO

Clara Garza pounded the steering wheel when her call to Ally went straight to voice mail for the third time. *Why doesn't she answer?*

She replayed the message her fifteen-year-old daughter had left over an hour ago, biting her cheek as Ally's carefree voice flowed through the Bluetooth. "Hey, Mom. I walked home to get my iPod. Jen's baking cookies for our road trip. I'll call you when I get back to her house. Love you. Bye."

"Damn it, Ally." Ally had been Clara's first call after the detectives left her office. Clara told her they should take a road trip up the coast for a girls' weekend and asked Ally to stay put until she got there in a couple of hours. Her spine stung as if on fire, tendrils of heat fanning out and leaving a trail of perspiration running down her back. *I should've warned her about her stepfather.*

Clara had missed her daughter's call while closing her accounts for Angels of Angeles and emptying a safe deposit box at the bank next to her office. She'd now been stuck in

3

Los Angeles afternoon traffic for an hour, plenty of time for Ally to walk the round-trip mile between houses.

"Where the hell is she?" Clara shouted as she flipped the visor down against the bright October sun, a slip of paper floating toward her. She let the note drift onto the passenger seat where it landed face up. Clara dropped her cell phone into her lap at the sight of Ally's handwriting and scooped up the small missive with one hand: *Have a radiant day, Mom. Love, Ally.*

Clara's eyes grew misty at the dragonfly Ally had drawn into the tail of the *y* in her name. She folded the slip of paper and stuffed it into the back pocket of her jeans, then picked up her phone wishing she had Jen's cell number. When the family's answering machine picked up, Clara blasted the horn at the endless red lights strung out before her.

God, had it only been two hours since the detectives knocked on her office door looking for her husband? The surreal conversation ran through her mind as she clicked on her blinker and inched her BMW into the next lane of crawling traffic.

"Mrs. Garza?" the tall, handsome man had asked.

"Yes." Clara's gaze shifted to the woman standing at his side. Her visitors both wore suits, the only difference being the woman's missing necktie.

"Detective Wilson," the man said as he flashed a badge. "This is my partner, Detective Hunt."

Clara's pulse rate spiked. "What can I do for you, Detectives?"

"We need to ask you some questions about your husband," Detective Wilson said. "May we come in?"

Clara stepped aside and then closed the door. "Please have a seat." She motioned to the leather arm chairs in front of her desk.

As they sat down, Detective Hunt pulled a black notepad and pen from her dark blue blazer. Clara thought she noticed a hint of pity in the detective's eyes.

Clara's shoulder muscles tightened and she resisted the urge to tilt her head from side-to-side to relieve the tension. "What's this about?"

"Do you know where your husband is?" Detective Wilson asked. His tone, like his posture, was all business.

"No. Why?" The shocking discovery she'd recently made jumped into her thoughts. *Could they be investigating Damian's strip club businesses or one of his family's other illegal activities? Did they know what she now knew, that Damian had been laundering money through her charitable organization, Angels of Angeles?*

Detective Wilson stared at Clara as if he could read her mind. "We've been investigating Mr. Garza for several months now and believe he's the Brentwood serial rapist."

The word rapist slammed into Clara like a sledgehammer to the gut and she gagged back bile as she bolted for the bathroom. After ridding herself of coffee and toast, she splashed cold water on her face and rinsed out her mouth. On the heels of what she'd learned a week ago, Clara knew Damian had disdain for women. But could a rapist be lurking beneath his Prince Charming façade? The implication horrified her.

"Mrs. Garza?" Detective Hunt's voice echoed through the bathroom door.

Clara stepped back into her office and glared at the two detectives, both of whom now stood facing her. Her mind had already accepted their accusations, but her heart struggled to believe the loving, caring man she'd married two years ago could be such a monster.

"I-I . . ." Clara fought back tears. "Do you have any proof?"

"Believe me, Mrs. Garza," Detective Wilson said. "Your husband is a brutal rapist."

Detective Hunt offered her a business card. "If you need help finding a shelter, or if there's anything else I can do, please let me know."

Clara's hand shook as she took the card. "Wh-what happens next?"

"We have an arrest warrant for your husband," Detective Wilson said as he and his partner headed for the door. "Hopefully, he'll be in jail by the end of the day, which will give you the weekend to find a secure place for you and your daughter."

Blaring horns dissolved the memory as traffic again rolled to a stop. To avoid rear-ending the car in front of her, Clara cut the steering wheel hard to the right. Tires chirping, she stomped on the accelerator and raced down the shoulder of the freeway. She honked at a frantically waving construction worker and narrowly missed an impact with a dump truck as she swerved around an asphalt paving crew. The oily fumes followed her as she sped down the exit.

When she'd unearthed the disturbing information about the Garza family, Clara had rented a condo for her and Ally. Now with the horrible accusation about her husband ringing in her ears, she prayed it wasn't too late to take her daughter and run as far away as possible.

She hooked a right onto a palm tree-lined street in her quiet neighborhood. A hint of sweet honeysuckle blew through her open window as she passed the local park. Clara grasped her phone from her lap and dialed Detective Hunt's

number and was soon being instructed to leave a message at
the beep.

"Jesus, doesn't anyone answer the damn phone anymore?"
She swallowed to clear her dry throat and spoke at the beep.
"Detective Hunt, it's Clara Garza. My daughter, Ally, isn't
where she's supposed to be." Clara hesitated. *She said to call
anytime.* "Can you meet me at the house? I-I'm worried."

She ended the call, her thumb hovering over the nine key.
What would she tell a nine-one-one operator—that her
teenage daughter hadn't called her back? She couldn't prove
Ally was in any danger. *Get a grip, Clara.*

Soon she and Ally would be on their way to Astoria,
Oregon where her closest friend, Devyn Corey lived. Damian
didn't know about Devyn and she didn't think he would look
for them in the sleepy coastal town. She'd almost told the
detectives about the damning evidence she'd uncovered
about Damian and his family, but had decided she might need
to use her knowledge as leverage against Damian.

A whisper of dread snaked through her gut. Damian would
be furious once he knew Clara had uncovered all the family
secrets. What if he already knew? What if his family's
corrupt influence kept him out of jail? What if he'd already
planned his revenge?

Clara punched the gas and swerved around a minivan in
front of her, sending her phone sailing off the passenger seat.

Two blocks later, she roared into the driveway, rammed the car into park and leaped from behind the wheel. She ran toward the house and threw open the unlocked front door. Her sweat-soaked cotton shirt clung to her like a body wrap designed to hold in fear.

Ally's piercing screams catapulted Clara past the elegant staircase and toward the back of the house. A vase shattered on the floor as she cut the corner of the hallway and collided with a table. Her daughter's bedroom door stood ajar and Clara stormed into the room.

"Noooo!" The word tore from her throat as she rushed toward the bed. "It's Mom, Ally . . . I'm here." Clara gathered her daughter's limp body in her arms. "Hang on, baby. I've called for help."

She laid Ally down on the bed, her shock morphing into anger as she faced her husband. "You bastard! I'm going to kill—"

Clara didn't see the gun until the muzzle flashed. As the blast banged off the bedroom walls and her ears buzzed from the concussion of the gunshot, she stumbled backward and stared down at the dark stain spreading over her chest. Spots danced before her, blurring with Damian's eyes, casting them in an evil red glow.

Then darkness.

CHAPTER THREE

Dread. The feeling consumed her.

Why? Clara struggled to remember. What was so dreadful? Why didn't she want to open her eyes?

Pain. Someone had hurt her. She forced her eyes open, mouthing a protest that died on a thick tongue.

"She's awake."

Devyn? The image of her dear college friend faded as Clara's subconscious dragged her back to oblivion, away from the dreadful thing that awaited her.

* * * *

"God, I'm thirsty," Clara croaked as she licked dry, cracked lips.

"You're awake." Devyn hovered over her. "How do you feel?"

"Like someone stuck a knife in my chest . . ."

The full weight of the anxiety that had suspended her in unconsciousness lifted. Images raced through her mind.

Ally. Damian. Gun.

"Ally, pl-please tell me—tell me she's okay."

She can't be dead. Please God. Please let it all be a nightmare.

Devyn's ashen face and tears answered Clara's pleading.

No. No. No.

"Clara, I-I'm so . . . so—"

"Noooo!" The word rode out on an agonizing wail. Clara cringed as pain ripped through her chest. The dreadful thing had been Ally's death. She closed her eyes, wishing she hadn't clawed her way to consciousness. She didn't want to live without her daughter.

No. It's a mistake. I need to protect Ally.

"Do you want something for the pain?" Devyn asked.

Clara shook her head. "I've got to get out of here." She sat up, her gaze bouncing from monitors next to the bed, to a white board with her name across the top, to flowers sitting on a window ledge.

"It's only been a couple of days. You need to rest."

Clara fumbled with the IV snaking from her arm. "I have to take care of Ally."

"Don't . . ." Devyn held Clara's hands. "Nurse!"

A nursed rushed in and pushed a button on the wall, then attempted to pin Clara's shoulders to the bed. "Mrs. Garza, you're going to pull your stitches open."

"Let go of me." Her vision narrowed and a twinge of nausea fluttered in her stomach as Clara tried to climb from the bed. "Ally needs me."

"Clara, listen to me." Tears streamed down Devyn's cheeks. "Ally's in a better place."

"What? No, no." Clara struggled against the nurse who pulled her back onto the pillows. "She's been h-hurt. I should be with her."

A second nurse appeared with a hypodermic needle in hand.

"Don't drug me," Clara pleaded as the nurse swabbed the IV port with an antiseptic wipe. "Pl-please don't . . . Ally needs me."

Ignoring Clara's pleas, the nurse slid the needle into a connector and pushed the plunger. Within seconds, Clara felt herself calming and drifting, drifting back to nothingness.

CHAPTER FOUR

Jackson Brady frowned at the picture of Damian Garza and then tossed the *LA Times* onto the passenger seat as the light turned green. He eased the battered Scout through the intersection and made a left-hand turn. Visiting Clara wasn't a good idea, but he couldn't help himself. He needed to know she was physically okay. He knew she'd never be the same mentally.

"Damn it!" He beat the dashboard. "I should've acted sooner."

He'd known Garza would kill again. Even though his sister had died by her own hand after the rape, Brady held Damian responsible for Iris's death.

He has to be stopped.

Brady braked for traffic and ran a hand over his three-day stubble. He hadn't slept well since Ally's murder, his sleepless nights filled with what he imagined to be the girl's horrific last moments and Clara's terror as she faced the barrel of Damian's gun. Familiar with the emotional baggage of guilt, Brady attributed his sudden need to protect Clara with his failure to save Iris. But he couldn't explain the persistent memory flashes of a Shakespearian quote his schoolteacher mother had taught him long ago: Love looks not with the eyes, but with the mind, and therefore is winged Cupid painted blind.

His first glimpses of Clara as he dug into her background in the process of learning all he could about Damian had stirred feelings he chose to ignore at the time. Still the more he discovered about her charitable organization, Angels of Angeles, and the difference she made in at risk kids' lives, the more he was drawn to her kindness . . . and beauty.

Just protect her . . . nothing more.

Brady turned into the hospital garage and waited as his entry ticket printed. He took the slip from the machine, pulled past the mechanical arm and found a parking spot. Sliding on black horn-rimmed glasses and loosening his tie, Brady angled his six-foot frame from the Scout, coughing when the exhaust fumes from a departing car engulfed him.

He knew from his recent reconnaissance that the police hadn't posted a guard at Clara's door, but two detectives hovered nearby, waiting for an opportunity to speak with her. He hoped his ambulance-chasing lawyer disguise would shield him from their attention as well as that of the two Garza henchmen who'd staked out Clara's room.

Brady shrugged into his rumpled suit jacket, snatched up his battered briefcase and headed for the elevators.

CHAPTER FIVE

Clara swatted at the hand on her forehead. "Go away." Her words pushed past dry lips. "Let me sleep."

"I'm sorry, Clara."

"Wh-what?" She opened her eyes as she tried to place the husky male voice. "Who . . .?"

"A friend." The man's whisper tickled her ear.

Clara blinked, attempting to bring his face into focus in the dim light. "I d-don't . . ." She inched away. "I don't know you." Gooseflesh erupted along her skin as she reached for the nurses' call box.

"Don't be afraid." He took her trembling hand in his before she could push the button. "I needed to see you and tell you that Damian will pay for what he did." He gently squeezed her hand, saying, "Trust me."

Then he was gone.

Clara scanned the blurred shapes in her hospital room. Listened to the muted sounds outside her partially opened door. Inhaled the spicy, woody aroma that lingered by her bedside.

She closed her eyes and slowed her breathing. She hadn't dreamed him; her visitor had been real. As Clara drifted back to sleep, she remembered his whispered promise.

Trust me.

* * * *

Clara brushed her hair and studied her skeletal appearance in the small mirror of the portable table. Had it only been four days since she'd been shot? Since Ally's death? Since her life had horrifically changed forever?

She frowned at her gaunt reflection and slapped the mirror shut. Her pulse ratcheted up a notch as she recalled her conversation with Devyn, who'd reluctantly told her what had happened after Damian's murderous spree.

"Your neighbor heard a gunshot and called nine-one-one," Devyn had said, holding Clara's hand. "Let's talk about this when you're stronger."

"No." Clara's lip quivered. "I want to know . . ."

Devyn blew out a breath. "Paramedics rushed you to the hospital."

"And Ally . . .?"

"The medical examiner completed the rape kit and she's now at the funeral home." Devyn swiped at a tear. "Damian fled and the house is a crime scene."

Hysteria had bloomed at the back of Clara's brain and she'd been sedated when her whimpering turned into a manic wail.

Now, as the familiar sensation of guilt consumed her, sparks of light flashed before her eyes and her cheeks warmed. The cacophony of the hospital blared in her ears and her chest felt heavy as she gingerly turned onto her side. *I should've died instead of Ally.*

Clara heard the door creak open and then Devyn's voice as she entered the room.

"Hey, are you okay?" Devyn touched Clara's back.

Clara nodded and turned over, a stab of pain stealing her air. Devyn wore capris and a peach-colored T-shirt that made her brown eyes appear darker. She held a bouquet of daffodils, their delicate spring scent wafting over Clara.

She'd rushed to Clara's side upon hearing the news of Ally's murder and Clara found herself comforted by the ministrations of her college roommate. Five years ago, Clara had been the supportive friend when Devyn's husband, Kevin, had died in a boating accident. At the time, both women were in their early thirties and found themselves sharing the unfortunate experience of losing a loved one since Clara's parents had died in a car crash during her first year in college. She knew Devyn would find herself overwhelmed with grief as Clara had when her parents died.

Clara also knew that the old adage, "time heals all wounds", wasn't true. The smell of gardenias, her mom's favorite flower, or the play-by-play of a football game, her dad's favorite sport, still brought tears to Clara's eyes. Clara knew all too well what waited for her as she faced a future without Ally.

"I'm just tired," Clara said. "Think I'll get some sleep."

Devyn glanced at the door. "Oh. Um . . ."

Clara cocked an eyebrow. "What?"

"The police are on their way up." Devyn fingered long strands of brown hair away from her face. "They've been hanging around waiting to speak with you, and your doctor finally gave them the green light. I can send them away."

"It's okay." Clara winced as she pushed herself up in the bed. "I might as well get this over with."

Devyn nodded, set the vase of flowers down and handed Clara the envelope.

Clara waved it off. "You read it."

Devyn slid the note card free. "It says, 'Have hope.' It's not signed, just like the card with the tulips."

Clara glanced across the room at the bouquet of pink tulips as the first anonymous message echoed in her mind: *Get well.*

"Trust me," Clara murmured.

"What?" Devyn asked.

"That's what my visitor said: 'Trust me.'" Clara reached for the note. As before, she didn't recognize the handwriting. She handed it back to Devyn and met her questioning stare. "I know you think I imagined him, but he was real."

"It was the middle of the night, you were heavily medicated and no one saw . . ."

A knock on the door ended Devyn's speculation and the two women turned their attention to the detectives entering Clara's room. One wore a rumpled department store suit, his badge hanging from a lanyard around his neck. The taller detective cut a more dapper figure in a dark suit that fit him as if it were tailor-made.

"Mrs. Garza," the tall detective said as he flashed his badge, "I'm Detective Hale. This is my partner, Detective Miller. We'd like to offer our condolences."

"Thank you." Clara swallowed to clear the lump in her throat and reached for a cup of water. "Please call me Clara," she said and took a sip.

Detective Hale smiled. "Do you feel like answering a few questions?"

As Clara simultaneously nodded and shrugged a shoulder, a sliver of pain shot across her chest. *As much as I ever will.*

"Detective Hunt, who rode in the ambulance with you, stated in her report that you kept asking her to stop Damian."

"I'm sorry. I don't remember talking to her." She smoothed a wrinkle from the bedspread.

"Understood." Hale's kind eyes met Clara's.

"Have you arrested him?" Hope echoed in her tone.

"No, we—" Detective Hale began.

"What?" Clara sat upright, the movement causing a firestorm in her chest. "Why not?" She thumbed the button on the morphine dispenser. "He raped and murdered my daughter!"

"Clara . . ." Devyn touched her hand, worry etched on her face.

"I'm . . . fine." Clara inhaled, exhaled.

"Maybe now's not the best time," Devyn said.

Detective Miller stepped closer to Clara's bed. "Look, you're the only person who can put Mr. Garza at the crime scene. Before we can obtain an arrest warrant, we need to get your statement."

"Can you tell us what happened?" Hale asked.

Clara nodded, then looked down and fingered a button on her bathrobe. "I . . ." Her lip quivered. "I came home and found . . . Ally." Tears trickled down her cheeks. "He ki-killed her." Clara swiped away her tears. "Then he shot me." She touched the bandage covering her wound.

Detective Hale looked up from his notebook and Clara met his concerned gaze. "So you didn't see Mr. Garza kill your daughter?"

Clara pounded the bed. "For Christ's sake, he was standing over her body!" Her voice cracked as she pushed the button on the morphine pump. "And he smiled at me when he pulled the trigger."

Detective Miller huffed and said, "But you didn't actually witness—"

Hale glared at Miller, cutting him off. "Now that you've positively identified your husband as the person who shot you, we'll arrest him as soon as possible."

Clara melted into her pillow as the morphine entered her bloodstream.

"I think we need to wrap this up," Devyn said to the detectives.

Clara focused a bleary-eyed stare on Detective Hale. "What can I do?" *Besides wish Damian dead.*

"Let us do our job." Hale nodded at Clara and then Devyn before striding from the room.

Miller shoved his notepad into his jacket pocket, nodded and then exited behind Hale.

Devyn patted Clara's hand before following the detectives into the hall.

Clara glanced out the hospital window at the late afternoon sunshine and her eyelids fluttered as the morphine coursed through her body.

If the detectives can't stop Damian, I might know someone who can. Trust me.

CHAPTER SIX

"What the hell were you thinking?" Ricardo Garza yelled at his son. A thread of spittle hung from the corner of his mouth.

Damian fought the urge to shrug his shoulders; instead, he looked down and shook his head. "I don't know, Father. That bitch pushed me too far, and I—"

"And you thought killing . . ."

"Clara knows too much and her daughter was—" Damian shouted.

Ricardo held up his hand. "I don't want to hear your excuses." He pounded his massive desk with a fist. "I believe a solution to our problems would be to turn you into the police myself!"

"Enough dramatics, Ricardo," Valencia Garza said to her husband. "You know you are not going to sacrifice Damian . . . no matter what he does."

Damian bristled at his mother's disgusted tone. He could feel her eyes on him, but he refused to meet what would surely be a condescending gaze. His father might feel a need to blame Damian for his misdeeds, but Damian knew what fueled his desire to punish women stemmed from his hatred for the woman who pretended to be his mother.

Damian had planned to punish Clara for sticking her nose into his private business affairs, stealing money from him and for talking to the police.

His intent had been to rape her as a parting gift before she slunk away to the dreary Pacific Northwest. According to the investigator he had following Clara, it looked like she planned to leave town and Damian knew she'd have to come home at some point to pack. The investigator had said his stepdaughter was staying with a friend so Damian had been surprised when Ally arrived at the house. Then his surprise had quickly turned to rage at the young girl's insolence. Initially, she had shown him respect. But lately she'd become willful and disrespectful, traits he attributed to her mother's suspicions of his extracurricular activities.

A warm flush traveled up Damian's neck to his hairline. Killing Ally had been the first time he'd acted recklessly. The first time he'd attacked a child. The first time he'd ended a life.

Well, he wasn't to blame. Ally's death was on her meddling mother's head. A vision of Ally struggling and calling for Clara flashed in his mind. Damian blinked to clear tears from his eyes and focused on his attorney.

"If I may," Alan Sanchez said. A year younger than Damian, the thirty-six-year-old attorney had earned Ricardo's respect after years of managing the family's legal issues with a cool confidence. "With regard to the serial rape charges, the prosecution's case is weak, which is why a judge released Damian on bond. However, when charges are brought for the crimes against Clara and Ally, bail won't be allowed. It has taken four days, but the police finally obtained a statement from Clara yesterday. Her eyewitness account will be the cornerstone of the prosecution's case."

Valencia tapped her nails on a marble-topped end table and said, "Clara is the only witness." Damian glanced in her direction as she crossed toned legs, leaned back into a burgundy leather arm chair and continued. "Can we discredit her with a background of drug or alcohol abuse?"

"That won't work." Damian glared at Valencia. She locked eyes with him, eyebrows slightly arched over her dark eyes. "No one will believe Clara has a substance abuse problem."

"Damian, please," Valencia said in a mock motherly tone. "Let your father and I decide the best defense for Alan to pursue."

Damian gritted his teeth, forced a smile and then said, "Fine, Mother. I will leave my freedom in your capable hands." He stood and took a couple of steps across the brightly colored Persian rug toward the door of his father's study.

"Sit your ass down!" Ricardo bellowed.

Damian shot a look at his father. A powerfully built man in his sixties, Ricardo Garza expected people to do as he said. His father sat taller in his chair, an attempt at intimidation, which had worked when Damian was a boy. Now that he topped his father's six-foot height by two inches, Damian no longer feared his father's physical anger. However, he did know better than to challenge his authority and suffer the consequence of losing his protection. Damian sat and crossed his arms.

"Alan, do you know if they have any evidence?" Valencia asked.

Damian already knew the laundry list of proof the police would claim he'd left behind in *his* house. *Fools.*

"The police have the bullet recovered from Clara." Alan adjusted his tie and directed his gaze at Valencia. "However, without the gun, it will be difficult to place the weapon in Damian's hands. Remarkably, the fingernail scrapings from Ally yielded little DNA. No fluids were found on her; however, the coroner did find a pubic hair containing a root on her body. I arranged for the recovered hair to be replaced with a tagless specimen. Without the follicle, the crime lab can't test for DNA."

"I trust the gun has been disposed of," Ricardo said to Damian.

"Yes." He met his father's stare and cringed at the contempt reflected in his dark brown stare.

"Which leaves Clara's testimony," Valencia said.

"Exactly," Alan said. "Combined with the circumstantial evidence, her testimony gives the prosecution a strong case."

"We need something on her," Valencia said. "Surely, Damian, there must be something Alan can use against her."

Damian smirked at Valencia and motioned for Alan to continue as he rose and walked to a credenza that doubled as a bar.

"Actually, there is." Alan pulled a manila envelope from his briefcase. "Damian arranged surveillance of Clara." He extracted several eight-by-ten photos and handed them to Valencia.

Damian poured a shot of tequila, tossed it back and poured another, before returning to his seat.

"The private detective took photos of Clara sitting in her car near some of Damian's strip clubs," Alan continued. "We can claim she hoped to catch Damian cheating—"

"In an attempt to void the prenuptial agreement," Valencia cut in as she flipped through the photos, sending a wave of her flowery perfume through the air.

"Yes," Alan said. "We can also lay the foundation for Damian's alibi."

Damian resisted the urge to hold up his shot glass in a toast and instead sipped the smoky liquid.

"Can you create an alibi quickly?" Ricardo asked Alan.

"Yes, but the cost will be high." Leather groaned as Alan shifted in his chair and straightened his Armani suit jacket.

"By all means," Valencia sniped. "Spare no expense."

Damian stiffened at the remark and gulped the last of the tequila. Valencia was the daughter of a real estate mogul who had fallen on hard times and wished to avoid filing bankruptcy. Ricardo had wanted her father's properties and the price for the land had been a marriage of convenience, which had greatly benefited Valencia, who spent Ricardo's money with vulgar abandon.

"Valencia, please." Ricardo shot a tired look at his wife and then returned his attention to Alan. "Continue."

Alan nodded. "We will create a paper trail placing Damian in a few hotels with a variety of women and have one of them serve as his alibi."

"I'm sure Damian knows plenty of tarts happy to oblige," Valencia said.

Damian wanted to cross the room and snap her neck, an urge that both surprised and excited him, but the feeling dissipated when Alan continued.

"The police have an arrest warrant for Damian," Alan said. "We need to act fast, because as I said, it is unlikely a judge will allow bail considering the seriousness of the charges." He leaned back in his chair.

"All right," Ricardo said. "Get started and find a defense attorney to represent Damian. A woman with a formidable track record. You will be her co-counsel, but I don't want her to know about your fact manipulation." He narrowed his eyes at Damian. "I want her to assume she is defending an innocent man."

"Yes, sir," Alan said. "I have already taken the liberty of hiring a divorce attorney and he filed a petition on Damian's behalf two days ago. I'd hoped to catch Clara off guard and have her served while in the hospital, but he tells me the court is backlogged. He understands our need for expediency in this matter."

"Excellent move, Alan," Valencia said. "Damian needs a speedy divorce in case this matter goes to trial and he is convicted of murdering Clara's daughter." She inspected a gleaming, blood red fingernail as she continued, "I imagine a divorce judge would relish giving Clara all of Damian's assets."

Damian flexed a fist and shifted in his chair. He knew Valencia would enjoy nothing better than seeing him locked away for the rest of his life. If it weren't for the ruinous scandal a guilty verdict would bring, Damian thought she'd volunteer to testify against him herself.

"Thank you, Alan. Please keep me updated." Ricardo nodded at the attorney and then shifted his gaze to his wife.

Damian couldn't help but look at his mother. She took a sip of her favorite chamomile tea and offered a prim smile before she spoke. "I think once this matter is behind us," Valencia said, "it would be a good idea if Damian took an extended trip out of the country." She set her teacup onto the saucer and the ping of fine china hung in the air.

Damian watched as she dabbed her mouth with a lace napkin and then folded her hands in her lap. Still beautiful at the age of sixty, she gave the impression that she was as fragile as her precious porcelain. Damian knew better. Valencia Garza was ruthless and calculating. Over the years, she had used her dark, seductive looks to her advantage, persuading many a man to do her bidding—or more specifically, her killing.

He hadn't known growing up that the woman he called mother loathed the very sight of him. Damian couldn't forget the day he discovered the family secret. His birthmother had

been a Mexican beauty who'd stolen his father's heart . . .
and Valencia had had her killed.

CHAPTER SEVEN

Jackson Brady watched the foot traffic in front of Café A'Latte from the bank lobby across the street. The lunch crowd hurried to and from their offices, talking on cell phones and jostling each other in their haste to navigate the busy sidewalk.

He checked his watch—another fifteen minutes. Brady scanned the bustling mob for Pedro Gomez, who most likely watched the same sidewalk from a different vantage point.

No trust among thugs.

"Good afternoon," the female employee said, her heels clicking against the marble floor as she approached. "Can I help you?"

Brady smiled and extended his hand. "Good afternoon. Thank you for offering, but I'm just waiting on my girlfriend for a lunch date." He saw a flash of skepticism in the young woman's eyes and widened his smile.

"Okay," she said. "Enjoy your lunch."

Brady waited for her to reach her desk, where she was drawn into a conversation with a customer, and then he made his exit. He rotated through the revolving glass doors and stepped into the warm fall air. The distraction from the bank employee had caused him to lose track of the activity across the street and a quick glance at the storefront revealed Pedro Gomez sitting at an outside table. He appeared to be alone, but Brady knew one or more of his goons wouldn't be far away.

Brady crossed the boulevard with a throng of pedestrians and headed for the coffee shop. Gomez had his head bent over a newspaper and looked up when Brady slid out a chair and sat down.

Gomez looked at his watch. "Right on time." A short, squat man, the Mexican looked more like a Guido than a Pedro. His pinkie ring flashed in the sunlight as he pulled a manila envelope from under the newspaper. "You want a latte? They serve the best in the city."

"No," Brady said. "What's up?"

"All business." Gomez smiled and slid the large envelope across the wrought-iron table. "We need you to dig up some dirt on Clara Garza and her friend Devyn Corey."

One of the goons arrived and set a latte in front of Gomez, steam from the large mug barely visible in the sunshine.

Gomez waved him off and the brute retreated after a slitty-eyed glare at Brady.

Brady raised an eyebrow. "What type of dirt?"

"On Clara we are looking for signs of infidelity." Gomez blew on the steaming cup and took a sip. "Senora Garza wants to discredit the *puta* and keep her from getting any of her son's money in a divorce."

Brady's jaw jumped at the slang word for whore, but his training kicked in and he held his tongue. *Marines don't show emotion.* Besides, the only way to help Clara was to immerse himself deeper into the Garza inner circle and that meant taking on whatever task the family doled out.

"Damian had her followed." Gomez tapped the envelope. "These are photos from his investigator." The Mexican took another sip and then wiped foam from his upper lip with a napkin. "Those idiotas missed a man visiting Clara in the hospital. Could be her amante. Si?"

Brady's stomach knotted and he concentrated on keeping his face void of emotion. "Did they get a look at the guy?"

"Si. But only from behind. Gringo, ugly coat . . ." Gomez snorted and cast a glare at his henchmen, who looked like Tweedle Dee and Tweedle Dum as they sat in chairs dwarfed by their size, arms crossed and a lack of intelligence reflected in their blank stares. "I need to know who this man is and if he is her lover."

"And the Corey woman?" Brady picked up the envelope.

"Every detail you can find. Damian knows nothing about her, except that Clara has been in touch with her recently."

Brady stood. "How soon do you want my report?"

"You got two days." Gomez slurped more coffee.

Brady nodded, ignored the henchman and walked away.

This should be easy since I already have files on Clara and Devyn . . . and the gringo I'm looking for is me.

CHAPTER EIGHT

Despite the hospital staff's dogged efforts to restore her to health, Clara began running a fever. They pumped her full of stronger antibiotics, watched her around the clock and methodically cleaned the smelly green ooze from her chest wound. Though Clara tolerated the treatments, she also welcomed the nausea and dizziness that had settled in. She was tired and heartbroken and hoped the infection ravaging her body meant the end was near.

Ally's waiting for me.

She would, however, miss her nightly dreams of the nameless, faceless man who mopped sweat from her brow and held her hand. Clara began to prefer sleep, drug induced or otherwise, just to feel his comforting presence. Despite her deep slumber, she never managed to stay asleep past his parting words. "Trust me," he'd say, and her eyes would fly open as if she expected him to be standing at her bedside.

A now nurse busied herself taking Clara's blood pressure and her doctor stood at the foot of the bed consulting her chart. He looked up. "We've scheduled you for surgery."

Clara shook her head. "No. I don't want another operation."

"Mrs. Garza . . ."

"Don't call me that," she snapped.

"She prefers Clara." Devyn took Clara's hand in hers. "Let's hear what the doc has to say. Then you can make your decision."

Clara cast a weary look at Devyn and then turned her attention back to the doctor.

"The bottom line is you need surgery. Now." His dark eyes held Clara's blurry stare. "You have necrosis—dead tissue—at the center of your wound. It needs to be removed. Then you'll need reconstructive surgeries to avoid further complications and to rebuild the breast."

"And if you don't operate?" Clara picked lint from the bedcovers.

"Clara . . ." Devyn squeezed her hand.

"You'll become septic and die," the doctor said.

The word *die* echoed in Clara's mind and she closed her eyes. *Just say no and the torture will end.*

"She'll have the surgery," Devyn said.

"I'm sorry, but Mrs. . . . *Clara* needs to give her consent."

Her daughter's face loomed large behind her eyes. *Ally needs me to live, to find justice for her.*

Clara blinked her eyes open. "Fine." She patted Devyn's hand. "Do whatever needs to be done."

Her doctor nodded, a faint smile on his lips. "You're scheduled for surgery this afternoon." He hung her medical chart at the end of her bed. "I'll see you in the operating room."

Devyn followed the doctor from the room, and Clara knew she'd ask all the necessary questions. Clara didn't want another surgery, but living did offer her the opportunity to make sure Damian paid for his crimes.

One way or another . . .

CHAPTER NINE

Damian slapped Kandee Kane on the ass. "Get off."

"You sure, sugar?" Kandee moved her hips and tweaked his nipples.

Damian gave her large tit a vicious twist. "Get. Off."

"Ow!" Kandee cried. She disengaged from his shrinking dick, climbed off the bed and slid into her robe.

Damian pulled the sheet across his waist and then stacked the pillows behind his head. They'd slept in, had a late breakfast and then entertained themselves in bed for the last hour. Kandee had all the right equipment, but despite the buxom blonde's efforts, he couldn't seem to climax.

He stared at Kandee's back and wondered if her neck would be as easy to break as Ally's had been. He didn't quite understand this new fascination, but he couldn't seem to suppress thoughts of killing again. Blood pulsated through his cock, bringing it to attention. Resisting the urge to stroke himself, he instead reached for the tumbler of tequila sitting on the glossy black nightstand.

He knew he couldn't harm Kandee, he needed her to be his alibi. He sipped the amber liquid, holding it on the back of his tongue long enough to feel the burn. He coughed and said, "Look, babe, I appreciate your efforts. I am just worried about my interview with the police tomorrow."

Damian hoped Alan Sanchez had worked the same magic he'd used to acquire bail after Damian's arrest for the rape charges. It had been over a week now and he wanted to get the meeting with the detectives regarding the new charges over as soon as possible. Clara had almost died from an infection, which would have put an end to this circus, allowing him to get on with his life. *Fucking bitch.*

Kandee shrugged a shoulder, reached for her cigarettes and turned. "Mind if I smoke?" She waggled a menthol light.

Damian hated cigarette smoke, but knew it would help her relax. "Make it quick and we'll go for a drive along the coast and stop for dinner somewhere."

Kandee dropped her cigarettes back onto the tall dresser. "Oh, can we go to Vic's in Santa Monica?" She dropped her robe and dashed into the bathroom. "What you need is a nice big steak. I'll be ready in a jiff."

What Damian needed was a decent lay. A wave of desire flooded through him as an image of Jia Dhal, aka China Doll, naked and gyrating on a dance floor, surfaced in his memory. Damian had wanted Jia to be his alibi, but Alan had insisted on Kandee. He claimed Jia's willingness to work as a dancer at Blissful Beauties in exchange for absolving her brother's gambling debts was one thing. Alan feared asking Jia, who hated Damian, to provide him with an alibi, and lie on his behalf, would provide the dancer with information she could bring to the police.

Damian drained the tumbler of tequila and swung out of bed. Alan had told him to be seen in public with Kandee and a relaxing drive up the coast, followed by a nice dinner sounded good. He padded across the soft cream-colored carpet of the penthouse bedroom and opened the heavy drapes to let in the midday sun. He crossed to the closet where dark suits hung neatly from the rod, but he wasn't in a formal mood. Instead, he reached for a charcoal blazer and a light gray button down. The weather had been in the low seventies, but he knew it would cool down at night, especially along the coast. Kandee had turned off the shower and he could hear her butchering Adele's newest song.

Cringing as she missed a note, he once again thought of Jia. Damian would much rather be seen in public with the intelligent Asian beauty. After their first tryst, he'd repeatedly invited her to dinner, but she always declined, claiming to be busy. Damian smiled as he selected a pair of black slacks. He knew what attracted him to Jia was the chase. As intelligent as she was gorgeous, Jia worked part-time for one of his father's business associates and was taking online classes toward an associate's degree in business management. Evidently, the American raised Jia aspired to assist other Chinese women with business startups and other endeavors.

Damian wanted to ravage Jia again, but his father had told him to leave the dancer alone. *I can wait . . . for now.*

"I hope Vic's has Death by Chocolate cake for dessert," Kandee said as she stepped from the bathroom, her hair turbaned in a towel. She wound her arms around Damian's neck, heat radiating from her skin, the smell of citrus filling his nose.

"Call and find out." Damian patted her ass. "I need to jump in the shower."

Kandee released him, let her hair down from the towel and shook out her long brassy locks. His cock responded to the sight of her voluptuous beauty as she made her call to Vic's and he stepped into the bathroom. He might feel like another go at Kandee after a big juicy steak and at least one bottle of wine.

He let the hot water wash over him as he leaned into the spray. Once they returned to the suite, and he'd screwed her again, he hoped Kandee would fall asleep. Damian knew the heat was on, but he had an overwhelming desire to roam the city streets in search of a new victim. He needed to feel the thrill of taking some unsuspecting female against her will.

He wiped steam from the large mirror and his birthmark reflected back at him as he dried off. The star-shaped patch was more defined than his real mother's bluish-gray blemish and Damian's rested on his bicep instead of the forearm like Estrella's. Of course, he'd only seen hers in an old photo, which could have distorted the birthmark. His stomach churned and a familiar obsession wormed its way into his mind . . . If his real mother had been the one to raise him, would he have developed the demons that haunted him now?

A knock on the door resonated through the suite as Damian wrapped the towel around his hips and stepped into the bedroom. Kandee stood trembling, holding her robe closed, and shot a nervous glance in his direction as he moved toward her.

Two men in dark suits stood waiting by the open door. They didn't need to introduce themselves; Damian knew they were Detectives Miller and Hale.

"Gentlemen." He gave them a tight smile. "All right if I get dressed first?"

"Sure, Mr. Garza," Detective Miller said. "Take your time."

Damian dropped his towel and pulled on the black slacks.

"Damian Garza," Detective Hale said. "You're under arrest for the rape and murder of Ally Marsh and the attempted murder of Clara Garza."

Kandee squeaked out a sob.

Damian slipped on the gray button-down.

"You have the right to remain silent," Hale continued.

Damian closed the last button, held up a hand and said, "I know the drill, Detective." He donned dark socks and stepped into black loafers. His cell phone chimed as he shrugged into the blazer.

Detective Hale produced a pair of handcuffs and Damian presented his hands behind his back. Damian's cell phone chimed again as Detective Miller marched through the opulent suite, opened the door and stepped into the hall.

"Babe." Kandee jumped when Damian spoke. "Answer my phone and tell Alan to meet me at the police station."

Alan better have a damn good reason for not calling sooner.

CHAPTER TEN

An orderly wheeled Clara through the hospital doors and into the early afternoon sunshine. The final surgery to repair her damaged breast had gone well, but it had kept her in the hospital for an additional week. Clara blinked at the brightness, savoring the warmth of the sun on her skin. As her eyes adjusted, she spotted Devyn leaning against a rental car.

Devyn smiled and walked toward them. She wore the same capris she'd had on the day before, which she'd paired with a new blouse—a recent purchase since she'd literally rushed to LA with only the clothes on her back. The shopping trip had netted new clothes for Clara too, black slacks and a tan blouse. Clara would've preferred to wrap her battered body and bruised soul in a pair of comfy sweats.

Dark smudges rimmed Devyn's hazel eyes and Clara thought her friend's five-six figure seemed thinner than when she'd arrived. *This nightmare has been hard on Devyn too.*

"Happy to finally be freed from the hospital?" Devyn asked as she helped Clara into the passenger seat.

"Definitely." Clara wrinkled her nose. "It smells like a florist's shop in here."

"It's nice, isn't it?" Devyn smiled.

A wave of cards, flower arrangements and balloon bouquets had arrived daily during her hospital stay. When one of her nurses mentioned how lucky Clara was to receive so much love, it led to a conversation about other patients who hadn't received any good wishes, or had visitors for that matter, so Clara asked the nurse to distribute her overabundance of flowers and balloons among the other patients. Clara knew people meant well when they sent their get well sentiments, asking if there was anything they could do for her, but Clara's first thought was always the same: Can you bring my daughter back?

On the backseat, a tall vase of yellow roses sat next to a spray of calla lilies, the last of the bouquets that had arrived anonymously, with the pink tulips and daffodils bookending the arrangements. She recalled each of the handwritten message that had accompanied the flower arrangements: *Get well. Have hope. Find peace.* A faint smile curved Clara's lips as she thought again of the whispered promise: *Trust me.*

Devyn slid behind the wheel of the SUV, cranked the engine and exited the parking lot. As she eased into the freeway traffic she glanced at Clara. "Lisa Hibbs from the DA's office called to say she'll meet us at the house."

Clara stared through the windshield at the never-ending ribbon of traffic ahead of them. Damian still hadn't been arrested for Ally's murder, but Lisa had told her the judge did order him to surrender his passport as a condition of his bail for the rapes charges.

He's too smug to run.

When she'd been served with divorce papers in the hospital, Clara had been tempted to sign them and be done with the bastard. But the paltry settlement offered was a joke and Clara decided to sue for all of Damian's assets. She toyed with the idea that she could liquidate his business interests, sell the house and then hire a hitman if Lady Justice didn't do her job.

Revenge for Ally.

"DDA Hibbs requested a few police officers for crowd control." Devyn zipped in and out of traffic. "Evidently, the media has staked out the place."

"Great." Clara shook her head. "Did you ask Lisa why they haven't arrested him?"

Devyn tapped the steering wheel.

Clara swung her gaze toward Devyn. "Well?"

"No." Devyn hit the horn and cut around a slow-moving car.

"Why?" Irritation dripped from the word.

Devyn shrugged her shoulders. "Why don't I take you to the hotel to rest? I can pack up your stuff."

"Thanks, but I want to be the one to gather Ally's things." Clara's frustration melted into tears. *My beautiful daughter's life reduced to cardboard boxes.*

"Um . . . the funeral home called . . ." Devyn said. "They're ready to hold Ally's services whenever you'd like."

"I'm not having a service." Clara wiped her cheeks with the palm of her hands. "Would you mind calling them and arranging for me to pick up her . . . her urn?"

Devyn cleared her throat. "I'll take care of it."

"I want to bring Ally to Astoria. She loved the Oregon Coast and I'd like to scatter her ashes there."

Devyn nodded and executed another lane change.

They made good time even though midday commuters clogged the freeway. Devyn followed the familiar route through Clara's old neighborhood. When the bronze weathervane jutting from the brick-red tile roof came into view, Clara sucked in air. She'd felt like a princess when Damian carried her across the threshold of the beautiful stucco mansion almost two years before. Their first meeting at a fundraising event for amateur astronomers invaded Clara's thoughts. Vivid images from that fateful encounter unfolded in her mind like flip cards.

Clara had been dabbing red wine from her sapphire blue off-the-rack sheath dress and raised her gaze to meet the force that had bumped into her. Dark, seductive eyes met hers and her cheeks colored under their intensity.

"My apologies," Damian said. "I have ruined your lovely dress."

"No, it's fine. I'm fine. I mean, the dress is . . ." She took a breath to cease her stammering.

"Damian Garza." He smiled and offered a business card. "You must send me the dry cleaning bill."

Clara shook her head. "That's not necessary. It wasn't very expensive . . ."

"Then it must be your beauty that creates such an exquisite vision." This time he flashed a suggestive smile. He signaled a waiter and ordered her another glass of wine before leaving her to contemplate his gallantry.

The mishap led to an apology bouquet, a lunch date, and eventually, dinner. An impromptu wedding in Las Vegas followed a whirlwind six-month courtship. Within a year, though, Clara thought she smelled cheap perfume on his dress shirts as she ready them for the dry cleaners. Of course, she'd question her suspicions when Damian always had a gift to distract her and explanation such as: "The sales girl at Macy's sprayed me with a sample when I was buying this for you."

When he stopped bothering with fabrications, Clara began to catch glimpses of the monster she'd married. Damian's charismatic personality faded with each passing day, revealing the devious person hidden within.

"Clara?" Devyn's concerned voice evaporated the memory. "You don't have to do this." She'd stopped the car a block from the house.

Clara slumped forward and sobbed into her hands. An agonizing moan escaped through her fingers. She'd brought her daughter into this home and exposed her to pure evil. Clara pounded the dashboard, her moan becoming a wail. When the stitches in her breast pulled, she gave the dashboard one final blow and leaned back against the seat. Devyn handed her a wad of tissue, and Clara sopped up her tears, taking a cleansing breath.

Please forgive me, Ally.

Up ahead, several cars lined the street in front of the house and a few people stood on the stone walkway. The Channel 2 news van rolled to a stop behind a police cruiser. Another local television station stood at the curb as if guarding the end of the sidewalk.

Vultures! Why can't they leave me alone?

"Look this way," Devyn said, taking Clara's chin in her hand. Clara held still as Devyn added concealer to the circles under her eyes and a touch of mascara to her lashes. Clara flipped the visor down and assessed her reflection in the small mirror. She wore her hair in a severe bun, which only served to emphasize her haggard appearance. Her once-vibrant brown eyes returned a lackluster stare, the reflected image a ghost of her former self.

"Are you sure you're up for this?" Devyn said. "I don't think we can avoid the press gauntlet."

"We'll be fine." A hint of resolve echoed in her tone. "Just say no comment and push past them."

"All right." Devyn eased the car away from the curb. "Let's get this over with."

CHAPTER ELEVEN

Detectives Hale and Miller ushered Damian into an interview room and tag-teamed him with pleasantries.

"Can I get you something to drink?" Detective Miller asked. "Coffee, soda, water?"

"No." Damian narrowed his eyes at the disheveled detective. "Thank you."

"Would you like to check on the status of your attorney?" Detective Hale added offering his cell phone. "I'm surprised he hasn't arrived yet."

Damian shook his head, his lips curving into a tight smile. "I'm sure he will be here soon."

"Anything we can do to make you more comfortable," Miller said, opening the door, "you just let us know."

Hale smoothed his silk tie. "We'll be close by."

"Thank you, gentlemen. I'm sure I will be fine until Mr. Sanchez arrives." Damian looked from one to the other as they departed the room.

He'd now sat stiff as a mannequin for over an hour in a hard chair, angled back from a grimy four-by-six interview table, in a ten-by-ten room he knew detectives called "the box." Damian wondered if the two detectives had watched him the entire time from the other side of the large two-way mirror. He cast a glance at the smudged dark glass that reflected the dim gray room back at him. He averted his gaze, resisting the urge to check his appearance.

Alan had better have a damn good reason for keeping him waiting. Damian knew the plan had been to turn himself in once Alan had hired Alexis Kent, a prominent defense attorney who'd lost only one case in the past five years. Alan described her as a beautiful, charming woman who made you feel like the only person in the room, which made the moment she legally ripped out your throat seem almost magical. Alan had planned for the three of them to have lunch the next day and Damian hoped he'd be eating something other than jailhouse gruel.

Commotion outside the door caught his attention and it banged open as Miller lumbered into the room. The sloppy detective sat down and plunked a mug onto the table. He placed a legal pad next to the cup, pen next to the pad and leaned back in his chair. "You're sure you don't want something to drink?" he asked.

"No. I'm fine."

"I thought since your attorney isn't here, we'd chat for a while." Miller slurped some coffee.

"I have nothing to say." Damian refrained from adding "you imbecile."

Miller grinned. "Okay, then I'll talk." He sat up in his chair. "This is some bad business you're in. It's one thing to go about raping women, but your stepdaughter?" He shook his head. "Then killing her . . ." He blew out a breath.

Damian concentrated on keeping his face a mask of indifference. His jaw muscle twitched, and he felt color rising in his cheeks, but he held the detective's gaze without flinching.

"You probably thought murdering your wife completed the perfect crime. No witness." Miller gave an exaggerated shake of his head. "Too bad she lived."

Damian mentally coached himself. *Stay calm. Don't respond. Ignore him.* But the urge to leap across the table and plant a fist in the detective's puffy face was becoming unbearable.

Miller scribbled on his pad and then looked up. "They teach us at detective school that you guys rape because it makes you feel in control. Like a real man. Right?" He tapped his pen on the pad. "But I can't wrap my brain around what you did to Ally." Miller shook his head. "What'd she do to deserve such rage?"

55

Ally's dark brown eyes, wide with fear, stared at Damian from a corner of his mind. Sweat beads dotted his upper lip and his stomach roiled. He hadn't meant to harm her, let alone kill her.

If she had just stayed away from the house.

"It's okay if you want to talk about it, Damian." Miller lowered his voice as he leaned toward the table. "It's just you and me here, and I'm a good listener."

Damian breathed deeply through his nose and shifted in his chair, his lips parting as he exhaled. "I don't have any idea what you are talking about, Detective. I suggest you ask my wife why her daughter found herself in harm's way."

Miller nodded and smiled. "Sure, I can do that." He made another note. "But don't you want to tell me your side first? You could help yourself, maybe even avoid the death penalty, if you just come clean."

Damian felt his self-control ebbing. He knew better than to say anything, but he couldn't stand the smug look on Miller's face. "The DA does not have a case, so I'm not too worried about the death penalty at this point."

"Well, you should be!" Miller boomed, pounding the table with a fist. "Once you lawyer up, it'll be too late to cut a deal."

"I have no intention of making a deal with a bunch of incompetents." Damian's tone rose to match Miller's. "You don't have any evidence to convince a jury that I'm a rapist or a murderer. Besides, I have an—"

"Damian! Not another word." Alan Sanchez stood in the open doorway, flanked by a stunning blonde and Detective Hale.

Damian glared at his attorney. "Where the hell have you been?"

Alan strode into the room and stood next to his client. "Gentlemen, this is Alexis Kent, Mr. Garza's defense attorney."

"Pleasure," Alexis Kent said as she joined Alan and Damian. "Detective Miller, I'm disappointed that you didn't abide by my client's request for counsel before questioning him—a matter I'll be sure to relay to the DA's office."

"I wasn't interrogating your client, Ms. Kent. We were just shooting the breeze." Detective Miller winked at Damian. "Right?"

Alexis smiled and placed a hand on Damian's shoulder. "I believe Mr. Garza was on the verge of sharing this information when we arrived." She waited a beat. "My client has an alibi for the day and time in question, which you may want to consider before you make the mistake of detaining an innocent man."

Miller and Hale exchanged a look as Miller picked up his pen. "Care to share this alibi's name and address?"

"Certainly." Alexis popped the locks on her briefcase and pulled out a document. "Here's a witness sheet with all the pertinent information. I believe you've already met Miss Kane and she's expecting to hear from you soon."

Miller scanned the form before passing it to Hale.

Alexis snapped her briefcase shut. "Now, if you'll excuse us, we'll be on our way." She nodded at the detectives and stepped toward the door.

"Thank you for the witness information, Ms. Kent," Hale said. "However, for the time being, we'll be holding your client on suspicion of rape, murder and attempted murder."

Damian went rigid. He couldn't go to jail. Alan had assured him he wouldn't have to spend time behind bars.

"After all," Hale continued, "you don't expect us to release your client until we've vetted this witness?"

Alexis glared at Hale. "I'd like a moment with my client."

"You got it, Counselor," Miller said as he stood. "Take a couple of moments."

Damian watched the detectives leave the room, and as soon as the door closed, he jumped from his chair, sending it crashing into the wall behind him.

"Damian, please control yourself," Alan said. "And for God's sake, don't say anything. They are watching and listening from the other side." He titled his head toward the two-way mirror.

"You said I wouldn't have to go to jail!" Damian sent spittle flying with each word.

"That was when we planned to meet with the detectives, which I thought had been arranged. I had no idea they had decided to arrest you instead."

"Fix this, Alan," Damian said through gritted teeth.

"Mr. Garza," Alexis interjected, "once the police have verified your alibi, they won't have any grounds to hold you. It's unfortunate that you'll have to spend a couple of days incarcerated, but there is nothing we can do about it at this point."

Damian glared at the blonde beauty and then turned his attention back to Alan. "I had better be released in forty-eight hours and cleared of these charges or you and I are going to have a problem." Damian tapped the attorney in the chest. "Understood?"

Alan Sanchez swallowed and nodded.

The door swung open, revealing the waiting detectives.

"We've got a nice cell ready for you, Mr. Garza." Miller smiled and did an elaborate wave. "Let's go."

Damian squared his shoulders and straightened his jacket. He knew he'd survive a couple of days behind bars, just as he knew those who had let him down would not survive his wrath. He also knew he'd have to be patient because, for now, he needed his attorneys.

With a last menacing glance at Alan Sanchez, Damian Garza followed the detectives toward his waiting cell.

CHAPTER TWELVE

Brady stood at his dinette table and sorted through the photos he'd taken of Clara soon after she'd married Damian. He frowned. *What good could she have possibly seen in such an evil bastard?*

He suspected his original foray into Clara's life had, at first, created his need to protect her from Damian, that concern slowly becoming . . . what, love? If he was being honest with himself, he'd finally realized he'd developed feelings for Clara as he tailed her from one charity event to the next. He looked forward to seeing her interact with the inner city kids she helped through her charitable organization, Angels of Angeles. Clara's smile as she handed out clothing, shoes or holiday gifts, made him want to join her efforts and bask in the warmth of her goodness.

Brady held up a photo of Clara and Ally at the Boys & Girls Club. The picture captured mother and daughter in a fit of laughter as they coached a mismatched pair of kids in the three-legged race during summer camp. The photo stirred memories of fresh-cut grass and grilling hot dogs. Brady's chest tightened as he set the picture aside and padded barefoot across his small kitchen. He grabbed a Corona from the refrigerator, popped off the cap and drained half the bottle.

The vision of her lying in a hospital bed jerked through his mind. His heart twinged as he thought about how close she'd come to dying from an infection. He'd wanted to visit her again, but didn't think he'd go undetected by Pedro's goons a second time.

Brady placed the beer on the eating bar next to his laptop and sat on a bar stool. He punched the keys, clicked on the file labeled DOSSIERS and waited for a blank form to appear on his screen. His background search had revealed Clara and Devyn were college roommates in Oregon at Portland State University, where both had obtained marketing degrees. Devyn had taken a job with the Astoria Chamber of Commerce, where she helped promote the wonders of the historic coastal city. She married Kevin Corey, a local fisherman, a year out of college, and they'd only been married three years when Kevin died in a boating accident off the Oregon Coast.

Brady sipped his beer and flipped open Devyn's file folder. Lying on top of was a screen shot from the *Daily Astorian,* featuring Devyn in an article that reported how the childless widow had used Kevin's life insurance to create a survivorship foundation to help other families who lost loved ones to the sea. He found it interesting that the two friends had marketing degrees they had both segued into charitable endeavors.

As Brady drained the bottle, he wondered whether Clara would move to Astoria after Damian's trial. His cheeks warmed at the thought and he rolled his neck as if he could dislodge the idea.

Clara had put her degree to use working as a junior marketing specialist for Thompson Creative in Los Angeles. He couldn't see her moving to a small town where advertising consisted of promoting the big sale at the dollar store, but he could envision her and Devyn combining their altruistic talents. Thompson Creative had eventually promoted Clara to advertising executive for Diverse Designs, a small chain of clothing boutiques that featured eclectic women's fashions. Unfortunately, her job had placed Clara on a collision course with Damian when she showcased the heterogeneous clothing collection organized a fundraising event for amateur astronomers.

"Then again, if she'd moved to Astoria to begin with, she'd never have met Damian Garza," Brady said to his computer screen.

Brady had hacked into Clara's email account as soon as she and Damian began dating. His goal had been to gather damaging information against Damian; instead, he'd learned that Clara and Devyn had maintained their friendship over the years. He'd discovered that Clara had reached out to Devyn as her life began to unravel, seeking a port in the storm she knew would soon engulf her.

Brady plucked another beer from the fridge and a bag of chips from the cupboard. *Dinner.*

As Devyn's financials loaded on his laptop, Brady's thoughts drifted to Clara. His imagination conjured a mental image of her sitting across from him, laughing as she had in the photo with Ally, sipping a glass of wine while they waited for dinner in some quaint restaurant flooded with candlelight.

"Jesus." Brady gulped down some beer. "Knock it off. The only dinner you'll enjoy with Clara Garza will be from a paper bag as you shadow her until Damian's behind bars."

He popped a salty chip into his mouth and began creating the dossiers for both women, which he would hand over to Pedro Gomez. Crafting backgrounds—a skill he'd perfected when he'd fictionalized his own—came easy to Brady. His stint in the Marines as an information analyst had taught him how to glean data from various sources and blend facts with enough false information to protect the privacy of the individual.

Brady didn't mind the monk-like existence he chose to lead after his sister's death. It was his penance for taking Iris to the party where she'd met Damian. His punishment for not stopping the bastard from stalking Iris and raping her.

But I led her into the lion's den.

He took a long pull from the Corona and fought the urge to hit something.

With revenge on his mind all those years ago, Brady had walked away from his life to pursue justice for Iris. After the Marines, he'd put his economics degree to work and amassed a small fortune as an investment advisor. His wealth allowed him to ditch his three-piece suits for jeans and T-shirts and become an investigator adept at gathering information. He cut ties with everyone in his life and changed his name, taking the name of the hero in the romance novel his sister had been reading when she died.

The siblings had never known their father, a drunk who ran off with another woman when Jackson was eighteen months old and just before Iris was born. Their mother worked two jobs, but always found time for her children. She instilled in Jackson a love for Shakespeare and strived to teach him compassion for others. Despite her efforts, Jackson fell in with the wrong crowd and eventually found himself in trouble with the law. Enlisting in the Marines had been his ticket out of a three-year stint in a juvenile facility for stealing a car.

The encouraging two-word notes his mother sent during boot camp ran through his memory: *Be good. Do well. You're great! Love you.*

Brady's new life became permanent after his mother died. He swallowed to clear the lump in his throat as he recalled his last conversation with her.

"Let her go, son." His mother had gripped his hand tightly. "Let Iris go and stop this nonsense." Her smile reached her eyes, which were cloudy from pain medication. "Promise me."

Brady kissed the top of her hand and blinked back tears. "I promise, Mama," he said.

"Good." She exhaled a rattling breath. "I'll tell Iris hello for you."

"Okay. I love you." His voice broke and tears fell onto her cheek as he kissed her.

"I love you too . . ." Her eyes held his, but he knew she no longer saw him.

"I'm sorry Mama, but I have to make Damian pay." Brady wiped away his tears. "I owe it to Iris."

Brady washed away the memory with a swig of beer. His mother had died five years ago, five years after Iris had taken her life.

He crunched a mouthful of chips and clicked on his computer's photo gallery. Ally's face loomed large on the screen. Long dark hair framed an oval face and her mother's eyes stared back at him from a picture he'd copied from her school's database. A dainty gold chain suspended a heart-shaped locket against her chest. He magnified the image, revealing the etching of a dragonfly on the front of the locket.

Guilt churned the beer and chips in the pit of his stomach. He'd had the better part of seven years to stop Damian, to stop him before he killed Ally. After Iris had taken her life, all Brady could think about was killing Damian. He researched poisons, hit men and how to make murder look like an accident. Then the dreams started—visions of Iris begging him not to avenge her death by taking a life, not to sacrifice his soul for her. She always said the same thing just before he woke: "You'll find another way, brother. Trust me."

Trust me.

Over the years, Brady had tracked Damian from New York to Mexico City, from Costa Rica to Los Angeles, with stops in between, watching and waiting for him to make a mistake. Damian left a trail of rape victims in his path, but none of them had pressed charges. Brady suspected they'd all been paid to stay quiet, but he also guessed they remained silent out of fear.

Once Damian moved to LA, his appetite for rape lessened, which Brady attributed to the string of strip clubs Damian now owned. He had a stable full of women to terrorize, women who considered violent treatment a hazard of their profession. As Brady worked his way into the corrupt Garza family, he soon learned that Ricardo Garza controlled his son's actions through bribery. If Damian stayed out of trouble, he had access to the Garza fortune for building his smut empire—and he stayed in his father's will.

After Damian married Clara, Brady noticed he visited his clubs less frequently. He huffed his disgust and shook off the thought of Clara in Damian's bed. *Don't go there.*

Brady closed Ally's picture and then opened the refrigerator in search of a more suitable dinner. Coronas, limes, lunchmeat, and cheese with a fuzzy layer of blue mold presented themselves on the cold metal racks. He rubbed his eyes as if the gesture would change the contents. Then he ran a hand over his stubble, closed the fridge door and looked at his watch. Devyn and Clara should be on their way to the Hampton Inn by now. Maybe he should get cleaned up, grab some dinner at the hotel bar and check on Clara.

No. I need to stay away . . . for now.

CHAPTER THIRTEEN

The late afternoon sun cast the circus milling in front of Clara's house in a golden glow. Devyn parked a few yards away, cut the engine and all eyes turned toward them. Clara stepped from the car, squared her shoulders and inhaled deeply.

"Ready?" Devyn asked across the roof of the car.

"Yes." Clara slid her sunglasses into place and marched toward the waiting spectators. Her peripheral vision caught a blur of blue linen that shape-shifted into a lovely young woman.

"Mrs. Garza," the dark-headed beauty said, her hand extended, "I'm Karmen Scott and I'd like to offer my services as your divorce attorney."

Devyn stepped in front of Clara. "This isn't a good time."

"It's okay." Clara touched Devyn's shoulder as she moved next to her. "I appreciate your offer, Ms. Scott, but I'm not quite . . ."

"Prepared? Well, you'd better be." Karmen adjusted her grip on a leather briefcase. "I've learned the Garza family attorneys are trying to fast-track your husband's divorce petition, claiming you haven't responded. If they're successful, you could effectively be cut off from your marital assets."

Clara cast a glance at the reporters trying to push past the two police officers keeping them at bay. She shoved the sunglasses to the top of her head and said, "Go on, Ms. Scott."

"Please, call me Karmen." She swept strands dark hair from her face. "Since you haven't responded to the petition, Mr. Garza's attorneys have requested a default divorce. If we act quickly, I can file your response and get you in front of a judge. Given the circumstances, I believe the courts will grant you temporary control of your community property."

Clara cut her eyes to Devyn, who shrugged and said, "Well, you do need an attorney."

Clara nodded. "All right, Karmen, you're hired."

"Great." The petite attorney dug in her briefcase, extracting pen and paper. "You're going to want to read my firm's contract before you sign it, but I took the liberty of drafting a simpler version for today." She handed the document and pen to Clara, then turned her briefcase sideways to serve as a makeshift desk.

Clara scanned the brief form, then scrawled her name across the bottom.

"I'll call my assistant and have her request a court date. I've cleared my calendar for this afternoon and have already drafted your response. How soon can you be at my office?"

Karmen's rapid-fire delivery clanged inside Clara's overtaxed brain. "You drafted a petition without any information from me?"

Karmen smiled. "Your charity work has touched many lives and most of the attorneys throughout the city of Los Angeles want Damian Garza to pay for what he did. Let's just say gathering the necessary facts for your response was a group effort."

A group effort. Anonymous flowers. A mysterious stranger. Are they linked somehow?

Clara looked past the young woman to the small crowd pacing the lawn. Watching. Waiting. "I can be at your office in two hours." She turned to Karmen. "How well do you *spin*?"

Karmen raised an eyebrow. "Very well."

"How would you like to speak on my behalf?"

"It would be my pleasure."

"Good. By the way, please refer to me as Clara Marsh. Clara Garza died three weeks ago."

"Understood."

"All right, ladies, ready to run the gauntlet?" Devyn gave Clara a measured look.

Clara did a head bob, dropped her sunglasses back into place, then fell into step behind Karmen, who marched confidently toward the waiting press. Clara breathed deeply and steeled herself for what she knew would be a gut-wrenching process. The crime scene tape had been removed, the house cleaned and Ally's bed discarded. But it didn't matter; the gruesome images from that day would be forever embedded in her memory.

As the three women reached the sidewalk, reporters swarmed them like bees in a flower garden. They shoved microphones toward Clara and bombarded her with questions.

"Clara, just a few minutes of your time."

"When are you holding services for Ally?"

"Mrs. Garza, how do you feel about your husband being arrested?"

Clara stumbled but stared straight ahead and followed Devyn, who shouldered her way through the crowd. As they stepped through the front door, Clara heard her attorney say in a firm tone, "Ms. Marsh has no comment at this time; however, I have a brief statement."

While Karmen addressed the media, Clara and Devyn entered the massive living room where they were met by DDA Hibbs.

"Good morning." Lisa smiled and stepped toward Clara.

Clara removed her sunglasses and blinked at the diminutive blonde. "Damian's been arrested?"

"Yes. A couple of hours ago," Lisa said. "He's claiming he has an alibi for the time of . . ."

"He's lying." A chill swept over Clara. *What if he's concocted a believable alibi?*

"My thoughts exactly." Lisa crossed her arms. "We're vetting his alibi and it's just a matter of time before his story unravels."

"How long before he makes bail?" Devyn asked.

"I'm hoping he doesn't make bail this time," Lisa said.

"He's going to do whatever it takes to stay out of jail." Clara dropped her purse onto the couch. "A false alibi is just the beginning."

Lisa's nostrils flared slightly. "Believe me Clara, we're prepared for any legal theatrics the Garza family might have planned."

Karmen breezed into the room, looking flushed but pleased with herself.

"Have you two met?" Clara looked from one attorney to the other.

Karmen extended her hand. "No, I haven't had the pleasure. Karmen Scott, Clara's attorney."

"Lisa Hibbs, DA's office." They shook hands and then Lisa turned back to Clara. "I took the liberty of procuring these for you a few days ago." She pointed to a collection of flattened packing boxes in the corner.

"Thank you." Clara managed a small smile.

Devyn inched toward an assembled box. "Someone's already packed a few things." She thumped a container with bold block lettering.

Clara stared at the words **ALLY'S THINGS** written in a familiar hand.

It can't be.

As if it had magnetic powers, the box drew her closer.

Don't look inside.

Clara lifted the cardboard flaps and peered within.

Oh God.

A photo of eleven-year-old Ally holding a bouquet of daisies lay on top of a stuffed unicorn. Her daughter's smiling face looked at her past a note taped to the black frame.

Don't read the message.

She couldn't stop herself.

The missive, in Damian's neat penmanship, read: *Ally . . . as beautiful as the flowers she holds.*

"Shit." Devyn slapped the flaps closed as Clara's knees buckled.

Tears blurred Clara's vision and a clammy film spread over her like a cocoon. The living room spun around her as she staggered toward the couch and fell onto the cushions. She dropped her head between her knees and took deep breaths.

God damn him!

"Clara." Devyn's concerned voice filled her ears. "Clara, are you okay?"

"She needs a glass of water." Karmen said, her footfalls suggesting she'd left the living room.

"I'll get a cold cloth," Lisa added.

Despite Clara's efforts, grainy, abstract clips jerked slowly through her mind like a defective home movie. The horrific memory of Ally's death began to consume her and tears blurred her vision.

"Damn you!" Clara shot to her feet. Grasped a crystal vase from the coffee table. Sent it crashing into the marble fireplace. "I'm going to kill you, you bastard!"

CHAPTER FOURTEEN

Damian tightened his grip on the neck of the tequila bottle. He'd nursed the fifth of liquor since his release from jail five days ago, sipping a little each day, waiting for his anger to dissipate. Waiting to leave Los Angeles. Waiting to be free from the control of others. He was tired of waiting.

Damian poured a shot and tossed it down, the burning liquid a reflection of his mounting rage. He wanted to strangle them all. Alan should have prevented his arrest. His father should have arranged for bail. Clara should have never meddled in his affairs.

Bitch.

Well, no one would meddle in his life once he escaped to Costa Rica. He hated that he had to wait before he disappeared, but Alan had advised he lie low for a week after his arrest. Just two more days. Since his father was footing the bill, he'd do as he was told.

This time.

Damian poured another shot, swallowed it, and reached for the phone. He stabbed a button on the keypad, then splashed the last of the clear liquid into his glass as the call connected.

A cheery voice filled his ear. "Room service. Lexi speaking."

"This is Damian Garza in the penthouse. Send up two bottles of Patron Silver immediately."

"Cer-certainly, Mr. Garza," Lexi croaked. "Any-anything else?"

Damian cringed as a recent headline from the *LA Times* ran through his mind: STRIPPER PROVIDES ALIBI FOR ACCUSED CHILD RAPIST/MURDERER, DAMIAN GARZA

"No . . ." Remembering the steak dinner he and Kandee had been denied, his mouth watered. "Wait. I would also like a ribeye, rare; baked potato, butter only; and a Caesar salad." Kandee wouldn't be joining him tonight since she and Alan were meeting with Detectives Hale and Miller. So far, the stripper had managed to maintain her fabricated alibi, but they had insisted on questioning her again.

"Okay. We'll send . . ." Lexi began.

"And two bottles of Bordeaux."

"All right. W-will that be all?"

"Send the tequila now." Damian hung up before Lexi could respond. Heat infused his skin, rising from his neck to his cheeks. He shoved up the sleeves of his black cashmere sweater and swiped sweat from the back of his neck. Lexi's fearful tone coupled with the humiliation he'd suffered at the hands of those asshole detectives brought on another wave of anger.

Instead of placing him in a holding cell, the cops had him processed and thrown in with the rest of the degenerates. Damian swallowed the tequila, then threw the glass against the wall. The thick tumbler thudded against the vellum, leaf patterned wallpaper and plunked onto the plush beige carpet.

"Shit." A shattering crash would have been more satisfying. He shook his head and picked up the stout glass as a knock resonated from the door. Damian padded barefoot across the room, jerked open the door and stared at his visitor. Her dark eyes seemed to dominate her oval face. She had to be a hallucination. Damian fought the urge to blink and instead held her gaze.

Jia Dahl lowered her eyes and asked, "How much trouble is my brother in this time?"

He is in trouble again?

"Come in and we will talk about it." Damian stepped aside and Jia brushed past him and into the suite. Her long jet-black hair danced down her rigid back as she marched to the couch.

"I can get a loan to pay off some of his gambling debts." Her words tumbled out, a pitch of panic in her voice. "But it won't be enough to cover everything and pay for the damages at the club. I'm also prepared . . ."

"Have a seat." Damian motioned toward a leather burgundy love seat as he sat on the accompanying couch.

Jia perched on the edge of the cushion and set her handbag on the floor next to her feet. She folded her hands in her lap, sat tall and met Damian's eyes with a determined stare.

Desire rose in his loins. She'd tried to downplay her beauty by dressing in a shapeless white blouse and loose fitting black slacks. Still, her exquisiteness stirred him and her defiance ignited his lust. A mental image of her luminescent naked body framed by the dark burgundy couch made him ache with discomfort.

Damian smiled, leaned back and crossed his legs. His chino's chaffed his bare skin, spurring his need. "As you may know, I have been somewhat out of the loop and had not heard about your brother's latest escapades. Tell me what has happened."

He noticed a look of relief cross Jia's face. She swallowed and then said, "He owes one of your loan sharks a hundred thousand, which makes his total debt to you over a hundred and fifty grand. I think I can borrow against my home for half the debt, and I can pick up extra shifts at the club, but . . ."

Her voice broke and she raised delicate fingers to her red lips.

Damian held up a hand. "I believe we can find a beneficial solution for both of us, Jia." She stiffened slightly and he suppressed a smile. "I would suggest, however, that you seriously consider distancing yourself from your brother's problems."

She lifted her chin and narrowed her eyes.

"I will instruct my men to cease making loans to your brother. As for the damage to the club, that is what insurance is for." He felt like a cat with a mouse, toying with his prize before consuming it.

Jia chewed her bottom lip and nodded.

A rap at the door was followed by a male voice. "Room service."

Damian stood. "I have ordered dinner. Can I get you something?"

"No." Jia stood as well, her tone dismissive. "We can discuss a payment plan another time. Enjoy your dinner."

Damian's jaw flexed. *You may not be interested in dinner, but you will definitely be participating in dessert.* "Sit. This will only take a minute." He managed to keep his tone pleasant. Damian stepped to the door and jerked it open as the waiter prepared to knock again.

"Good evening, sir." He smiled. "I've brought the alcohol you ordered." The waiter wheeled in a cart containing the tequila, red wine, two crystal wine glasses and two diamond-cut tumblers. He nodded at Jia and then turned, opened the black check presenter and handed Damian a pen.

Damian scrawled his name across the bill. "How long until my dinner is delivered?"

"Your cart was being prepared when I left, sir," the waiter said removing the seal on the bottle of Patron. "It shouldn't be long."

"Fine. That will be all." Damian waved off the waiter with the check folder and handed it back.

The waiter departed as Damian uncorked the bottle and poured tequila into each tumbler before turning to Jia.

"We are not quite finished." He moved closer, inhaling the fresh scent of orange blossoms. "Drink this. It will help you relax." He offered her the heavy glass.

"I don't drink tequila." Her lip curled slightly and she took a step back. "I really should be going."

Damian tossed down his shot and set the empty glass on the end table. "You knew when you came here that I would want more than your money." He offered the shot of tequila again. "Perhaps some liquid courage will make paying off your brother's debt a tad more tolerable." Damian seized her wrist, his grip tightening until she opened her hand. He grinned and placed the tumbler in her palm.

Jia glared at him as her fingers wrapped around the glass. She took a deep breath and then swallowed the shot. A cough escaped her lips as Damian took the empty tumbler.

"What do you have in mind?" she rasped.

"Take off your clothes and I will show you."

"Room service," a young female voice called with a light tap on the door.

Damian held Jia's wide-eyed stare for a beat, then turned and crossed to the door. He cracked it open and stuck his hand through the small space.

"Give me the check and leave the cart in the hallway," he barked at the young server.

"Y-yes, sir." She handed him the bill.

Damian signed and thrust the black case back at her. She barely looked at him and scurried down the hallway to the elevators. He watched her until the doors closed, and then he flipped a switch on the wall that would prevent the elevator from returning to the penthouse floor.

He wheeled in the food cart, the aroma of the bloody steak filling the room and parked it next to the small glass dining table. Damian leered at Jia and said, "You should eat something to keep up your strength."

"I told you I can raise part of the money and that I'll dance more at the club." Jia jammed her hands onto her hips. "I'm afraid that's all I have to offer."

Damian strutted toward her. "Then you should have phoned in your offer instead of coming here." He reached for the top button of her blouse.

Jia slapped his hand away. "Don't touch me."

Damian threw his head back and laughed—then, in one single motion, he ripped open her blouse. Jia gasped and Damian lunged at her. He pinned her against the wall, smothering her lips with his before a scream could leave her mouth. His hands deftly removed the torn blouse, then her bra. Jia fought to free herself and Damian chuckled when her knee missed its mark.

He rammed a leg between her knees and pinned her arms above her head, then traced a path along her alabaster skin with his lips to her breasts, perfect orbs begging him to suck them dry.

"Let go of me, you bastard!" Jia snarled.

Damian barely heard her. He focused on controlling himself. He wanted her more this time than the first time she'd found herself in his bed. She'd been willing then, compliant in an effort to save her brother from a few broken bones. Once Jia became a favorite dancer at the club, bringing in influential clients, his father had instructed Damian to treat her with respect.

Jia squirmed as he rolled a nipple between his fingers. "You should have gone to the old man for help."

"His assistant sent me here. You know he's going to be pissed when I tell—"

He bit her breast and she cried out. Her insolence made him want to enjoy the ride even more, to be so consumed by his need for her that his release would be explosive.

After raising her nipples to firm buds, he let go of her hands and tossed her over his shoulder. Jia beat his back with her fist. She kicked her legs and sent her shoes flying, her efforts stoking the fire of lust burning in his loins. Damian pushed open the bedroom door, dropped Jia onto the dark gray comforter and sucked in a breath at the sight of her half-naked body. She flipped onto her hands and knees and scrambled toward the edge of the bed.

Damian grabbed her by the waist and yanked at her slacks, the button and zipper giving way. He pulled slacks and panties down to her knees, crippling her movement. He slapped her on the ass, sending her face down onto the comforter as he pulled off his sweater.

"Get away from me, you monster!" The thick quilt muffled her cry.

"Why are you fighting me?" Damian tossed his shirt aside, clutched her feet and tugged off her pants and lacy underwear. "You know you enjoyed yourself last time."

"Screw you," Jia hissed as she tried to crawl away.

Damian gripped her legs and flipped her onto her back. "Lie still, damn it, and I will not hurt you."

Jia's breathing came in jagged bursts, her firm tits rising and falling with each breath. Damian stared at her, surprised at the spark of defiance still in her eyes, as he shucked off his pants. He inhaled deeply to suppress the urge to take her. He sat next to her on the bed and ran his hands over her body, her silky smooth skin soft under his palms.

She recoiled and tried to inch away. Damian planted a hand next to her, effectively hemming her in with a strong arm. "Shall we take this slow and enjoy ourselves." He leaned down and covered her lips, his tongue probing her mouth.

"Ouch!" He touched his bitten lip, then backhanded her across the face. Blind rage consumed him, exploding in a need to subdue Jia. He climbed on top of her and forced her legs apart. Once again, he trapped her arms above her head. Damian lowered his hips and probed Jia's softness, eliciting a cry of protest. He couldn't wait any longer—it was time. He leaned down and rammed his tongue between her lips, his hips poised to thrust his dick deep inside of her.

His cell phone rang. Damian hesitated. Stared into Jia's cold, dark eyes. Slid inside her. Kissed her as the incessant ringing continued.

"Shit." He snatched up the phone from the bedside table. Alan's name and number flashed on the screen. He felt himself grow limp as he hit the answer key. "What the hell do you want?"

"Kandee cracked and has been arrested for obstruction of justice. The detectives are going to arrest you again or you can turn yourself in." Damian heard contempt in Alan's voice. "It's up to you."

"How long do I have?" Damian climbed off Jia, who wrapped herself in the comforter.

"The detectives gave me a fifteen-minute head start. I am in the lobby, but the elevator's been switched off."

"Be down in ten." Damian pulled a robe from his closet and tossed it onto the bed. "Did you call my father?"

Jia covered herself and gathered her clothing.

"Yes. He and your mother will meet us at the Brentwood police station, along with Alexis Kent."

Damian flinched at the mention of his mother. "How bad is it?"

"Without an alibi, you are pretty much screwed."

Jia fled into the bathroom and closed the door as Damian disconnected and set the phone on the dresser. He climbed into his pants and pulled on his sweater. He pulled socks from a drawer and then his loafers from the closet. Damian tried the bathroom door. It was locked.

"Open the door."

No answer.

"Jia, I have a proposition for you. Open the damn door."

"Go screw yourself!"

Damian reared back and kicked in the door. Jia stumbled backward.

"Don't you need to go?" She'd donned her slacks and clutched the robe around her shoulders.

Damian moved closer. "Do not breathe a word of this and your brother's debts will be absolved."

Jia glowered at him and strode into the living room. Damian followed and gripped her arm as she picked up her bra and shredded blouse.

"Did you hear me?" He tightened his grip.

"I hope you rot in jail." She jerked her arm free, stuffed her ripped clothing into her purse and stepped into her shoes.

"There is more." Damian placed his hands on her shoulders, pulling her to him. "Stand by me at trial . . . and your brother lives."

Her pupils dilated slightly and he could tell she chewed the inside of her cheek. Without a word, she wrenched free of his grasp, flung opened the door and stomped into the hallway.

Damian Garza glared at the wasted dinner sitting on the delivery cart, flipped the elevator switch and then followed the ramrod straight figure of Jia Dahl.

CHAPTER FIFTEEN

Jackson Brady arrived early at Casa Lupita, ahead of the happy hour crowd. He sat in a booth at the back of the restaurant with a view of the door. After his first meeting with Pedro Gomez, Brady wanted to be the one holding court this time.

He inhaled the spicy aroma of Mexican food as he took a warm chip from the basket, dipped it in salsa and popped it into his mouth. A half-empty margarita sweated rivulets that ran down the stem of the colorful glass, soaking a cocktail napkin.

The restaurant became Brady's favorite after he settled in LA. He enjoyed the brightly colored decor, authentic cuisine and close proximity to his apartment. When Gomez suggested Casa Lupita, Brady recognized the implication. Gomez wanted him to know he had no secrets, that the Family had done their due diligence and knew everything about Jackson Brady.

Everyone has secrets.

It had taken him a year to move up the ranks in the Garza organization. After playing errand boy and filling in as a bouncer at Damian's clubs, Brady was finally tapped to dredge up dirt on Quan Dahl. A gambler who couldn't stay away from the poker tables, Quan had a temper and he had busted up more than one of Damian's clubs. Brady felt sorry for Quan, and his older sister, Jia, who happened to be one of Damian's obsessions. But the Dahl siblings weren't his problem.

Brady sipped his margarita as bells on the door jangled. Pedro Gomez stepped into the restaurant and smiled when he spotted Brady. The squat Mexican appeared to be as wide as he was tall, and the illusion only served to emphasize his dark beady eyes.

"Senor Brady, you started without me." Gomez sat across from Brady. Tweedle Dee and Tweedle Dum slid into a booth close to the door.

"Can I get you a drink?" Brady lifted his glass in a mock toast. "It's Margarita Monday."

Gomez nodded. "Si, si."

Brady waved at the waitress, pointed at his drink, then held up two fingers.

"What do you have for me?" Gomez took a tortilla chip and snapped it in half.

Brady slid the files across the table. "Not much."

Gomez cocked a bushy eyebrow and popped the chip into his mouth.

Brady continued. "I'm guessing you didn't expect me to find much on Clara that you don't already know." He paused and finished his margarita. "The only black mark I could find in her past was getting knocked up in college. She doesn't have any addictions or other skeletons in the closet."

"And the Corey woman?" Gomez scooped salsa onto his chip and shoved it in his mouth.

Brady leaned back against the bench seat. "Devyn Corey was widowed after three years of marriage. She now lives off of her deceased husband's life insurance and a percentage of the fundraising dollars from her foundation, Survivors of the Sea. Her parents are in their late seventies and live in Boca Raton, Florida. Corey doesn't have children or siblings—or any vices as far as I can tell."

Brady fell silent as a waitress delivered their margaritas.

She smiled at him. "Can I get you anything else? Some happy hour nachos, maybe?"

"No, thanks, Jill." Brady flashed a grin. "We're good for now."

A year ago, Jill had become his waitress with benefits after a night of tequila tasting left him vulnerable to her offer to see him home. He'd kept the pretty brunette at arm's length until that night. But now he enjoyed her company every few weeks.

Jill nodded at Brady; cast a furtive glance at Gomez, who leered at her; and then hustled away.

Gomez chuckled, stirred the ice in his margarita and stared at Jill's ass as she retreated. "I know what she can get for me." He shifted his gaze back to his margarita and lifted the multihued glass, his thick, stubby tongue protruding in anticipation of the salt-rimmed edge. After a salty slurp, Gomez said, "And the guy who visited Clara in the hospital?"

Already annoyed with Gomez's slimy remark about Jill, Brady's shoulder muscles tightened. He shrugged, picked up his margarita and took a sip. "As far as I can tell he's just another ambulance chaser looking to make a quick buck."

Gomez's dark eyes watched him as if looking for a sign he was lying.

"He could have been wearing a disguise."

Brady nodded. "I suppose anything's possible."

"Did you check the security tapes from the hospital?" Gomez asked.

Heat pricked the back of his neck, but he managed to keep his face relaxed. He didn't need to check the tapes, because he had been Clara's late night visitor. "No, but I managed to get a good description from one of the night nurses." Brady produced a small notebook from his jacket pocket and flipped it open. "Medium build. Average-looking, with short blond hair. Black-rim glasses. Dark jacket and slacks."

Gomez smirked. "Sounds a bit like you."

Brady managed a smile. "That's me, average Joe."

A crowd of co-workers from the office building across the street spilled through the door, their raucous voices filling the previously quiet restaurant. The group claimed a large table and Jill began taking drink orders.

Gomez turned his attention to the group for a minute, but then focused on Brady. "Keep looking for this man. It would please Senora Garza immensely if Clara has a lover."

"You're the boss." *Shit.* Brady jotted a note in his spiral notebook.

Gomez's phone vibrated and he glanced at the screen. "Bueno." Gomez nodded and listened. "Si." A frown accompanied another head nod. "Treinta minutos." Gomez rose from his seat, as did his two goons.

Gomez's body language told Brady something had happened. "Bad news?"

"Let me know when you have a name for Clara's visitor," Gomez said over his shoulder as he made his way to the exit.

"Will do," Brady called after him.

Pedro Gomez exited the restaurant as the rowdy group erupted in a chorus of "Finally!"

Brady shifted his attention to the muted TV hanging in the corner of the bar and the caption scrolling across the bottom of the screen: BREAKING NEWS: DAMIAN GARZA BACK IN JAIL FOR THE MURDER OF ALLY MARSH.

CHAPTER SIXTEEN

Steaming mug of coffee in hand, Clara settled into the weathered beach chair. Comforted by the briny sea air and the white noise of the surf, she focused on the thin line of the horizon. Clara often wondered if her daughter waited for her there, where the sea met the sky. She leaned her head back, closed her eyes and let the vision bloom in full color. Fifteen-year-old Ally, her arms stretched forward in greeting. Angel wings fluttering in the ocean breeze. A beautiful smile gracing her face.

Happy birthday, sweetie.

The tears she'd learned she had no control over, wet Clara's cheeks as she blew a kiss heavenward. The weak February sun peeked over the roof of the rented Malibu bungalow, sending diamonds of light dancing across the ocean. Clara smiled as she imagined the beautiful sight to be her daughter's response.

A seagull squawked overhead and, despite the warm sun, a chill washed over Clara. Another loud, harsh cry from the gull seemed to voice Clara's dread. After four months of waiting, her day in court had finally arrived. The fluttering in her stomach accelerated to match the frenzied flight of the gulls swooping down to snag sand crabs from the beach. She would finally come face-to-face with Damian, finally be able to point her finger at him and declare him a murderer.

Clara wished her day in court hadn't fallen on what should've been Ally's sixteenth birthday. She rolled her head, her neck muscles popping, and then toed the deep sand, locking her chair in place.

DDA Hibbs had done everything she could to reschedule Clara's testimony. Unfortunately, Damian's attorneys had countered Lisa's every move, but thanks to Karmen's efforts, Clara had been awarded control of their marital assets pending a verdict.

Clara's ringing phone sent the gulls soaring into the sky. She pulled the phone from her sweater pocket, checked the caller ID, and answered on the third ring. "Good morning, Devyn."

"I wish you'd pickup sooner."

Clara flinched at the edge in her friend's tone. "Devyn, you have to stop worrying. No one can access this property. It has more fences, gates and security systems than most celebrity homes."

"Yeah, well, all Damian needs is for you to vanish, then *poof*—no more eyewitness."

Devyn had been Clara's rock since Ally's murder. She'd been by Clara's side when she spread Ally's ashes along a rocky cliff overlooking the Pacific Ocean. She'd accompanied Clara on each trip from Astoria to LA for meetings with the detectives, the attorneys and Clara's appearances in divorce court. Devyn had rented this bungalow in Malibu, arranged for extra security measures and stocked the fridge and cupboards with food and essentials.

"You didn't have to stay in the city last night," Clara chastised.

"I know. I thought you'd like the morning to yourself," Devyn said.

"Are you coming with the car this morning?"

"Yes. The driver's picking me up at seven, which should put us at your door by eight-thirty."

"Right. I'll be ready."

"Okay, see you soon."

"Devyn . . ." Clara chewed her lower lip. "I . . ."

"You can do this. I'll be in the courtroom. Just keep your eyes on Lisa or me. Focus on the celebration you've planned for Ally this afternoon. This will be over soon."

"Yes." Tears pooled in Clara's eyes. "I can. For Ally."

She ended the call and cast another glance toward the horizon, where a bank of clouds had taken up residence. The ominous clouds reflected her feelings of apprehension. She sucked in a salty breath, exhaled and headed for the shower.

Standing in the hot spray of the shower, Clara thought back to when she discovered she was pregnant. Ally's father had wooed her for months with poetry, long walks in the park and romantic dinners—finally worming his way into her heart. He'd stripped her of her defenses and clothing, with three little words: "I love you."

At first, Clara ignored the symptoms, convincing herself she had the flu. When reality set in, she contacted the wayward frat boy, who came from wealth and privilege. His solution to their predicament was to pay for an abortion.

Appalled at his suggestion, Clara had said no. Ally arrived one month after Clara's college graduation and the two moved to Los Angeles. As mother and daughter began their new life together, Clara took a job as a receptionist with a marketing firm, eventually becoming a junior marketing specialist with a few of her own clients. Clara excelled in her career and Ally blossomed into a delightful preteen.

Then she met Damian Garza, a monster disguised as Prince Charming.

The memory faded into the corners of her mind as she toweled herself dry. She'd never listen to her heart again. Never trust another man. Never fall in love.

Clara dressed as Lisa had instructed: black suit over a cream-colored blouse. She accented the ensemble with black heels, gold stud earrings, and Ally's locket. A touch of minimal makeup accompanied her French twist hairstyle. Lisa wanted to project a mother in mourning. Clara wanted to wear her red suit, a power color that said she wasn't afraid of Damian Garza.

As she transferred lipstick, antacid and tissue from her well-worn purse to a black leather clutch, Clara recalled last night's news coverage of the media-banned trial: "Damian Garza stepped from the court house this afternoon looking as if he's been on vacation instead of locked up for the past four months," a woman reported for Channel 2. "Mr. Garza continues to proclaim his innocence." Her belief in Damian's claim echoed in her tone.

Stupid bitch.

With a few minutes to spare, Clara stepped through the front door. A bouquet of pink roses and baby's breath filled a crystal vase sitting at the edge of the porch. Her pulse raced at the sight of Ally's favorite roses clustered in the familiar vase.

It can't be.

She'd smashed that vase against Damian's fireplace months ago.

He's here.

She spun around, searching for him.

Don't read the card.

Clara picked up the vase.

Toss it in the trash.

She snatched the card from its stand. Her breath caught at the familiar writing.

> *My thoughts are with Ally on her sixteenth birthday, and with you on this sad occasion—and always.*

"Shit!" Clara's hands shook as she read the message again. She knew even with a guilty verdict; Damian would continue to torment her. She knew she'd always be at his mercy. She knew she couldn't live with that fear.

Clara knew she needed to take action.

CHAPTER SEVENTEEN

Damian Garza sat at the table listening to Alexis Kent explain her defense strategy to his father. Ricardo nodded in agreement, but Damian knew his father's flushed face was an indicator of building anger. Valencia sat next to her husband and studied her manicure as if their discussion bored her.

Damian smoothed his black and gray striped tie and adjusted the cuffs of his crisp white shirt. The expensive poplin felt cool against his skin, a welcome sensation after four months of wearing scratchy prison garb. He wore his favorite charcoal-gray suit, which complimented his dark coloring.

With arms crossed, Alan Sanchez stood next to a large window that offered a bird's eye view of the city of Los Angeles as it crept west toward the Pacific Ocean. Damian knew Alan felt a sense of security after Ricardo told Damian not to harm the attorney. He glared at Alan, who avoided eye contact and tapped his fingers on the mahogany table top.

It is only a matter of time before I am free to do as I want.

"Damian, please," Valencia said, tearing her gaze away from her blood red nails to hold his dark stare. "That is distracting."

Damian folded his hands in his lap. "Sorry, Mother." Sarcasm dripped from his words.

"Ms. Kent." Ricardo held up a hand. "Will attacking Clara seem cruel to the jury?"

Alexis shrugged. "Possibly, but we need to create doubt about Clara's credibility and her motive for accusing Damian."

"If only Ms. Kane had kept the lie alive." Valencia's mock concern set Damian on edge and his clenched jaw made his teeth ache.

Despite her attorney's efforts, he couldn't believe Kandee caved and admitted she wasn't with Damian at the time of Ally's murder, which led to his arrest.

Through his mind, Damian reran Alan's visit when he brought the disconcerting news.

"Without an alibi," Alan had said from the other side of the visitor's window, "no judge is going to allow bail. Alexis is due back in two days. Maybe she can wave her magic wand and free you." The attorney delivered his monologue standing and didn't wait for Damian's response before departing.

After Alan left, Damian had sat staring at the thick marred glass as if it were a crystal ball that would provide a different message.

During the four months he'd sat in jail waiting for a trial date, his only visitors had been Ricardo and Alexis, both intent on setting him free.

A sultry scent floated over Damian, bringing him back to the conversation at hand. He inhaled deeply as Alexis flipped her hair off her shoulder, wishing he had the attorney writhing naked in his bed. He exhaled, shifted in his chair and refocused on the ongoing debate about his defense.

"A setback for sure." Alexis lifted her chin slightly. "I would have advised against a fake alibi if I'd been consulted."

Damian glowered at Alan, who watched Alexis with an impassive stare.

"The damage is done," Ricardo said. "The question is how badly will Kandee's testimony hurt Damian?"

"I think we can use the DA's offer of probation in exchange for her testimony to our advantage." Alexis consulted the notepad in front of her. "By putting Ms. Kane on the stand, the DA opens the door for cross about her affair with Damian."

Alan spoke for the first time, "And with Ms. Dahl's testimony to Damian's philandering, Alexis should be able to paint a picture of Clara as a scorned woman intent on making Damian pay for her daughter's death."

"Thank you, Alan," Alexis said without looking at him. "The goal today is to discredit Clara in the eyes of the jury and create a sense of doubt as to Damian's guilt."

Damian and his father had discussed this strategy and the elder Garza worried the tactic would only serve to create sympathy for Clara. Ricardo didn't share the specifics but implied that he'd arranged for at least two jurors to vote not guilty, on the off chance Alexis didn't achieve an acquittal on her own. And even though the serial rape charges against Damian had taken a back seat to this trial, Ricardo had begun the process of paying off witnesses and corrupting evidence, hoping to get those charges dismissed.

Damian hated not being in the loop. Not being in control. Not having a say about his fate. But his father was footing the bill, so he had no choice but to do as he was told.

For now.

A knock at the door caused all eyes to look past Damian.

"Yes," Alexis said.

Kevin Long, her co-counsel, poked his head in. "You wanted to know when Mrs. Garza arrived."

Alexis nodded.

"She's here with DDA Hibbs in a witness room down the hall."

Damian fought to control the smile that crept to his lips. *I hope she enjoyed my gift.*

"Thanks, Kevin," Alexis said. "Let me know when we're due in court."

"Will do." Kevin's head disappeared through the opening and he closed the door.

Alexis stared down Damian. "Do you have something to add?"

Damian sipped from a water glass, held her gaze and then responded, "No, Counselor. I believe you have everything under control." Alexis Kent was the type of woman he loathed but felt an overwhelming ache to subdue. Her cool confidence only served to heighten his burning desire to strip her of her smugness.

"I know that look," Valencia said. "What have you done, Damian?"

Damian narrowed his eyes at Valencia, but kept his tone conciliatory. "I have no idea what you are talking about Mother."

"What the hell could he possibly do from behind bars?" Ricardo glowered at his wife. "For Christ's sake, Valencia, leave the boy alone."

Valencia raised an eyebrow, her nostrils flaring slightly. "I simply do not want Ms. Kent blindsided by any actions Damian's managed to orchestrate from jail."

An image of Clara discovering the vase of pink roses flashed through his mind, bringing another tight smile to his lips, which he hid with another sip of water.

Valencia turned to the family attorney. "Alan?"

"To my knowledge, Damian has not done anything that will jeopardize our case."

"See, Mother." Damian flashed a broad smile. "I have done nothing to—"

The door opened again after a sharp rap and a court clerk popped his head in. "Ms. Kent, we're ready to begin." Kevin Long hovered behind the officer.

"We'll be right there." Alexis placed her notepad into her briefcase. "Damian, please do yourself a favor. Don't look at Clara, sneer at the jury, or show contempt for the judge. Keep your—"

"I know the drill, Counselor." Damian concentrated on creating a docile look. "Keep my face void of emotion."

There will be plenty of time to express myself once this fiasco is over and I plan to start with you.

CHAPTER EIGHTEEN

With each passing minute, the off-white walls of the witness room closed in on Clara. She clicked Ally's locket open and closed as she paced the small space, taking inventory of stains on the carpet, scuff marks on the walls, scratches on the table. Occasionally, she stopped to stare out a lone window to the street below. A crowd of curious bystanders who couldn't find seats in the gallery blended with news reporters who'd been banned by the judge. The throng pulsated with a buzzing noise that drifted up to the closed window. They, like Clara, waited for word from the proceedings. If only Devyn could text her from the courtroom with an update.

Lisa Hibbs had planned to put Clara on the stand first thing, but Alexis Kent had filed a motion for dismissal based on the prosecution's lack of physical evidence—no DNA or murder weapon, and no witnesses, except a vindictive wife and mother. Lisa told Clara the stall tactic was meant to put her on edge before she took the witness stand.

Mission accomplished.

Karmen Scott pushed through the door. "How are you holding up?"

Clara answered with a shoulder shrug. "How much longer will I be trapped in here?"

"Judge Bailey is hearing arguments from both sides. It shouldn't be much longer." Karmen dropped her briefcase into a chair and adjusted the collar of her dark blue suit jacket.

Clara changed the subject. "Did the judge dismiss Damian's motion to restrict my access to assets?"

"Yes and no." Karmen opened the briefcase, extracted a folder and placed it on the small conference table. "Judge Sanders released your savings account, but denied our request to sell any assets."

"What about my name change?"

"I'm sorry, Clara, but it's been delay—"

A knock at the door interrupted their discussion. Blood drained from Clara's face and her head spun. She gripped the back of a chair to steady herself.

It's time, time to face Damian.

The door swung open, and Sloan Carter, Karmen's co-counsel, entered toting a tissue-wrapped bouquet. The cloud of white obscured her young face, leaving only a halo of brown curls visible behind the arrangement. She set the package in the middle of the table and handed the envelope to Clara.

Clara recoiled and crossed her arms. "Wh-who gave those to you?"

"They were delivered to the office." Sloan looked at Karmen, who was focused on Clara. "Are you okay?" Karmen stepped toward Clara.

Clara shook her head and took a step back. "Damian left a vase of roses at the bungalow."

"What? How?" Karmen stood hands on hips. "Did you call the police?"

"N-no," Clara said.

"What did you do with them?"

"Devyn gave them to Detective Hale."

"He should have delivered them to forensics by now," Karmen said. "God, I hope he left DNA or prints."

Sloan pointed at the vase of flowers. "Should I take these to the guard?"

"Let's see who they're from first." Karmen looked at Clara. "Do you want me to read the message?"

Clara held her breath and nodded.

With a tissue, Karmen slid the note card free and read the words aloud: "Be strong."

Clara exhaled at the familiar two-word message. She pulled the tissue away to reveal deep purple irises standing at attention in a simple vase. Their faint, sweet aroma mingled with a familiar masculine scent. *Trust me.*

"Looks like you have a secret admirer." Sloan gathered the tissue and tossed it into the trash. She missed the look of recognition between Clara and Karmen. To date, they had yet to discover the identity of her anonymous well-wisher, whom Clara also believed to be her mysterious visitor.

The door opened after a slight knock. "Mrs. Garza, they're ready for you," the court clerk said, his kind eyes meeting Clara's.

Clara's stomach lurched as the room began to spin. She put her palms flat on the table and sucked in air.

"She'll be there in a minute," Karmen told the clerk.

He nodded and pulled the door closed.

"Clara." Karmen stepped close and put her arm around Clara's shoulders. "You can do this."

Clara covered her mouth as bile rose in her throat. Sloan raised the tissue-filled garbage can and placed it under Clara's chin. The remnants of her morning coffee swirled in her gut. Clara gagged as acid bubbled up and burned the back of her throat. She closed her eyes, breathed through her nose and willed herself to relax. Clara heaved a sigh as Ally's smiling face flashed behind her eyelids. *You've got this, mom!*

Clara blinked at Sloan and then met Karmen's worried gaze. "I'm ready." She fingered the heart-shaped locket.

Ready as I'll ever be.

CHAPTER NINETEEN

From the back of the courtroom, Jackson Brady listened as Alexis Kent lobbied for a dismissal based on the lack of evidence against her client. He watched her move confidently across the well, crossing from the jury box and back again. He noticed with each pass she made brief eye contact with a different set of jurors, smiling to punctuate the points she made.

Brady had learned the statuesque blonde liked expensive suits and designer shoes. She was the type of woman men noticed across a crowded room and women generally hated on sight. To Brady, Alexis Kent represented the enemy, despite her beauty.

Damian's parents watched the proceedings two rows back from the defense table. His father hadn't missed a day, but his mother attended sporadically. Damian never acknowledged their presence, which Brady found curious.

He could also see Lisa Hibbs's tiny frame perched on the edge of her chair as if prepared to leap at the first opportunity to object. The only sound he heard, besides Alexis's voice, was the rapid clicking of the court reporter's keys. Brady thought Judge Bailey looked like a hawk watching a field mouse, tracking Alexis as she repeated her trek from the jury box to the defense table.

Kay Bailey was the youngest sitting judge in Contra Costa County. Brady's background check on the judge revealed a reputation for being fair, although she appeared to side with the prosecution most of the time. He'd heard Bailey generally displayed no sympathy for the defendants who came before her and he hoped she'd feel nothing but contempt for Damian Garza.

Brady scanned the jury box, making a mental note of each juror's reaction. Most of them appeared to be listening intently to Alexis's presentation, with a few taking notes. Despite the relentless news coverage, Judge Bailey had decided not to sequester the jury, a decision that had made it easier for Brady to contact jurors four and nine.

Pedro Gomez had instructed Brady to gather dirt on the twelve jurors and two alternates for comparison to the information the jury consultant, hired by the family, had found. Of the fourteen, numbers two, four, nine and eleven had mountains of debt, but only four and nine had addictions that fueled their bottomless financial pits.

Gomez told Brady to deposit nine thousand dollars into two jurors' bank accounts and Brady chose jurors two and eleven. The amount wouldn't raise a red flag at the bank, but Gomez could use the deposits to blackmail the jurors if necessary. Brady knew it wouldn't come to that because the prosecution would know about the bribes before the jurors did. And once DDA Hibbs knew about the tampering, she'd be obligated to tell the judge. Since Brady hadn't contacted the jurors directly, he hoped the judge would replace them with the alternates instead of declaring a mistrial.

Assuming the judge would then be compelled to sequester the jury for the remainder of the trial, Brady decided to add his own touch and sent jurors four and nine anonymous letters with copies of a Swiss bank statement that showed a balance of fifty thousand dollars in each of their names. He had eradicated the account number and all other information, making it impossible for the jurors to withdraw the money until they'd earned it.

His letter explained the money was from a concerned citizen who wanted to see justice done and he went on to say that he wouldn't presume to tell the jurors how to vote. He simply hoped after they'd heard all the evidence, they would see clearly that Damian Garza was guilty. Such clarity, the note said, would reward the jurors for their efforts.

The hundred thousand dollars had come from his retirement fund and if everything went according to plan, Brady would finally be able to retire from his pursuit of justice for Iris. For Ally. For Clara.

Brady tugged at his suit jacket and squirmed on the hard bench. He knew he was breaking the law, but what choice did he have? If the Garza family would stop at nothing to see Damian acquitted, then he had to play defense. The urge to kill Damian with his bare hands swept over him again. Murder would have been a simpler, more permanent solution, but Brady knew he wouldn't be able to live with himself.

For the first time since he'd begun pursuing Damian Garza, Brady sensed victory. Of course, his plan depended on Clara's participation, which meant he still had his work cut out for him.

She has to trust me.

Alexis's confident tone interrupted his musings. "And that is why I move for a dismissal of all charges against my client." She smiled and took her seat at the defense table.

"Thank you, Ms. Kent, for your complete dissection of the prosecution's case," Judge Bailey said. "However, I believe there is sufficient evidence to proceed. Motion to dismiss denied."

Alexis sat erect in her chair and the only indication that she'd suffered defeat was her light pat on Damian's shoulder.

Judge Bailey shifted her focus to Lisa. "Call your next witness, Counselor."

"The prosecution calls Clara Garza to the stand." Lisa motioned to the clerk standing by the courtroom's double doors.

Brady smoothed his tie and inhaled the faint hint of lavender as Clara entered the room. He fought the urge to turn and look, but the rest of the gallery, with the exception of Alexis, hadn't managed the same control. All eyes stared toward the back of the courtroom.

Brady watched Damian as he sat taller in his chair and narrowed his eyes, his body tense as if he intended to pounce. Brady's neck muscles tightened—if Damian moved a muscle, Brady would be on him in an instant.

I would kill him to protect Clara.

CHAPTER TWENTY

The packed courtroom blurred in Clara's vision as she marched straight to the witness stand. Her pumps clacked loudly on the hardwood floor, sounding more confident than her trembling legs felt. She sat down and sucked in air as she took in the sea of faces staring at her. Clara fingered Ally's gold locket, touching the etched dragonfly before she clicked the clasp open and then shut. Her pulse accelerated as she scanned the crowd for Devyn. When Devyn smiled at her, Clara expelled the breath she'd been holding.

The hulking bailiff, who'd been swearing her in, cleared his throat and repeated his question. "Do you swear to tell the truth, the whole truth and nothing but the truth?"

"I do." Clara rubbed her sweaty palms together.

"Please state your name for the record."

"Clara Garza." The name tasted bitter on her tongue.

DDA Hibbs rose from her chair and approached the witness box. Her emerald-colored suit seemed to darken her green eyes.

"Good morning, Clara." Lisa flashed a confident smile.

"Good morning." Clara held the deputy district attorney's gaze and worked the locket. Open. Close.

Just breathe.

"Clara, I know this is difficult, but can you take us through the events on October seventh of last year?"

They had practiced her testimony repeatedly. Clara would recite a monologue outlining the events of that horrific day. Lisa coached her to keep her answers short and to the point when the defense cross-examined her. She'd said it would be okay to become emotional but important to remain in control.

"I'd been unable to reach my daughter, Allyson, and I went home to check on her. When I arrived, I . . . found her . . . in her room . . ." A sob choked off her words. Clara took a breath and popped the locket again. Open. Close. Open.

Lisa stepped closer and Clara held her concerned gaze. "And you saw the defendant on top of your daughter?" Lisa asked.

"Objection. Leading the witness," an authoritative female voice said.

Don't look.

Clara couldn't help herself and Alexis Kent came into full focus. The defense attorney met and held Clara's eyes. Clara caught sight of movement next to the attorney. Again the warning in her head, but she had to look her daughter's killer in the eye.

"Sustained," Judge Bailey responded.

"Clara, can you tell us what happened when you entered Ally's room?" Lisa prompted.

Damian's dark eyes bored into Clara's and she went rigid as if encased in a straightjacket of fear. His lips curved in an evil sneer. Her heart slammed against her rib cage. Damian arched an eyebrow, his trademark sign of contempt. Clara wished she'd brought a gun.

"Mrs. Garza," Judge Bailey said, "please answer the question."

Clara blinked at the judge and nodded. She raised her chin and returned Damian's stare, then focused on Lisa. "Damian was . . . standing next to my daughter's bed. She . . ." Clara's mouth went dry. She swallowed and opened her mouth, but the words wouldn't come.

"Do you need a minute?" Lisa poured a glass of water and handed it to Clara.

Clara sipped the water and then shook her head. "No. I-I'm fine."

Lisa nodded. "All right, please continue."

"Ally was dead." Clara worked the locket. Close. Open. Close. "I tried to save her, but . . . but . . ." Tears clouded her eyes. "The last thing I remember is being shot."

"Clara, can you identify the man who shot you?"

"Yes. The defendant." Clara wanted to stand and point and scream his name, but instead said in a firm voice, "Damian Garza."

"Thank you, Clara." Lisa gave her a reassuring smile. "Your witness, Counselor."

Despite her determination not to cry, tears slipped from Clara's eyes. She quickly scanned the gallery and spotted Devyn, who flashed a thumbs up.

"My condolences, Mrs. Garza. Would you like to take a break?" Alexis asked as she crossed the well to the witness stand.

Clara thought the defense attorney looked as if she'd just finished a photo shoot for a glamour magazine. "Thank you, no." Clara's jaw muscles tightened as she bit off the words and clicked the locket open, then closed

Alexis smiled. "Are you aware that there were several home invasions in your neighborhood during the time of your daughter's murder?"

"Yes," Clara said.

"In fact, didn't your husband report some items stolen from your home's garage?"

"So I've been told." Clara narrowed her eyes as the defense attorney continued.

Alexis turned to the jury box. "And you're aware the police have arrested a man in connection with these burglaries who is similar in height, weight and coloring to Mr. Garza?" She turned and took a step toward Clara, who gave a slight nod. "Isn't it possible that in your concern for your daughter's safety, you didn't get a good look at the assailant? That possibly the man who harmed Ally is the burglar who's been arrested?"

Clara shook her head. "No, it's not possible."

"Do you own a dark blue BMW?" Alexis asked as she moved to the defense table.

"Yes."

Alexis picked up a stack of photos and said, "Defense exhibit F." She handed a set to the bailiff, dropped another set onto the prosecution's table and then stepped to the witness stand. "Mrs. Garza, can you confirm that this is you, in your car, parked in front of the Luxe Hotel?"

Clara shot a look at Lisa, who studied the pictures. Lisa's creased brow sent a shiver up Clara's spine. They knew the defense had photos of Clara's car, but it had not been made clear what, if anything, the implication of the photos could be.

"Mrs. Garza?" Alexis Kent moved the stack closer to Clara.

She cast a quick glance at the photo. *The bastard had me followed.*

"Yes."

Alexis revealed the next photo.

"And you also parked across from the Four Seasons Hotel?

"Yes."

A third photo. "Do you know this woman, Mrs. Garza?"

Clara glanced at the photo of a buxom, brassy blonde. "No."

Another photo. "What about this woman?"

The petite Asian female looked familiar, but Clara couldn't place her. "No."

Alexis picked up the photos and tapped them straight against the rail of the witness stand. "You're sure you don't know either of these women?"

"I'm sure." The locket slipped from her sweaty fingertips.

"Yet we have proof that you had your husband and Ms. Kane under surveillance." Alexis held up the photo of the trashy blonde for Clara to see. "As well as he and Ms. Dahl." She exchanged the photos. "Can you explain why you were spying on Mr. Garza and these women?"

"Objection." Lisa stood. "Your Honor, this line of question has nothing to do with the defendant raping and murdering a young girl."

"It goes to the witness's state of mind, Your Honor," Alexis countered.

The judge tapped her pen for a few seconds. "I'll allow it. But make your point quickly, Counselor."

Alexis nodded and turned to Clara. "Mrs. Garza, can you explain why you were spying on your husband?"

"I wasn't spying on him. I couldn't care . . ." Clara bit her lip to keep from finishing the sentence.

"You thought your husband was cheating on you so you followed him hoping to,"—she formed quote marks with her fingers—"catch him in the act."

Lisa came to her feet again. "Objection."

Alexis spoke across Lisa's objection. "Pictures don't lie, Mrs. Garza."

"Objection!" Lisa repeated, her tone an octave too high.

"Withdrawn," Alexis said before Judge Bailey could respond to the objection, then fired her next question, "Mrs. Garza, do you patronize the hair salon, Mane Style?"

The question caught Clara off guard. "Y-yes."

"And your stylist is Vivienne Kimber, correct?"

Vivienne? What could she have to do with this?

Clara's mouth went dry. "Yes."

"Are you aware that Jia Dahl is also a client of Ms. Kimber's?"

From the salon—that's where I've seen her. "No."

"According to Ms. Kimber's schedule, you and Ms. Dahl had back-to-back appointments on several occasions. Didn't you in fact see Mr. Garza meeting Ms. Dahl at the salon and become suspicious of their relationship?"

"N-no. I've never met—"

The defense attorney cut in again as sweat beads bloomed across Clara's forehead.

"An affair would nullify your prenuptial agreement, would it not?" Alexis directed the question at the jury with a palms-up shrug. "Which would mean a much larger divorce settlement for you . . ."

"Objection," Lisa said from the prosecution's table.

Alexis ignored the objection. "Aren't you simply a scorned wife looking for revenge against a cheating husband?" Alexis flashed an accusatory look at Clara.

"Objection! Counsel is badgering the witness."

"Sustained," Judge Bailey said. "Move along, Ms. Kent. And kindly refrain from continuing your cross until I've made a ruling." The Judge gave her a warning look.

"Yes, Your Honor." Alexis turned and faced the jury box. "Mrs. Garza, how much do you stand to gain without a prenup in a divorce from my client?"

"Objection!" Lisa Hibbs shot to her feet. "Relevance."

Alexis turned to the judge. "It goes to credibility, Your Honor."

"Judge, this isn't a divorce hearing," Lisa said. "Ms. Kent is contaminating the jury with information that's irrelevant to this matter."

Clara's attention bounced between the two attorneys.

"It's our contention, Your Honor,"—Alexis stepped closer to the bench —"that Mrs. Garza's potential gain is motive for falsely accusing my client."

Lisa bolted from behind the prosecution table. "Seriously? Your Honor . . ."

"Yes, seriously." Alexis shot a look of disdain at Lisa.

"Enough!" Judge Bailey banged her gavel. Clara jumped in her seat and cut her eyes to the judge, who motioned to the battling attorneys. "Approach."

The attorneys stood an arm's length from each other in front of the bench as Judge Bailey leaned forward and lowered her voice. "Ms. Kent, you will cease this line of questioning. If you have questions of this witness in defense of your client, ask them. Otherwise, move on." Judge Bailey waved her fingertips at the attorneys and they retreated to their respective tables.

"Ms. Kent?" Bailey said, her hawk-like stare fixed on the defense attorney.

"One more question, Your Honor." Alexis squared off to the witness box. "Mrs. Garza, I noticed you're not wearing your wedding ring." She now faced the jurors. "Can you tell us what has happened to—"

"Objection!" Lisa jumped to her feet once again. "This is—"

Clara gripped the arms of the witness chair to keep from standing as well as she shouted over Lisa, "I donated the ring to an auction because I do not want anything that reminds me of the monster who murder my daughter!"

Silence blanketed the court room and all eyes were focused on Clara who glared at Damian.

"The defense is done with this witness for now," Alexis said, ending the stare down, "but requests the right to recall her at a later time." Alexis took her seat and focused on the notepad in front of her.

"Noted." The judge shifted her steely gaze to the DDA. "Ms. Hibbs?"

"Redirect, Your Honor?"

Judge Bailey nodded and Lisa moved slowly toward Clara. "Clara can you tell us to whom you made the donation?"

"To the Boys and Girls Club." Clara had wanted to throw the two carat wedding set into the ocean, which is also where she'd like to have sent Damian to a watery death, but logic prevailed and she donated the five-thousand-dollar ring instead.

"It's late in the day, Counselors, let's resume at eight o'clock Monday morning. The jury is excused." Judge Bailey rapped her gavel. "You're excused too, Mrs. Garza."

Clara blinked at the judge and nodded. Bailey gave her a sympathetic smile before turning her attention to the bailiff.

Caught up in the heated exchange between the attorneys, Clara had lost sight of Devyn. Now, in the chaos of the crowded gallery, she couldn't find her friend. Sweat trickled between her breasts as she scanned the spectators for a familiar face. Lisa had her head bent in conversation with her co-counsel, Sloan Carter, and Karmen Scott spoke with a court clerk at the back of the courtroom.

As Clara extricated herself from the witness box and continued to search for Devyn, she found Damian watching her. He smiled at her as he buttoned his suit jacket. An innocuous smile to most, but to Clara his smile radiated a smug confidence.

She took a halting step toward the defense table and in a flash of fantasy saw herself crossing the well and slapping Damian's face. She heard herself threaten to remove his testicles with a soup spoon. She imagined leveling a gun at him and watching his smile dissolve into a tight line of fear as she pulled the trigger.

In reality, Clara stood stock still as if her subconscious knew better than to react. Her blood boiled and she balled her hands into fists.

Damian held her stare, his smile dimming slightly when Alexis spoke to him. Clara shifted her gaze to the attorney, who glanced at Clara and then gripped Damian's arm and signaled for the guard.

It was Clara's turn to smile as the guard cuffed Damian's hands behind his back and guided him from the courtroom. She lifted her chin as he cast a last searing look in her direction before the guard propelled him through a side door.

Clara's rage melted and she swayed on her feet as if her dissipating anger were liquefying her muscles.

"Clara?" Devyn took her by the elbow. "Come on—let's get out of here."

CHAPTER TWENTY-ONE

Thankful to be free of the town car that had delivered her and Devyn to Malibu, Clara inhaled the briny ocean mist. Blinking back tears as the salty sea air stung her eyes; she rested her palms on the weathered pier railing and exhaled slowly. Testifying on Ally's birthday, and coming face-to-face with her daughter's killer, had stripped her of her resolve not to cry.

Holding a balloon bouquet in one hand, Devyn offered Clara a tissue and stood next to her as she released the strain and sorrow of the day in a flood of tears.

Clara sighed a last sob and turned to Devyn, who rotated a pink balloon to reveal a scribbled message:

Your mom's fine, but misses you tons.

Love you, Auntie Devyn

"I thought Ally might enjoy a little news from home."

Devyn handed Clara a balloon and a purple sharpie. The marker quivered in Clara's hand as she contemplated her message. She wanted to tell her daughter so many things.

More than she could possibly write on the face of a balloon. Her throat tightened as the tip squeaked across the latex surface:

Miss you lots and love you more. Happy 16th

Birthday, Ally! Love, Mom

"Ready?" Devyn fingered the white ribbon streaming from her balloon.

Clara nodded, kissed her balloon and let go. Tears stained both women's cheeks as they watched the ocean breeze carry the bright orbs across the sea toward the horizon.

Devyn sniffed and cleared her throat. "Let's get a drink."

"Rain check?" Clara fingered Ally's locket. "I'd like some time alone."

Devyn hesitated. "Do you have your Taser?"

Clara patted her jacket pocket. "Yes."

Devyn scuffed a wooden plank with her toe. "You're sure?"

"I'll be fine." Clara attempted a smile.

Devyn sighed. "Okay. See you in bit."

Clara watched Devyn weave her way through sightseers on the crowded pier until she disappeared from sight. Clara returned her gaze to the ocean and scanned the horizon for Ally's birthday balloons. She hadn't expected to see them and took comfort in the idea that Ally had reached down from the heavens and snatched them from the sky.

When Devyn had suggested releasing balloons as a way to celebrate Ally's birthday, Clara warmed to the idea. She'd grown tired of being wrapped in a cocoon of mind numbing grief and soul consuming rage. In an effort to regain a semblance of balance, she'd begun reading books with inspiring stories about families who'd helped rape victims reclaim their lives. Clara had slowly come to terms with the fact that she could no longer help Ally, but maybe she could make a difference for other victims of violence.

The sun drifted closer to the sea as Clara replayed her day in court. Anger bloomed on her cheeks as she recalled Alexis Kent's accusations.

Scorned woman my ass.

Damian's face swam before her eyes and Clara gripped the rail, the rough wood biting into her palms. She wished she had the courage to permanently remove Damian's smug smile.

"Beautiful view, isn't it?"

Clara stiffened as she cut her eyes to the man next to her. She took in his profile; strong jaw line, close cropped hair, muscular frame. He turned toward her, his gray eyes reflecting the setting sun, and her heart fluttered. At first she was confused, then annoyed.

He's not that good-looking.

"No comment." Clara waved him off and looked back across the ocean.

"I'm not a reporter, Clara."

A whisper of familiarity resonated in her mind and Clara turned to search his face for clues.

He leaned on the rail, his attention on the sea. "Quite a day in court."

Court—that's where I've seen him. Clara fingered the Taser in her suit pocket. "Do I know you?"

He looked at her. "We haven't officially met. But we have a common problem. Damian Garza."

Clara noticed he flinched as if saying the name caused him pain. "I'm fairly certain you and I have nothing in common, but if you've come with a proposition to kill him, you're hired." The thought of Damian dead by someone's hand other than her own appealed to her.

"You can't afford the cost."

"You underestimate me, Mr. . . .?"

"Jones." He faced her and extended his hand.

Clara met his gaze and saw her agony reflected back at her. She shook his hand and desire flared in long-dormant parts of her anatomy. Her skin tingled from his touch and Clara blushed as she pulled her hand free of his grip.

"Jones . . . That's original." A nervous laugh escaped her. "Well, Mr. Jones, I'd be tempted to pay the price no matter how steep."

"Oh, I don't doubt you have the money." He cocked an eyebrow "It's your soul that can't afford the price."

Maybe I'm beyond caring about my soul. "Why are you here?"

"I have information about the jury."

"And what?" Clara squared her shoulders. "You want money?"

"No. I need you to deliver a message to DDA Hibbs."

Clara moved to step past him. "Deliver it yourself."

"I can't do that." He caught her by the elbow. "I helped bribe two jurors."

Clara glared at him and then looked at his hand on her arm. He tightened his grip slightly before releasing his hold.

"If your goal is to see Damian acquitted, we have nothing further to discuss."

He shook his head. "That's not my goal."

Clara crossed her arms. "And?"

"Let's just say I'm playing for both teams. The Garza family hired me to assure an acquittal—"

Clara gripped the Taser and pushed past him. "Goodbye, Mr. Jones."

"I'm also working for a conviction."

Clara turned and caught a glimpse of sorrow on his face.

"We want the same thing, Clara. We both want Damian to pay for his crimes." He looked down, then out across the ocean.

"Why are you interested in seeing Damian convicted for murdering my daughter?" Clara noticed his jaw muscles jump before he cleared his throat.

"Because he raped my sister and he's never been punished."

His words slammed into Clara like a fist to the gut. She leaned over the railing as a wave of nausea washed over her. How many women had Damian violated? How many lives had he destroyed? How could she have been so blind not to see the evil bastard she married?

Brady placed a hand on her shoulder. "Clara . . . are you okay?"

Clara nodded. "I'm sorry about your sister." Concern etched his face and for a moment she thought he was going to wrap her in his arms.

"Me too." He uttered, his voice was rough with emotion. "I-I wish I could have stopped him from—"

Tears welled in Clara's eyes and she put up a hand. "What . . . do you need me to do?" Participating in jury tampering was a criminal act, but a crime that registered far below the act of murder.

He handed her a slip of paper. "These are the names of the jurors who've been paid to vote not guilty. I believe the judge will replace them with the two alternates instead of declaring a mistrial."

Clara cocked an eyebrow. "Why would she do that?"

"It's the easiest solution."

"And the two jurors who are supposed to push for a guilty verdict?"

"They haven't received any money, so technically they haven't been bribed."

"Then how do you know they'll vote guilty?"

"Let's just say they have an incentive to do so."

They locked eyes in a stare that made Clara uncomfortable as her gaze settled on his lips, parted slightly, as if expecting something.

Mr. Jones broke the silence. "Tell the DDA an anonymous source gave you the names."

Clara's heart skipped a beat. *Anonymous, just like the notes delivered to the hospital.*

"Yes, of course." Clara swallowed and folded the note into a tiny square. "What if your plan fails and Damian goes free?"

"I have a back-up plan." His soft smile reached his eyes. "Trust me."

CHAPTER TWENTY-TWO

"Let me be perfectly clear," Alexis Kent said as she paced the small meeting room inside the Los Angeles County jail. "You will follow my instructions to the letter and refrain from interacting with any of the witnesses, especially your wife—"

"All I did was smile at her," Damian interrupted, "and the jury had already left the room."

Alexis stopped pacing and leaned palms down onto the table. "Mr. Garza." She glared at Damian. "I don't give a damn if you're innocent or guilty, but I do care if I lose."

Her silk blouse puckered just enough to reveal a glimpse of tantalizing cleavage. Damian dropped his gaze to enjoy the alluring mounds of flesh shimmering with sweat.

Alexis rolled her shoulders back and thrust her breasts forward improving his view. A rush of blood brought him to life and his flesh rubbed against the rough cotton of his prison issue boxers.

"Like what you see?" A hint of mint drifted out on her breathy tone.

Before Damian could respond, Alexis stood up and adjusted her blouse.

"Then I suggest you do exactly as you're told." She met his dark stare. "Or I'm going to file a motion to withdraw as your attorney and the only breasts you'll be ogling will be the man boobs of your cellmate."

Damian smiled at her as he leaned back in his chair and crossed his arms.

"Alan Sanchez is competent but he's not a criminal defense attorney." Alexis crossed her arms in matching posture. "And given the nature of this case . . ." A smile played across her blood-red lips. "I doubt you'll be able to hire another attorney in this city."

Damian looked into her electric blue eyes and wondered what they would look like filled with fear. "Ms. Kent, I do not like being threatened." He focused on controlling his anger. "Also, I believe it is unlikely a judge will allow you to resign." He shrugged. "Given the nature of the case . . ."

Alexis blinked and checked her watch. Damian sensed her weakness and wished he could bend her over the small table and teach her a lesson.

Once I am free.

Damian waited for Alexis to meet his stare again and when she did he thought her eyes looked darker than before.

"I'm not afraid of you, Mr. Garza." Alexis swept her hair back off her shoulders. "Rest assured I will make good on my threat."

Damian lunged across the table and seized her wrist as she reached for her briefcase. He pulled her toward him, their faces inches apart. "You should be."

The door banged open and a guard placed Damian in a chokehold. "Let go of her and sit your ass down," he barked.

Damian struggled and the guard compressed his windpipe. Damian released Alexis and threw his hands up in surrender. The guard gave one last squeeze and shoved Damian back into his chair.

"What the hell is going on?" Alan Sanchez asked from the doorway.

"Nothing." Alexis rubbed her wrist. "Damian and I had a slight difference of opinion regarding a new defense strategy." She smiled at the guard. "Thank you that will be all."

Alan cocked an eyebrow at Alexis. "New strategy?"

"Yes." Damian scowled at Alan who had barely glanced his way. "I am afraid my enthusiasm regarding Jia Dahl as a witness got the better of me." Damian shifted his attention to

Alexis, enjoying the look of confusion on her face. "My apologies, Counselor."

"Jia Dahl?" Alan's bewildered face mirrored Alexis's.

"Yes." His anger under control, he plastered a placid facade on his face. "Surely you recall suggesting Ms. Dahl testify about the conversation she overheard Clara having with her hairdresser. Ms. . . . what is her name again?"

"Vivienne Kimber," Alan said.

Damian nodded. "Alan, please give Alexis the abridged version?"

Damian knew he'd caught Alan off guard. Blackmailing Jia into testifying about a fictitious conversation had been vetoed by both Ricardo and Alan. Damian didn't care; neither of them faced the death penalty. He'd been patient, but enough was enough. The time had come for him to take matters into his own hands. Jia Dahl loved her brother and Damian knew she'd do anything to keep him alive.

Alan stared at Damian and cleared his throat. "Yes. But I thought we decided that Ms. Kimber would most likely deny the conversation ever happened."

The tips of Damian's ear burned and he wanted to scream at Alan to do as he was told. Instead, he steepled his fingertips and shrugged.

"Why am I just now hearing about this conversation?" Alexis pulled a notepad from her briefcase and sat down.

Damian held Alan's gaze before the attorney looked away and took a seat.

Good boy.

"Prior to Ally Marsh's death, Ms. Dahl claims to have been waiting for her appointment at Mane Style while Clara received services from Ms. Kimber." Alan mopped sweat from his brow and then tucked his handkerchief away. "She stated Clara told her stylist that she was sick of Damian's cheating. When Ms. Kimber suggested Clara leave Damian and file for a divorce, Clara complained she would get practically nothing due to the prenuptial agreement she signed."

Alan paused and straightened his tie.

Damian placed his hands flat on the table and leaned forward. *Not a bad off-the-cuff liar.*

"And why do you think Ms. Kimber will deny this exchange happened?" Alexis asked.

Damian bit the inside of his cheek to keep from jumping into the conversation.

"Clara and Ms. Kimber have been friends for years, which could cause her to dispute any conversation that paints Clara in an unfavorable light."

"Still," Alexis looked up from her notes. "I'd like to speak with Ms. Dahl. Alan, let's bring her in tomorrow at two pm."

"Fine, I will arrange it." Alan cast a nervous glance at Damian. "You should also know Ms. Dahl is one of Damian's dancers."

Alan had rushed the last sentence, his utterance a blur of sound in Damian's ears. The word *dancer*, however, had resonated loud and clear. Damian's jaw ached as he gritted his teeth.

Bastard.

"I see." Alexis looked from Alan to Damian, keeping her focus on Damian when she spoke. "Alan, is this another attempt to suborn perjury from one of Damian's employees?"

Alan hesitated, then responded in a firm tone, "No. But I thought, given the incident with Ms. Kane, you should know Ms. Dahl's history with Damian before you meet with her."

"Thank you, Alan." Alexis stuffed her notepad into her briefcase before snapping it shut and standing. "I'll have my investigator start digging into Ms. Kim—"

"That is not necessary." Alan shifted forward in his seat. "I have already done a background check and can get you the information by Monday."

"Great, but Monday's not soon enough." Alexis pushed her chair in. "Walk me out and I'll explain why."

Alan stood, but Damian remained seated, leaning back in his chair.

Alexis met Damian's cold stare with an equally cool gaze. "I trust we have an understanding about my earlier advice?"

Damian managed a conciliatory smile. "Absolutely, Counselor."

"Good." Alexis nodded. "Alan?"

"I have some business matters related to one of Damian's clubs I need to discuss with him." Alan smoothed his jacket. "I will call you after I have spoken with Ms. Dahl."

"Fine. Please deliver the Kimber information by noon tomorrow." Alexis gave a curt nod before signaling the guard she was ready to leave.

The conference room door clicked shut and silence filled the room. God he wanted to rip Alan's throat out and watch the attorney's life pump through the gaping wound, but Damian knew if he moved one muscle the guards would repeat their earlier restraint tactics. He flinched in surprise when Alan rammed his chair into the table and began pacing the room.

"Are you fucking nuts?" Alan shouted.

"Control yourself and watch your tone," Damian warned.

Alan ran his hands through his hair, dragging them down over his face as he shook his head. "You do not seriously think a woman you tried to rape is going to aid in your defense do you?"

"Sit down," Damian commanded.

Alan lapped the small room before sitting in Alexis's vacated chair. He loosened his tie and slumped back.

Damian lowered his voice. "I think if Jia is interested in keeping her brother alive, she will do exactly as she is asked."

"And what will keep her from going to the police as soon as she is presented with your proposition?"

"You are going to arrange for her brother to disappear until the trial's over and she has served her purpose."

"Okay, say she agrees to perjure herself for you, what is going to stop her from going to the police after the trial?"

Damian stared at Alan. He wanted to say because she'll be with me far away from here. But Damian knew Jia would never agree to run away with him.

Alan began shaking his head and sat taller in his chair. "I will not be party to killing her or her brother." He stood and headed for the door. "You will have to find someone else."

The thought of killing anyone who stood in the way of his freedom didn't bother Damian, but he knew he needed Jia and her brother. And, for now, he needed Alan. "Alan, you know my father will be disappointed if you do not help me."

Alan's hand rested on the doorknob, but he didn't respond.

"Here is what I would like for you to do." Damian's tone was pleasant, as if he were asking for a favor. "Arrange a trip for Quan Dahl to Puerto Rico. Get him a room at the Condado Plaza with a half million-dollar line of credit. Call Alfredo, the floor manager, and explain our situation, he will take care of everything else."

Alan turned and nodded.

Damian drank in the resignation he saw in Alan's eyes. "Before you speak with Jia, call our bank in the Cayman's and open an account in her name and prepare a wire for a million dollars. After you tell her what we need, you can give her a copy of the wire, which of course we will fulfill after she testifies, along with a copy of an open plane ticket to the Caymans. Tell her once she is on her way, we will arrange for Quan to join her."

Alan returned to his seat and began taking notes. Damian thought the attorney seemed smaller than he had a few minutes ago, which sent a wave of pleasure coursing through him.

"Now, about Vivienne Kimber."

"Our preliminary background check did not turn up anything we can use against her."

"Then you have your work cut out for you." Damian paused. "Because if I am convicted, I will not have any further need for you . . . or any reason to keep you alive."

Alan met Damian's dark stare, and when the attorney's eyes filled with dread, Damian flashed a triumphant smile.

CHAPTER TWENTY-THREE

An undercurrent of illegal activity flows through the underbelly of Los Angeles. Two years ago, Brady had tapped into this slimy resource looking for the perfect smalltime crook to introduce him to the Garza organization.

Shane Sackett turned out to be that guy. A legitimate business owner, Shane, or as he was known on the street, SOS, operated a successful print business. *Print This!* customers could do everything from making plain black and white copies, to printing business cards, to producing spectacular color brochures. The print shop used state of the art machinery and housed old print presses that could recreate aged documents as well as new ones. Should you have a need for fake documents, Shane Otis Sackett was your man.

Brady had already purchased all the necessary documents needed to match the identity he'd adapted long ago. Initially, he had wondered whether the twenty-something kid sitting across from him was capable of delivering pizza let alone creating documents worthy of Homeland Security scrutiny.

When Shane did a background check after their first meeting, Brady was pleased to know his documents were solid. But there was a glitch; Brady's cyberspace profile didn't quite match his paper history.

"Hey, man," Shane said at their third meeting. "You should know there are holes in your background."

Brady waited a beat, measuring whether Shane's knowledge would pose a threat or come in handy.

"It's no big deal." Shane uncapped a water bottle. "When I ran a web search on you, nothing popped up about your time in the Shasta County lockup for assault."

Sweat beads dotted Brady's temples. "Maybe Shasta County isn't part of the World Wide Web yet."

Shane shook his head. "I checked and they've been online for the past five years."

Brady resisted the urge to wipe away the sweat trickling down the side of his face.

"I can fix it for you," Shane said. "For a price, of course."

"How exactly?" Brady held Shane's stare. "I thought paper was your specialty."

Shane nodded. "Yep, I'm good at paper. But in today's world, you have to make sure internet searches reveal the same information as a paper trail. I dated a chick who's a master hacker and she taught me a few things. If I can't handle a job, I hire her."

"How much?" Brady didn't care about the cost, but asking was part of the dance.

"Five g's if the fix is easy." Shane took a pull from a water bottle. "If we have to get Abby involved, the cost goes up."

Brady had forked over five thousand dollars for Shane and Abby to work their magic and waited three months for his introduction to one of the Garza family soldiers.

And so here he was, back at the beginning, needing SOS's help in creating a new identity.

Brady stepped into the interior of *Print This!* and a wall of cool air, mingled with the scent of toner, paper and linseed oil, engulfed him. A young Hispanic girl smiled at him from behind a work counter. "Can I help you?"

"I have an appointment with Mr. Sackett."

"Oh, si." She nodded. "I will tell him you are here. Uno momento." She held up a finger and disappeared through a pair of double doors.

Brady glanced around the shop, taking in stacks of paper boxes and a Canon copier with instructions listed in both English and Spanish on how to operate the commercial beast.

The counter clerk popped back through the doors and returned to her stapling project as Shane appeared behind her, carrying a large box with UCLA MEDICAL CENTER marked on the side.

147

"Hey, Bro. What's up?"

Brady offered the chin lift version of hey. "I need a quote."

Shane placed the box on the counter and waved Brady toward the back. "Let's talk in my office."

The two men trekked through print shop's work area to a small office in the back. Shane pointed to a chair facing his desk as he took a seat. At six-five, Shane Sackett was a formidable figure. Large biceps strained against the sleeves of his black T-shirt. He'd let his close-cropped hair grow out and wisps of dark bangs curled across his forehead.

"Haven't seen you in a while." Shane tilted back his oversized chair.

Brady met Shane's curious stare. "Been busy."

"I'll bet." Shane laced his fingers behind his head. "This Damian business is crazy."

Brady nodded. "It's a mess all right."

"What's the project?"

"I need to know the timeline and cost for a new identity."

"For you or someone else?"

"Just inquiring." Brady didn't want to admit he might need to disappear if his plan worked and Damian was found guilty.

Shane shrugged. "Standard packet . . . Ten days, ten grand."

"And for a twenty-four hour turn around?"

"You worried about the trial?"

Brady's turn to shrug. "Maybe."

Chair legs banged against the floor when Shane leaned forward. "Twenty grand, but I'm going to need at least a forty-eight hours' notice."

"Fine." Brady stood. "I'll get back to you."

"You involved with Garza's plans to take care of Clara permanently?"

Brady hoped his surprise didn't show on his face. "What's the time frame?"

Shane gave a palms up shrug. "Any day."

Shit! "I hadn't heard." Brady saw conflict in Shane's eyes and focused on keeping his expression neutral. "What's it to you?"

"I met her once at Always Welcome, where I coach youth basketball." He rubbed the stubble on his chin. "Nice lady. Someone should warn her."

"I'm guessing she's safe under the protection of the police." Brady turned toward the door. "I'll be in touch . . ."

"Hey, man." Shane shot to his feet. "You know the police are no match for whoever Garza's hired, beside he's probably paid off whoever's guarding Clara. Maybe I should warn her myself."

Brady shook his head. "No, you shouldn't. Find someone else."

Shane nodded. "Okay, how about you?"

CHAPTER TWENTY-FOUR

Smog blanketed Los Angeles Saturday morning, defusing the sun and creating a vacuous climate that emphasized Clara's sense of unease. She hadn't slept well, tossing and turning as images of Mr. Jones replaced the faceless visitor who'd stroked her hair during her hospital stay. The words *trust me* had echoed through the endless night. Concerned eyes above full, sensuous lips haunted her dreams. Clara longed to trust someone, but knew it would be foolish to trust a man she'd just met. *To trust any man.*

Lisa placed a cup of coffee in front of Clara and sat across from her, the large mahogany conference table gleaming in between them.

"Sloan." Lisa looked at her co-counsel. "What did our investigator find?"

"Hannah discovered an interesting connection between Jia Dahl, aka China Doll, and Kandee Kane." Sloan consulted her notes and continued. "They're exotic dancers at a club called Blissful Beauties. Ms. Kane has an attorney and wouldn't answer any questions. Hannah's left several messages for Ms. Dahl, but no response so far."

Lisa asked, as she made a note on her legal pad, "Did you call Ms. Kane's attorney to setup a meeting?"

"Yes. Mason Stewart." Sloan smirked. "Lawyer to the beautiful and brainless hasn't responded."

"Call him again and tell him we're interested in making a deal for his client's testimony."

Sloan stood and headed from the room. "On it."

"Clara," Lisa said. "How well do you know Vivienne Kimber?"

"She's been cutting my hair for over ten years." Clara fingered a lock of hair. "I doubt she's part of Damian's lie."

"Still . . ." Lisa leaned back in her chair. "The salon's appointment book shows back-to-back visits by you and these strippers."

Clara rubbed her temples. "I've never met them."

"We're going to need to speak with Ms. Kimber." Lisa touched a pen to her chin. "I think she'll be more comfortable coming to the office if you invite her."

"All right." Clara reached for her cell phone. "How soon-"

"Today," Lisa said as Sloan stepped back into the conference room.

"After lots of bluster," Sloan rolled her eyes, "Stewart agreed to make his client available today at five."

Lisa consulted her watch and looked at Clara. "It's noon. Ask Vivienne to come in at two, I want speak with her before interviewing Ms. Kane."

Clara scrolled through her phone's address book, found the salon's number and pressed SEND. Anxiety crashed through her mind flipping over stones of worry. Damian was guilty, but what if the jury believed the scorned wife theory? What if the judge didn't replace the bribed jurists? What if, God forbid, Damian was acquitted?

Trust me.

A female voice echoed in her ear. "Mane Style. How can I help you?"

"Vivienne Kimber, please."

"I'm sorry; she's with a client. Can I have her return your call?"

Clara hesitated. "This is an emergency and I need to speak with her now."

"Can I tell her who's calling?" The faceless voice bordered on impertinent.

"Her doctor."

"One moment, please."

Clara waited through the classical hold music, then Vivienne's concerned voice filled her ear. "Doctor Bishop?"

"No, Vivienne. It's Clara Garza." Her words rushed out. "I need you to come to the district attorney's office today." She held her breath. "I need your help."

"Clara . . ." silence then, "I don't think I can help you."

"Please, Vivienne . . ."

"Tell her she can come in voluntarily or I'll subpoena her," Lisa said loud enough to be heard through Clara's phone.

Silence again.

"Vivienne?" Clara said.

"I heard her. I can be there around six."

"How does two o'clock sound?" Clara asked.

"Better than a subpoena." The line went dead in Clara's ear.

Clara dropped her phone into her purse and dug for the aspirin bottle.

"Clara?" Sloan said.

"Yes." She continued searching her handbag.

"What can I get you from the deli?"

Clara looked at Sloan. "Nothing, thanks. I'm not hungry."

Sloan glanced at Lisa. "I'll get some turkey sandwiches. Be back in a bit." She picked up her legal pad and exited the conference room.

The note Brady had given Clara lay at the bottom of her bag next to the aspirin bottle. Clara withdrew both items. She popped the cap off the bottle, shook out two tablets and downed them with a gulp of warm coffee.

"I know you're under a lot of stress, Clara," Lisa said. "Please don't worry; we're doing everything we can to ensure Damian goes to prison."

"About that." Clara fingered the note and met Lisa's green eyes. "An anonymous note was slid under the gate in Malibu." The lie tasted bitter on her tongue.

Lisa extended her hand for the note and Clara laid the note in her palm. "I think this means there's been jury tampering."

"Shit!" Lisa scanned the message. "Damn it. Even if this isn't true, the judge will have to consider a mistrial."

Mistrial? Clara licked dry lips with an ever drier tongue. "Wh-what about the alternate jurors?"

"There's no way to be sure only these two have been bribed." Lisa rose and paced around the table. "I have to present this to the judge." She looked at her watch again. "Put the note back in your purse. I want to get this meeting with Vivienne over first and have Hannah start checking juror bank accounts for a money trail."

Sweat seeped from Clara's skin. "What if there isn't one?"

"There's always a trail, we just have to find it."

"Then what?"

"Then it's up to Judge Bailey." Lisa sighed. "Thank God she's a judge who can't be bribed. This might just piss her off enough that she'll want to proceed with the trial. She banged a fist on the conference table. "Screw the almighty Garza family!"

Lisa's slamming fist competed with the pounding in Clara's head and she rubbed her temples again.

Screw the family and they'll want revenge. Fine, but I'll have mine first.

CHAPTER TWENTY-FIVE

Damian Garza sat on a cement stool, staring through the thick security glass at the empty seat on the other side. His visitor had taken a call and stood with his back to Damian. A guard stopped behind Damian, leaned over him and rapped on the partition.

Flavio Vargas turned, cell phone still pressed to his ear, and nodded.

"If he's not off in a min—" the guard began.

Flavio ended the call. "My apologies." He offered a slight head bow. "Something that could not wait."

The guard tapped Damian on the shoulder with his baton. "You've got ten minutes."

Damian acknowledged the guard with a nod, his eyes still on his visitor. He'd never met Flavio Vargas but had heard a great deal about him over the years. Legend had it that young Flavio had been teased by his schoolmates for his blond locks, an uncommon trait for Hispanics and the reason for his undesirable moniker, to the point that he shaved his head.

When his tormentors shifted their focus to his now-bald pate, Flavio endured their taunting day in and day out . . . until they began to disappear one by one.

Flavio sat in the visitor's stool, perched on the edge as if he didn't plan to stay long.

Damian lifted the wall-phone and waited for his guest to do the same.

Flavio picked up the receiver and looked at the ear piece with disgust. "Senor Garza, since our time is short I will make my report brief."

"Fine."

"The matter you inquired about has been considered and I believe is well within my company's scope of expertise."

Damian nodded.

"Also, I believe the fee you suggested will be adequate to cover all three phases as well as any unexpected costs."

"I am still committed to paying a bonus for an expedited completion of these projects." Damian wanted to add that he'd also pay a bonus to assure the excessive pain and suffering of his targets, but no one told Flavio Vargas how to do his job. The hitman specialized in tortuous kills that resembled sinister accidents, which would have to be enough to sate Damian's need for revenge.

"Understood. I do not anticipate any issues that will prevent our meeting your requested end dates, except, of course, your instructions to cease and desist." Flavio stood and smoothed the front of his suit jacket. "Unless you have any further questions, my firm will send you a final bill after the completion of these ventures."

"No. I believe we are in agreement." Damian didn't stand, but met Flavio's pale blue eyes. He hated being in a position of submission to anyone. However, he knew better than to show disrespect for an assassin, even one in his employ.

"Good. I hope your stay in this . . . facility ends soon." Flavio hung up the wall-phone and, wiping his hands with a handkerchief, headed for the exit.

Damian replaced the receiver, stood and strode from the room. A large metal door slammed shut as he entered the corridor leading to his cellblock. The decibel level of the block reached him before he stepped through the last set of gates. Prisoners filled the common area, eating lunch, watching television and playing cards. The aroma of chicken pot pie mingled with the scent of stale garlic bread and Damian's stomach growled despite the disgust that wrinkled his nose.

He stepped through the gate and weaved his way through the throng, making eye contact with no one. The hardest thing to adjust to in prison was the constant presence of others. What he missed most though, was the ability to study his beloved *estrellas* at night. He'd spent his first few nights of incarceration mentally projecting the constellations on the ceiling of his cell, but found the exercise only served to fuel his rage for those who'd placed him behind bars.

In the four months he'd been incarcerated, Damian had managed to stay out of trouble. Of course his family name helped and even the generals of the different prison gangs steered clear of him. His only run-in had been with a member from the *Los Niños Muertos* intent on making a name for himself. The kid, who'd cornered Damian in the laundry room during one of his shifts, had demanded cigarettes in payment for protection.

"It does not matter who you are, senor, you still must pay." The scrawny twenty-year-old flashed a toothbrush honed into a sharpened point and held out his hand.

"You are wrong." Damian continued folding towels. "It does matter who I am, especially to you."

The kid brandished the shiv, his hand shaking and took a step back. "I-I am not afraid of you."

Damian was on the young man in a flash, breaking his wrist as he stripped him of the makeshift weapon.

"Mierda!" The young man cradled his injured arm as he backed into the wall. "You broke my hand."

"No. I broke your wrist and if you ever threaten me again . . ." Damian relished the look of terror in the kid's eyes. "I will break your neck and you really will be a dead boy. Comprender?"

The young gang member nodded. "Si, si, Jefe."

Damian later heard through the prison grapevine that the kid claimed to have slipped and fallen in the yard. From that point on, neither the would-be gang hero, nor any other inmates crossed Damian.

As Damian navigated the common area, a voice called out behind him.

"Hey, Garza."

Damian knew who spoke without turning and motioned for him to follow.

"What do you want, Malik?" Damian stepped into his cell.

"You said ya wanted to know if any new fish has arrived that's got a thing for rape."

Damian gave the gaunt black man his full attention. "And?"

"Young guy came in yesterday." Malik shifted from foot to foot. "Got popped for raping and torturing his girlfriend."

"What type of torture?" Damian crossed his arms and leaned against a small metal table anchored into the cement floor.

"Some sorta cross-like brand on her leg." Malik rubbed his stubbly chin.

"Is he in holding?"

"Yeah, for a couple of days, till he's processed."

"Can you arrange for him to be my cellmate?"

"Sure, sure." Malik scratched his forearm, inspecting his skin as if he'd opened a wound. "It's gonna cost a bit."

"Find out how much and I will think about the new guy."

"Got it." Malik turned to leave.

"Malik." Damian loathed having to depend on a tweaker in need of a fix, but he'd learned early on that Malik Amari had the uncanny ability to procure any information Damian wanted. "What do you need?"

"Me?" Malik's thin smile showed a row of rotten teeth. "Nothing, man. I'm good."

"Fine. Let me know if that changes."

"Sure, sure." Malik nodded his goodbye.

Damian already knew he wanted the new guy for his roommate, but maintaining a posture of indifference was important to maintain his illusion of self-sufficiency. He wanted his fellow inmates to see Damian Garza as a man who didn't need anyone or anything.

CHAPTER TWENTY-SIX

Vivienne Kimber paced the small waiting area of the District Attorney's Office. Her long auburn hair danced down her back as she scanned the sparsely furnished room and her eyes narrowed when she spotted Clara.

Clara wiped sweaty palms on her capris and crossed the well-worn carpet. "Thanks for coming, Vivienne."

"Like I had a choice." Vivienne hitched her purse higher onto her shoulder.

Clara cocked an eyebrow. "I don't understand why you don't want to help me."

Vivienne pursed her lips and then heaved a sigh. "Because I'm afraid of the Garza family and you should be too."

Clara jammed her hands onto her hips. "What I'm more afraid of is that Damian will get away with killing my daughter!"

The two women squared off, unaware of the small group listening to their heated argument.

"Ladies," Lisa said as she approached, "let's take this discussion into my office." She held open a door that led to an internal hallway. "Thank you for coming, Ms. Kimber." Lisa angled around her desk, temporarily back-lit by sunlight streaming through a large window that offered a sprawling view of the city. "Please, sit."

Vivienne sat and smoothed wrinkles from her floral-print skirt as Clara sat in a matching utilitarian chair.

"We need to clarify a few points that arose during Clara's testimony yesterday." Lisa glanced from Vivienne to Clara and back again.

"As I tried to tell Clara on the phone." Vivienne sat taller. "I don't believe I can help. I don't know anything and I really don't want to get involved in this . . . situation."

"I understand," Lisa said, "but let's go over a few things to be sure you don't have any useful information."

"All right." Vivienne shifted in her chair and crossed her legs.

Lisa slid a glossy eight-by-ten picture across the desk. "Do you recognize this woman?"

Vivienne shook her head. "No."

Clara stared at the photo of Kandee Kane; her bouffant, reddish-gold hair curved around a face caked with make-up and Clara stiffened at the sight of the amber pendant plunging into the cleavage of her massive breasts. *That's my necklace.*

"You've never been her hairstylist?" Lisa tapped her pen on her pad.

Vivienne snorted a small laugh. "God, no. Her dye job is appalling and the color is all wrong for her complexion."

"Ms. Kane claims you're her stylist and that on several occasions she had back-to-back appointments with Clara in your salon."

"That's absurd." Vivienne cut her eyes to Clara. "Do you know her?"

"No. She's the stripper who tried to provide Damian with an alibi."

The color drained from Vivienne's face. "A stripper at Blissful Beauties?"

"Yes." Lisa raised an eyebrow. "Why?"

"Our new receptionist used to dance there." Vivienne frowned. "Mane Style was sold a couple of years ago, and the new owners have made changes, most of which haven't been good for business."

Lisa's pen scratched across the page of a legal pad. "Who are the new owners?"

"The Estrella Corporation," Vivienne said.

"Shit!" Clara jumped to her feet. "That's Damian's corporation."

"How do you know?" Lisa said.

"It's a long story but trust me—he owns Estrella Corporation." Clara paced the small office. Damian loved stars and constellations. When they were first married, they used to lug his massive telescope to Joshua Tree national park so they could spend the evening gazing at the estrellas.

Lisa turned her attention to Vivienne. "Do you know Jia Dahl?"

Vivienne shook her head. "The name doesn't sound familiar."

Lisa consulted her notes. "She's a colleague of Ms. Kane's and dances as China Doll at Blissful Beauties."

"Sorry." Vivienne shrugged. "I don't know her."

"What's the name of your new receptionist?" Lisa asked.

Vivienne wrinkled her nose. "Paisley Pashun."

Clara stop pacing. "Jesus, it sounds like the salon is becoming an extension of the strip club."

Vivienne stood. "Look that's all I know. Can I go now?"

"Wait . . ." Clara placed a hand on Vivienne's arm and looked at Lisa. "Don't you think she needs protection until she testifies?"

"What?" Vivienne held up her hands. "Are you nuts? I'm not testifying; I don't know anything!"

"That's why we need you to testify." Lisa leaned back in her chair. "You don't know these women, which shoots down the defense's theory that Clara knows them or that she saw Damian with them at your salon."

"You can't make me testify!" Vivienne crossed her arms.

"Yes, I can." Lisa stood behind her desk. "And I can have you arrested if you refuse to cooperate. It's your choice, Ms. Kimber. Spend the night at a hotel or in jail.

"Trust me, Vivienne," Clara said. "You want to choose the hotel."

CHAPTER TWENTY-SEVEN

Clara stared through the window at the sea of traffic surrounding the town car as the driver headed for Malibu along the busy Pacific Coast Highway. It had been a long day and she yearned for a hot bath and a glass of red wine. Maybe several glasses would put her in a blissful wine coma. Clara sighed. Probably all she'd accomplish is a hangover.

She'd been unable to sleep Friday night thanks to Damian's pink roses delivery, the hellish day in court and Mr. Jones' surprise visit to the pier. Devyn had welcomed Clara home with her favorite dinner of shrimp fajitas and a pitcher of margaritas. After dinner, they finished the margaritas as they sat in weathered beach chairs and listened to the pounding surf. This morning after coffee, Devyn left for Astoria where her presence was required at a board meeting for her foundation Survivors of the Sea.

Clara checked her watch again, mentally estimating where Devyn might be in her trek home. She'd expected Devyn to call after her plane landed in Portland but guessed she planned to call once she was en-route to Astoria, a trip that could be daunting in February. Clara imagined Devyn navigating the winding Oregon coast highway through rain, wind and possibly snow.

The setting sun bled a burnt-orange hue into the ocean as the town car came to a stop at the gates of the bungalow. Lisa had arranged for a patrol car to be stationed at the beach house after Damian's flower magic trick and the sight of the well-marked car gave Clara a small measure of comfort. The security gates swung open as one of the officers climbed from the vehicle and marched toward the town car.

"Ms. Marsh," the driver said through the lowered window.

"Right." The officer nodded at Clara and waved the car forward.

"Will you need me tomorrow?" the driver asked as he pulled through the gate.

"No, thank you." Clara smiled at his reflection in the rearview.

He came to a stop and hopped out to open Clara's door. "Have a nice night, Ms. Marsh."

"Thanks." Clara stepped from the car. "You too."

She unlocked the front door and the aroma of Italian spices enveloped her as she stepped into the entryway. "Devyn?" Clara locked the door. The dining room, visible through a set of French doors on the other side of the office, was awash in soft ambient light.

"Was your flight canceled?" Clara set her purse on the foyer table, kicked off her flats and padded across the cool tile floor toward the kitchen. "Devyn?"

No answer. Clara stopped in her tracks. Her chest tightened and her pulse beat out a warning.

Weapon. She grabbed a wrought-iron candlestick and backed slowly toward the door, snagging her phone before she turned and came face-to-face with Mr. Jones.

Clara swung the candlestick, but he caught her forearm and wrestled the decorative weapon from her hand.

"Shit! How the hell did you get in here?"

"About that." Jackson Brady placed the candlestick back on the entry table. "You're going to need to beef up your security."

"I'm calling the police." Clara pushed buttons on her phone. "There's a car just outside the gate."

Brady took the phone from her trembling hand. "You can call them after dinner. I'm hungry." He brushed past her and disappeared into the kitchen.

Clara stepped toward the front door, but hesitated. *If he wanted me dead, probably he wouldn't be cooking dinner.*

She spun around and marched after him. "Who the hell are you?"

Brady handed her a glass of red wine and then returned to tossing a green salad in a large wooden bowl.

Clara wanted to guzzle the wine. "What are you doing here?"

"I'll explain everything while we eat." He hefted a large serving dish and headed toward the dining room. "Bring the salad."

Clara one-handed the bowl and followed him. Two place settings of nautical-themed china adorned the antique table. A fire burned lowed in the fireplace located on the far side of the living room. Brady took a seat as Clara placed the bowl in the middle of the table. He refilled his glass and then he offered her the bottle. She shook her head as she sat and crossed her arms.

"What's your real name? Why are you here? How the hell did you break into my house?"

Brady dished a helping of spaghetti onto her plate and then served himself. "Jackson Brady." He reached for the salad bowl and repeated his serving ritual. "As I said on the pier, we both want to see Damian pay for what he's done."

Clara reached for her wine glass. "And breaking and entering?"

"I scaled the fence from the neighboring property. Covered the razor wire with a heavy blanket." He forked in a mouthful of spaghetti, holding her stare as he chewed and swallowed. "Then bypassed the security system. The lock on your bedroom window was easy to manipulate."

Clara held his gaze for a moment before breaking eye-contact and taking a small bite of salad.

"The security system is good but outdated. I just crossed a couple of wires . . ."

"I get the picture." Her had shook as she finished off her wine. *Had Damian used the same methods to leave the vase of roses on the porch? I can't stay here . . .*

"Your spaghetti's getting cold."

Clara pushed her plate away. "I'm full." *I need to get rid of Brady and move to a hotel.*

He dipped a breadstick into a pool of sauce. "What did DDA Hibbs say about the jury tampering information?"

Clara saw his lips moving, but didn't hear what he said. She couldn't stop thinking about running. *This house isn't safe.*

"Clara." As if sensing her fear, he held her hand in his. "You're safe with me."

"Damian left roses on the porch . . ." her voice cracked, "he could've killed me?"

Concern clouded his eyes. "I'm not going to let anything happen to you."

Clara nodded and reached for the bottle of wine. Brady's fingers brushed hers as he picked up the bottle and poured her half a glass. A warm sensation bloomed within her, calming her anxiety and melting the edges of the icy walls she'd encased herself in.

"So what did DDA Hibbs say about the information you gave her?"

Clara sipped some wine. "She said she'd have to tell Judge Bailey immediately."

"Good." He sipped from his glass too. "Let's hope the judge puts the alternates in place of these jurors."

"Lisa plans to have her investigator look for a money trail."

Brady nodded, leaned back in his chair and stared across the room as if seeing into the future. Clara took the opportunity to study him. While not drop-dead gorgeous, he was attractive in a ruggedly handsome way. She guessed him to be forty-something, even though his taut physique suggested a younger man.

She wanted to ask about the sadness in his eyes. She wanted to smooth the pain lines etched in his forehead. She wanted to trust him. Instead, her flight instinct returned, reminding her she needed to flee. She pushed her chair back. "Thanks for dinner. I'll show you out."

"You can show me where some blankets are for the couch."

"You're not staying here." She took her plate and headed for the kitchen.

Brady followed her with his own dishes, which he placed in the sink on top of hers. He turned and stepped toward her, and Clara instinctively backed away, bumping into the counter. "I'm not leaving," he said.

"Fine. Stay. I'm checking into a hotel." She moved to step around him.

Brady closed in, pinning her against the cold marble edge. She held up a hand as he reached around her, retrieving another bottle of wine. His breath warmed her cheek as she palmed his chest and shoved. She might as well have been trying to move a brick wall. His lips parted in a slight smile as she tried to push him again.

"You can't stay here." Her tone lacked conviction.

"Let's discuss it by the fire." He left the kitchen, leaving her weak in the knees.

Brady poured wine into their glasses, pulled a picture from his back pocket and handed the photo to Clara.

She studied the pale face framed by long, blond hair. "Who's this?"

"He's the hitman who's been hired to kill you." He set the wine bottle onto the coffee table.

Clara fell onto the couch, thankful she didn't land on the floor and studied the photo. "How do you know he's a—a hitman?"

"Trust me." Brady sat next to her. "You're in danger. That's why you're not leaving and I'm not leaving you alone until this trial is over, Damian's gone to prison and you're safely out of the country."

CHAPTER TWENTY-EIGHT

The doorbell rang and Clara jumped to her feet.

"Are you expecting someone?" Brady said.

She headed for the front door. "No, I—Shit! Devyn."

He followed close on her heels. "Wait."

"It's the police," Clara said over her shoulder.

"How do you know?"

"Because I haven't heard from Devyn." She reached for the deadbolt. "Something must've happened."

Brady grasped her arm, his voice low. "Ask who it is."

Clara nodded. "Who's there?"

"Ms. Marsh, it's Officer Frey." His deep voice resonated through the closed door. "Ms. Hibbs asked us to check on you. Is everything okay?"

"Yes." She cut her eyes to Brady. "Why?"

"We need a visual confirmation. Can you open the door please?"

Brady stepped closer, leaned over her shoulder and looked through the peephole. "Ask to see his badge," he whispered.

Clara jumped when the officer spoke again.

"Ms. Marsh?" Frey's tone suggested annoyance.

"I recognize his voice." She reached for the door knob again.

Brady placed his palm against the door and shook his head.

"Can you show me your badge?" Clara chewed a finger nail.

"Sure." A tinny click followed his answer.

Brady spied through the peephole again, then nodded as he stepped into the office and closed the door.

Clara pasted a smile on her face, flipped the deadbolt and opened the front door.

"Ma'am." He nodded. "Is your cell phone working properly?"

"What?" *Shit.* "Why?"

"Ms. Hibbs became worried when you didn't answer your phone."

Clara palmed her forehead. "Oh, the battery must be dead." She hoped the grin on her face masked her irritation at Brady for taking her phone. "Thank you, Officer. I'll call her right now."

He smiled for the first time. "Have a good night."

"Thanks. You too."

Officer Frey nodded and headed back to his patrol car. Clara locked the door and whipped around.

Brady waggled her phone. "The battery is dead."

Clara snatched it from his hand and stomped into the office in search of her charger. When she returned to the living room she discovered a stack of blankets and pillows sitting on the floor next to the couch. Clara snapped her phone into a charging case, which brought her screen to life, showing she had two texts each from Devyn and Lisa, and two voice mail messages.

Devyn's first text said she'd arrived home safely. Fifteen minutes later, her text indicated she was clearly worried: *Clara, where the hell are you? Why haven't you called me?*

Lisa's texts echoed Devyn's concern. Clara switched to her voice mail and listened to Devyn's, which said, "Shit, I'm calling Lisa." Lisa message said she'd called the police.

Clara checked her watch. It had been over an hour since Devyn's first text. She dialed Devyn's number and texted Lisa while waiting for her friend to answer.

"Jesus, Clara! Where the hell have you been?"

"I'm fine. My phone died and I . . . I took a bath and forgot to charge it."

"You hesitated. You're lying."

Clara's cheeks colored as Brady walked in carrying a tray with coffee cups, cream and sugar. He cast a glance at Clara as Devyn's voice boomed from the phone.

"What the hell's going on?"

Clara met Brady's cool stare, then said, "Remember the man from the pier?"

"Yes. Why—wait he's there?"

"Yes."

"In the house? Are you crazy? You don't know him! What if he works for Damian and he's there to kill you?"

"Devyn, calm down. He has information . . ." Brady held his hand out for her phone. "He wants to speak to you."

"Clara, don't—"

"Ms. Corey," Brady said. "I know it's a lot to ask, but for now you're just going to have to trust me."

"Bullshit!" Devyn's voice roared from the phone. "You either leave, or I'm calling nine-one-one and reporting you as an intruder—"

"No, you're not. You're going to pull up an article on the internet, and once you've read it, call Clara back."

Clara finished off her glass of wine as she listened to the exchange. She watched Brady pace the living room, nodding his head and uttering an occasional yes. She couldn't explain why, but she felt safe in Brady's presence . . . she trusted him.

"I'm sure we'll still be up," Brady said before he disconnected and placed the phone on the coffee table. He picked up his wine glass, sat on the couch, his eyes focused on the fire.

Clara took a seat on the opposite end and poured a splash of wine into her own glass. She stole a glance at Brady who took a sip and continued to stare at the once again a low bed of embers.

"Tell me about your sister," Clara said.

Brady stood and added another log to the fire. "I find it odd that this house still has a wood burning fire place. Doesn't the owner know Southern California has a pollution problem?"

With his back turned to her, Clara couldn't help but notice his strong back, narrow hips and blue jeans that hugged a firm butt.

Brady prodded the dying fire and a flicker of life flamed up the sides of the dry wood. He moved to the sliding glass door and stared into the night as if he could see the undulating ocean pounding the dark beach below. Clara wondered if he too imagined meeting his sister at the elusive horizon, just as she did her daughter.

"Damian raped Iris when she was a freshman in college."

He turned and faced Clara, the sadness in his eyes a reflection of her own sorrow. Tears burned Clara's eyes. She took a breath and waited.

Brady drained his glass and returned to the couch. "I convinced her to file charges, but the NYPD didn't feel they had enough evidence to arrest Damian." He ran a hand over his close cropped hair.

Clara pushed a tear from the corner of her eye.

"The attack destroyed Iris. She dropped out of school and became a shut-in." His voice broke and he poured wine into his glass.

Clara wanted to reach out and touch his arm, offer some form of comfort, but she remained still. She knew his agony could not be hugged away.

"That's when I began tracking Damian. I found another victim, Sandy Hicks. She worked as a dancer at a club Damian owned. Her rape kit turned up a pubic hair that matched Damian and an arrest warrant was issued, but before the police could pick up Damian, Sandy died in a car accident."

Clara sucked in a breath.

Brady looked at her and nodded. "Yes, I think he had her killed."

"Bastard," Clara said.

"Iris committed suicide a month later. She couldn't live with the shame or the fact that Damian had marked her for life."

"Marked her?" Clara cocked an eyebrow.

"He carved a crude falling star into the inside of her upper thigh."

"A-a star?" *Estrellas. Damian was obsessed with them.*

Brady nodded. "He branded Sandy with the same mark."

"Are you sure Iris really . . . committed suicide?"

"No. She overdosed on prescription sleeping pills. The only red flag is she downed the pills with alcohol. Iris wasn't a big drinker and I've always wondered if someone forced fed her the vodka."

"I'm so sorry."

Brady fixed her with a stare that seemed to run the gamut of emotions; anger, sorrow, guilt. "I'm the one who's sorry."

"What?"

"I've been following Damian since Iris's death." He drained half his glass of wine. "He's always been one step ahead of me, leaving rape victims in his wake in foreign countries off and on for years. Jamaica, Brazil, Aruba . . . I finally convinced a young woman in Aruba to report her rape, but the police claimed they didn't have enough evidence to proceed."

"Did something happen to her as well?" Clara didn't want to know, but had to ask.

Brady shook his head. "I don't know. I couldn't locate her after the police voided her complaint." He reached for Clara's hand, covering it with his. "I suspected Damian of the Brentwood rapes. I should've acted sooner. If I had . . . Ally might still be alive."

Clara's throat constricted. "It's not your fault."

He shook his head. "I should've stopped him permanently, but I thought building a solid case against him was nobler than killing him."

Clara turned her hand palms up and grasped his tightly. "I should've handled my suspicions of Damian differently too." A tear escaped and trailed down her cheek.

Brady leaned in and brushed the tear away with his thumb. His touch filled Clara with peace. His gaze traveled to her mouth and her lips parted in expectation as if they had a will of their own. He moved closer, his musky scent stirring anticipation throughout her body. Brady searched her face as if looking for an objection, his hand now cradling her head, his fingers tangled in her hair. Clara reached up and touched the stubble on his cheek. The gesture seemed to be the encouragement he'd been waiting for. His lips touched hers.

This probably isn't a good idea.

The warning thought dissipated with the sound of her ringing cell phone.

CHAPTER TWENTY-NINE

Brady couldn't take his eyes off Clara. She stood staring into the dark night, speaking in hushed tones. He watched as she tucked hair behind her ear and his eyes traced her jaw line as it curved into the softness of her neck. A flicker of desire sparked at the thought of kissing that particular spot. He sucked in air and lifted the fireplace poker. Before he could tend to the smoldering fire, Clara switched ears, and shifted her weight from one foot to the other, the slight movement causing her hips to sway. Now the fire wasn't the only thing smoldering.

Clara nodded at whatever her caller had said. Brady assumed the voice on the other end belonged to Devyn. He stood poker in hand, mesmerized by Clara's beauty. Heat flushed his face as the urge to gather her in his arms pulsed through him.

"Okay," Clara said. "I'll tell him."

She disconnected and turned, meeting his schoolboy stare. Brady hoped the color had dissipated from his cheeks.

"Devyn?" He coughed to clear the huskiness from his voice.

"Yes." Clara moved to the coffee table and poured a cup of now lukewarm coffee. "She said she's sorry to hear about Iris and offered her condolences."

Sorrow seized Brady's heart as he nodded and added a log to the glowing embers. He pushed thoughts of his sister from his mind and turned his attention back to Clara. She was gone. He blew out a sigh, picked up the coffee tray and headed for the kitchen. No sign of her there. He set the tray down as his libido conjured up an image of Clara returning to the living room, stunning in red lace lingerie, inviting him to join her in the bedroom.

Jesus.

Still clad in slacks and cotton blouse, Clara appeared at the edge of the living room. "I thought you might need an extra blanket," she said as she placed a lighthouse-patterned quilt on the arm of the couch.

"I'm sure I'll be fine." He took a step toward her and she retreated behind the couch.

Clara nodded. "All right. See you in the morning." She picked up a book from the end table and exited the room.

"Shit," Brady muttered as he took the pillow and jammed it up against the arm of the couch. The fire popped and crackled as a log settled into the embers, sending a puff of smoke into the room. The smoky scent mixed with a hint of Clara's sensual floral perfume that lingered in the air.

He removed his ankle holster, slid the .38 free and placed the gun on the table. After kicking off his boots, he plopped down onto the soft cushions and lay back. He tucked his hands behind his head and ran the almost kiss incident through his mind. Had he misinterpreted Clara's signals? She'd responded to his touch by holding his hand. By touching his cheek. By embracing his lips.

When Devyn's phone call interrupted the moment, Clara had probably realized she'd crossed a line with him and decided getting involved on any level would be a mistake. And she'd be right. They needed to focus on their common goal—seeing Damian punished for his crimes.

Brady closed his eyes and Clara's face swam into focus. His heart stuttered and he could almost feel her lips meet his. The image disintegrated with a chirp of an incoming text message.

The screen on his phone read Shane, followed by his message: *Got message. Docs ready in 2 days. Later.*

Brady keyed in his response: *K. Talk tomorrow.*

He'd called Shane this morning and green-lighted the new identities for himself and Clara. She might not want to run once they accomplished their goal of sending Damian to death row, but he'd be ready if she did. His phone chirped again.

Shane had sent a new message: *Rumor VGs days are numbered. Know who?*

Brady sat up and read the message again. He shook his head.

Why would Damian order a hit on Valencia Garza?

CHAPTER THIRTY

Damian Garza couldn't sleep. He stared at the ceiling of his cell, illuminated from light filtering through the small window of the pod door, his mind a rolling tape of unresolved issues mingled with plans of retribution for those who had betrayed him.

Night sounds from other inmates bled through the thin walls of his cell, causing his agitation to flare. His thoughts jumped from strangling the snorer in the cell next to his, to knifing the mumbler two cells down who uttered nonsense throughout the night, to snapping the neck of the child molester across the hall who equated himself to being just like Damian.

Anxiety morphed into rage. He should never have been incarcerated in the first place, let alone jailed in the section of the Twin Towers that housed perverts and pedophiles. The bitches he'd raped had gotten exactly what they deserved, what they'd asked for.

Ally's smiling face projected back at him from the grey ceiling. Her voice filled his head.

"It's okay, Damian, I forgive you."

Damian gritted his teeth. Covered his ears. Closed his eyes. His breathing became ragged and his chest tightened.

Jesus, I need a drink.

He focused on the act of pouring a tumbler of tequila. Held the imaginary glass to his nose and inhaled the remembered smoky scent of the amber liquor. His throat burned as if he'd actually tossed down a shot.

Damian's mind shifted to his new cellmate. He'd only had two days to decide if he wanted Billy Boyd for a roommate. The Towers were usually overcrowded and it could be a matter of days or weeks before a new wave of scourge arrived. Besides, Damian liked the idea of controlling who shared his cell and had instructed Malik to make the arrangements. The tweaker had come by after dinner with the news.

"It's fixed," Malik had said. "Kids moving in with you tomorrow."

Damian nodded and motioned Malik into his cell. "How much?"

"Thing is," Malik bobbed his head and continued to gnaw his nail, "it's a bit more than normal."

Damian cocked an eyebrow. "Because . . .?"

"Cause it's you that wants the kid." The skinny Peeping Tom actually cringed as if he thought Damian might hit him.

"How much?" Damian faced him hands on hips.

"Ten g's."

"The usual account?"

"Yep, yep. Same account."

"Fine. I will have the money transferred by the end of the week."

"K. See ya." Malik gave a half wave and moved to leave.

"I am adding five thousand for you personally."

Malik's shuffle came to a halt and he stared openmouthed at Damian. A sour odor rode out on Malik's breath and he blinked a couple of times.

"But I better not find out you have already charged me double."

Malik wagged his head. "No, no. Wasn't even taking a cut this time."

Damian had smiled and waved Malik away.

The snorer let out a loud rumbling breath as Damian pummeled his pillow into a ball under his head and thought about Billy Boyd. The kid had carved a cross into his girlfriend's thigh, which piqued Damian's interest since he liked to brand his women as well. He'd finally created the perfect *estrella* on the thigh of the last bitch. It helped that she'd passed out from the initial pain—providing him with a still canvas. The five-point star was beautiful and he'd been especially pleased with the curling tails that he engraved down her thigh.

He'd paid each one of his conquests handsomely to keep their mouths shut. Most of them were strippers or hookers. Occasionally, though, he craved an interlude with an innocent female. Unfortunately, money didn't always keep them quiet and they had to be silenced permanently. But until Ally, Damian had never done the deed himself.

Damian didn't know anything else about his new cellmate, but knew that would change once he moved in. Damian intended to use Boyd as a pawn in his plan to seek revenge against those who'd set this fiasco in motion and who'd done nothing to extricate Damian from his current situation. Flavio would see to it that Valencia and Clara paid with their lives, but Damian wanted others to suffer and then live in fear of his retaliation.

He yawned, stretched and closed his eyes. He had just enough time for a power nap before the wake-up bells signaled a new day in hell.

CHAPTER THIRTY-ONE

Clara's back radiated heat as if Brady still watched her. She leaned against her closed bedroom door and recalled the image of his reflection in the living room window as she talked to Devyn. Goose flesh erupted along her skin with the memory of the emotions she saw play across his face. Longing. Lust. Embarrassment.

Getting involved with this man would be a mistake—a fact her mind hadn't quite convinced her body to accept as the same feelings pulsed through her. She stripped off her clothes and slipped on a white cotton top sprinkled with dark purple dragonflies and matching purple shorts. Heat lingered in Clara's cheeks as she imagined crawling into bed and snuggling into the crook of Brady's arm.

It had been a long time since she'd touched a man. Since she'd wanted to be touched by a man. She trembled as she recalled Brady's fingers in her hair.

"Stop it." Clara shook her head and marched into the bathroom. Face washed, teeth brushed, she reached for the bottle of Ambien. Should she sedate herself with a man in the house? Who seemed only to have protecting her in mind. Remembering the feel of his lip against hers answered the question. *Probably not a good idea.*

Clara returned the sleep aide to the shelf and decided on a couple of ibuprofen to abate the wine headache building in her temple. She swallowed the tablets with a gulp of water, padded to the bedroom door and touched the lock. Clara smiled and doubted a locked door would stop Brady from entering her room.

She threw the bedcovers back, stacked the pillows and looked at the book in her hand. Since Ally's death, Clara had read countless books offering insight into healing after the violent death of a child, all of which suggested one-on-one counseling. After her encounter with a well-known psychiatrist ended, once he told Clara she would never move forward until she admitted her failure as a mother, Clara embarked on her own quest for redemption. She joined several support groups and found comfort in sharing her story and volunteering to counsel others. She read books written by women who'd recovered from rape. Her current selection had been written by a mother who discovered her new husband was molesting his step-daughters. Clara brushed the dragonfly etching on Ally's locket with her fingertips. While nothing could bring her peace after Ally's horrific death,

Clara found solace in learning how other women survived similar tragedies.

She placed the biography on her nightstand and selected a romance novel from a disorganized bookcase. Her eyelids grew heavy before she finished the first chapter. She switched off the light; her last thought before falling asleep was Brady's warm lips against hers.

* * * *

Clara's eyes flew open and she shook her head. She couldn't breathe.

"It's me," Brady whispered, his hand covering her mouth. "The alarm's been disabled and someone's outside the house. Come with me."

Clara nodded and climbed out of bed.

Brady led her into the master bathroom where a nightlight cast shadows over the fixtures. He pulled back the shower curtain and motioned for her to step inside and lie down.

Every nerve in her body vibrated with the urge to run, but Clara did as instructed. Brady put a finger to his lips and slid the curtain closed. Darkness enveloped Clara as she lay against the cold porcelain, breathing in the scent of musty mildew and staring at the slightly illuminated ceiling. She closed her eyes and tried to listen, but her pounding heart filled her ears.

Her mind raced with solutions, landing on her phone. If she could get to her phone, she could call the police, who would notify the officers stationed in the car parked in front of the house.

Why hadn't Brady summoned the police?

Clara bolted upright when gunfire erupted from the back of the property. She cocked her head and strained to hear any other sounds. Nothing.

Her mind raced with different scenarios. The police discovered the intruder and shot him. They shot Brady. Brady shot the intruder. The intruder shot all of them, making her his last target.

"Shit." Clara stood and reached for the shower curtain. A floorboard creaked and she froze. The curtain flew open and she almost fainted.

Brady took her by the arm. "You need to get dressed." He helped her step from the tub and hurried her from the bathroom.

Clara stumbled behind Brady. "What happened?"

"I'll explain later. Put some clothes on. We need to go."

Her shaking hands found a pair of jeans sitting on top of the dresser. She pulled them on over her pajama bottoms and then pulled a sweatshirt from the same pile of clothes. She crammed her feet into a pair of sneakers and snatched her cell phone from the nightstand.

Brady held his hand out for the phone. Clara hesitated, then placed her phone in his palm. "You have to leave it behind," he said tossing the phone onto the bed.

"What the hell." Clara stepped toward the bed.

He took her hand. "Leave it."

Brady led her from the bedroom. Clara quick stepped to keep up with his long strides as they made their way through the dark house. He seemed to have perfect night vision as he headed for the sliding door off the living room. Clara bumped into him as he came to a stop and stared out the slider, his head swiveling from side to side.

"We're going down the bluff. There's a trail, but it's still a steep descent so hang on and I'll guide you. Don't speak until I do. Understand?"

She bobbed her head.

Brady slid open the door and led Clara into the dark night. The roaring ocean boomed in the distance and wind ruffled her hair. She crouched low like Brady as they scurried across the small backyard to the security fence. He tossed the blanket he'd used before over the razor wire, laced his fingers together for her foot and then hoisted her to the top of the fence. Clara struggled but managed to pull herself up and over, dropping down onto the soft sand.

Brady landed next to her and took her hand as they headed for the edge of the bluff. A half- moon hung low in the sky amidst a blanket of stars and the celestial orbs seemed to be lighting their way. When they stopped at the edge, she sucked in air as she stared down the side of the cliff. Seagulls screeching into the night seemed to echo her fear as the briny smell of the sea washed over her like a rogue wave. Brady squeezed Clara's hand and they began their descent. Sea grass brushed against her pant legs and she stumbled in the shifting sand, grabbing onto his arm for support.

The thunder of crashing waves greeted them when they reached the bottom. Brady tightened his grip and picked up the pace as they raced into the night.

CHAPTER THIRTY-TWO

Even tired and disheveled, Clara left Brady breathless. Light
from the rising sun spilled through the grimy window of the
Blue Whale Diner, casting a glow over her as she sat staring
at him. Clara hadn't said a word. Not as they fled up the
beach to the vacant lot where he'd parked his Rent-A-Wreck.
Not during the two hour drive down Highway 101. Not as
he'd wiped away their fingerprints and ditched the car in a 7-
Eleven parking lot just north of Oceanside.

She'd listened intently, occasionally tracing a water stain
on the chipped blue tabletop, while Brady had told her
everything, including the fact he'd left his former life behind
after Iris died and become obsessed with Damian. He
outlined his role in the Garza organization and explained how
he planned to use his inside access to see Damian punished.
When he apologized again for not stopping Damian before he
murdered Ally, Clara had parted her lips as though to speak,
but chewed her bottom lip instead. He explained he had sent
her the flowers with encouraging notes and visited her in the

199

hospital in an effort to assure her she wasn't alone in her quest for justice.

Now, as the diner began to fill with the morning rush and the smell of bacon wafted through the air, Clara looked out the window, across the highway, toward the Pacific Ocean. He studied her profile and wanted to offer a comforting caress. Clara jumped as the waitress thumped her pad with a pencil and shifted her gaze from Clara to Brady.

"You sure I can't get you something to eat?"

"No, thank you." Brady handed her a twenty-dollar bill. "Keep the change."

The waitress flashed a gapped toothed smile. "Thanks, hon. You two have a nice day."

His phone chirped with an incoming text from Shane. *B at ur place in 20.* Brady stood and offered a hand to Clara. "We need to go."

She ignored him, stepped from the booth and pushed through the diner door. Her anger baffled him, especially since he'd just saved her life? Still, he hated the idea of her being upset with him and pang of guilt washed over him as he trailed after her.

Brady took her elbow. "This way."

Clara jerked her arm free and stopped. "Where are we going?"

Her irritated toned echoed in his ears. "I have a house within walking distance of here. You'll be safe there."

"Safe?" She stomped her foot. "Are you kidding me?"

"Look, I know you're upset, but we need to get off this road."

"Someone tried to kill me!"

"Technically he tried to kill me." Brady fought the urge to grab her hand and drag her after him. "Coming?" He headed up the highway.

"Fine. But I'm calling the police when we get there."

Brady didn't respond. Now wasn't the time to tell her the police already knew about the shooting since the assailant had shot the policemen posted outside the house. They undoubtedly scoured the area looking for Clara, so he'd have Shane get word to DDA Hibbs that Clara was safe.

Mentally he checked his list of belongings, confident he hadn't left any trace of himself in the Malibu bungalow. He had learned over the years to touch as little as possible in public places. All the dishes they'd used had been run through the dishwasher and he'd wiped down the fireplace poker. Brady couldn't think of any surface that might yield his prints.

"How much farther?" Clara asked.

"We're here." Brady stepped from the roadside onto an overgrown trail and glanced over his shoulder to see if she'd followed. "My place is at the end of this path."

Crunching gravel turned into grainy sand as they made their way toward the sea. Brady had bought the property in the name of one of his aliases; to serve as an escape when he needed time away from the Garza organization. The rundown cottage sat on a rocky cliff overlooking the ocean, which provided built-in protection, but he'd installed a security system as an added safety measure. It never occurred to him that he'd be bringing someone here, and he worried about the lived-in look he knew he'd left behind after his last visit.

Brady stomped sand from his boots as he unlocked the front door and held it open for Clara. She marched into the small entry way, her sand-coated sneakers leaving debris in her wake. He threw the lock, reset the alarm and then followed her into the living room.

Clara, backlit in light from the huge picture window that framed an idyllic view of the bluff and ocean beyond, faced him with her hand extended. "Your phone."

"Thirsty?" Brady headed for the small kitchen and pulled two bottles of water from the refrigerator. He offered her one of the bottles, but Clara glared at him, her hand still palms up.

"Sit down." He sat on a well-worn maroon-colored couch. "We're going to call Devyn, but we need to talk first."

Clara crossed her arms, cocked a hip and glared at him. Brady held her stare and motioned toward a matching overstuffed chair. Clara lifted a T-shirt from the arm of the chair, dropped it to the floor and perched on the edge of the cushion.

He set one water bottle on an ancient coffee table, took a swig from the other and replaced the cap. "The policemen protecting you are dead."

Clara blinked at him and his chest constricted at the sight of fear in her eyes. He leaned forward, forearms resting on his knees, water bottle turning in his hands. "I wounded the assailant, but he managed to get away. You're safe for now, but you need to disappear."

Clara jumped to her feet as a knock at the door sounded simultaneously with a chirp from his phone.

Glancing at a text from Shane, Brady stood and said, "It's a friend of mine." He retreated to the front door.

"Hey, man." Shane stepped inside. "You're right; you'd never know this place was here."

"You walked?" Brady asked as he headed back to the living room.

"Yep and your rental's on its way back to the lot." Shane came to a stop beside Brady.

"Clara, this is Shane Sackett. Shane, Clara Marsh."

Shane offered his hand. "Pleasure to see you again."

Clara tilted her head as they shook hands. "Sorry, I—"

"We met when you donated gym equipment to Always Welcome."

A hint of a smile curved Clara's lips. "Yes, I remember, you're the basketball coach."

Shane nodded, sat on the couch and placed a large manila envelope on the coffee table, while Clara reclaimed the overstuffed chair.

"There's water in the frig." Brady picked up the envelope and slid a stack of documents free.

"Thanks, I'm good." Shane pointed at the papers. "All her new docs are there."

Brady flipped through a passport, examined a birth certificate and social security card, and lastly inspected a driver's license. He said the name silently to himself: *Mary Edwards.*

"What's going on?" Clara's gaze darted from Brady to Shane.

Brady handed her the papers. "This is your new identity."

She folded her arms.

"Clara, whoever Damian hired to kill you isn't going to stop until the deed is done. And if by some miracle, I fatally wounded him last night, Damian will just hire another hitman."

"I'm not going anywhere until this trial is over and he's behind bars." Clara sat taller.

Brady held her angry stare. God, she was stubborn. He blew out a sigh. "Fine. But you agree to leave town after the trial?"

She raised an eyebrow. "Define leave town."

"Shane has some ideas." Brady picked up his water bottle and took a long drink.

"Clara, I've researched some suitable places for you." He took a list from the pile of papers and handed it to her. "I know you speak a bit of Spanish and you once said in an article you'd like to learn Italian."

Clara scanned the short list of destinations: Spain, Costa Rica, Belize, Italy, Cayman Island.

"Of course," Shane continued, "we can look at stateside locations, but Brady thought it best you relocate outside the US."

Brady nodded. "It's better if you move somewhere that will make it difficult for Damian or his family to find you."

Shane offered Clara a second document. "These are some professions for you to consider."

As Clara perused the list, Brady's phone chirped. He looked at the display screen and read the message from Pedro Gomez: *Clara Garza missing. Find her!*

Brady went to an old bureau nestled on one side of a stone fireplace. He extracted three cell phones from a drawer, tossed one to Shane, and said, "Do you have an untraceable gun?"

Shane shook his head, and Brady moved to an antique roll-top desk on the opposite side of the fireplace, pushed up the slatted wooden panel and spun the lock on a small safe. He withdrew a handgun and a box of ammo and closed the safe.

"The phone's charged. I need you to call Lisa Hibbs and tell her Clara's safe."

Clara shot to her feet. "I want to call Lisa and I need to call Devyn."

Brady exchanged a look with Shane and then handed the second phone to Clara. "All right. But it's important you don't tell them where you are or who you're with."

"Like I know where I am." Clara pushed the phone's ON button. "And I'm telling Devyn I'm with you." She headed into the kitchen.

"What's up?" Shane asked.

"The Garzas know she's missing and want me to find her." Brady typed *On it* into his phone and hit SEND. "I can probably stall Pedro for twenty-four hours, but then he's going to expect an answer."

"What's the plan?" Shane checked the gun and then tucked it into the back of his jeans.

"While I work on persuading her to leave the country, I need you to get a line on the hitman."

Shane nodded. "Got it. We're going to need more phones, want me to pick up a few?"

"Yes." Brady pulled out his wallet and handed Shane a hundred-dollar bill. "Get six if you can."

Shane pocketed the money and headed for the door. "I'll text you when I'm on my way back."

Brady followed and peeled off another hundred. "Pick up some groceries too?"

"Yep." Shane took the bill and stepped outside.

Brady locked up and returned to the living room, where he found Clara looking out the window, arms hugging herself, sobbing quietly.

"Clara, I . . ."

"They didn't answer," she said to the window. Anger sparked in her eyes when she turned to face him. "You're crazy if you think I'm going to run."

He gritted his teeth and waited a beat. "And you're crazy if you think I'm going to let something happen to you."

"I have to see Damian convicted."

"I understand, but you won't see anything if you're dead." Brady wanted to fold her into his arms as tears trailed down her cheeks. "Clara, I know you're scared. That's why—"

"I'm not scared, damn it!" Clara swiped her cheeks. "I'm helpless. Helpless to protect Ally. Helpless to stop Damian. And I'm sick of being helpless."

Brady stepped toward her. "That's why you need to disappear." He wanted to thumb away her tears. "Damian's not going to stop."

"Then teach me to defend myself." Clara fingered the tears from her eyes.

Brady rubbed his chin stubble. "All right, but first you have to agree to disappear."

"I'll agree to consider it." Clara turned back to the window and resumed her self-hugging posture.

Brady watched her shoulders heave as she dissolved into tears again. He moved behind her and placed his hands on her shoulders. She turned into his embrace, burying her face in his chest. Her touch sucked the air from his lungs and all he could do was whisper into her hair. "It's going to be all right."

She lifted her face to him. "Promise?"

Brady covered Clara's lips with his in response. His need to protect her blurred with his desire to take her, and he couldn't stop himself from gathering her in his arms and carrying her to the bedroom.

CHAPTER THIRTY-THREE

Damian stared across his cell at the small clock sitting on the corner of the battered desk. Only thirty-five minutes of visiting hours left. Damian had thought he'd be the first called to the visitors' area where he'd find Flavio waiting with news that his first assignment had been completed. Instead, he'd passed the day sulking in his cell, watching his new roommate read a self-help book on litigation.

Billy Boyd had barely spoken to Damian since he'd moved in two days ago. According to Malik, Boyd's attorney had petitioned for a new trial claiming evidence from the first trial for raping his girlfriend had been compromised by the police department. Damian wondered if the blond bumpkin from Oklahoma had the means to pay for contaminated evidence. *Doubtful.* The crime scene investigators most likely screwed up and gave the kid's lawyer the break he needed.

Another glance at the clock showed five minutes had passed.

"Garza," a guard barked.

Damian looked at the muscle-bound hulk, but didn't speak.

"You got a visitor." The guard motioned for Damian to step from his cell.

Damian climbed from his bunk and followed the guard through cellblock's common area, where a television blasted a *Law and Order* rerun and a group of inmates played cards at one of the tables. The guard ushered him through the door into the visitors' room and pointed to a cubicle. Damian stepped into the small space and glared at Alan Sanchez's through the thick glass. He sat and held Alan's glare before the attorney finally took a seat. Damian picked up the wall-phone and waited for Alan to do the same.

The two men continued their dueling stares a minute longer. Then Alan asked, "Did you order a hit on Clara?"

Damian couldn't believe his ears and narrowed his eyes at his attorney. The last thing he needed was for the prison officials to get wind of him ordering the execution of his wife.

"Fine." Alan shifted on the hard stool. "I can guess your answer. You should know she is missing from the rented house in Malibu. Two policemen are dead and someone was injured. They are typing the blood to see if it matches Clara's."

Worry tugged at the back of Damian's mind. If Flavio had been successful, he would be here instead of Alan. The police would have discovered Clara's body, an investigation determining she'd died from some type of accident. Instead, Alan Sanchez sat watching him with a contemptuous glare.

"I have no clue what you are talking about." Damian kept his tone even. "And I do not appreciate your accusing me of such an abominable idea."

Alan smirked at Damian and shook his head. "Fine. You did nothing and you know nothing." He straightened his tie. "Clara's not the only one missing. I am unable to locate Jia."

Damian's worry edged into panic. "When was the last time you spoke to her?"

"Two days ago, when I presented your generous offer and she agreed to assist in your defense."

Anger consumed Damian's panic as he leaned into the glass partition. "Watch your tone and your allegations, Mr. Sanchez."

Alan stood, phone still to his ear. "I also know there has been a hit order on your mother."

Damian's jaw muscles jumped as he gritted his teeth.

"You will be happy to know she is fine and has gone into hiding." Alan's lips curved into a sneer as he hung up the phone. He tugged his suit jacket into place, turned on a heel and exited through the visitors' door.

Damian replaced his phone, stood and followed a guard from the room. The guard let Damian back into the common area, the door closing behind him with a thud. A cacophony of sound from the milling inmates bounced off Damian as his mind raced with possibilities. Had Clara somehow fought off Flavio and escaped? He shook his head. She would've had to kill Flavio; a feat Damian didn't think she was capable of. Had Flavio subcontracted the hit on Valencia? It wasn't what Damian had paid for, but possibly the hitman had a good reason.

He had better have a damn good reason for everything . . . or be dead.

Billy Boyd looked up from his book as Damian entered the cell, his eyes meeting Damian's briefly before returning to the page.

Damian paced the small cell, turning scenarios over in his mind. Clara didn't have the skills to take on a trained assassin. She had to have had help. But who? And where the hell had Jia disappeared to? Why would she agree to be his alibi and then vanish? Did his father also suspect he'd ordered the hit on Valencia?

What the hell is happening?

After ten laps, Damian flung himself down onto his bunk.

"Trouble in paradise?" Boyd asked without looking at Damian.

Damian cut his eyes to his roommate. "Excuse me?"

Boyd laid his book down, sat up and said, "You look like a man who's just been screwed without the benefit of dinner first."

Damian glared at Billy Boyd, then closed his eyes. Alan Sanchez's smirking smile flashed behind his lids as the kid's annoying southern drawl echoed in his ears. He nostrils flared as a pungent order swirled around him. He stole a look at Boyd to see if the kid ate something offensive, but he had stuck his nose back in his book.

Damian licked his lips, surprised at the salty taste of his own sweat. He sniffed again and cringed as he realized the repulsive scent filling his nostrils was his own fear. For the first time since this nightmare had started, Damian couldn't shake the feeling of pending doom.

He blamed Clara. If she hadn't snooped in his business and talked to the police, her daughter would still be alive. Damian conjured up the mental image of pouring a shot of tequila and took a deep breath as he imagined the burn of the alcohol at the back of his throat.

The pretend drink offered him a small measure of calmness as he reassured himself that his plan would work. That soon he'd be released from Hotel Hell. That if Clara had somehow survived Flavio, then he would take great pleasure in killing her himself.

CHAPTER THIRTY-FOUR

Clara relished the feel of Brady's strong arms as he carried her into a dimly lit bedroom. His musky scent stirring her longing as he placed her gently on the bed. She gripped the shoulders of his T-shirt, pulling the shirt over his head.

Brady leaned in and kissed her. A slow lingering kiss that fanned the fire in her loins. His lips moved to her neck, but he pulled back when she whimpered. He searched her face. "Are you sure?"

Clara responded by lifting the hems of her sweatshirt and pajama top up, and freeing herself of both garments. She heard Brady's breath catch before she saw desire etched on his face.

He came to her, her arms intertwining with his as she worked to remove the remainder of his clothing. His hands seared her skin as he tugged off her jeans. Her heart fluttered when a sliver of light bounced off of his taut physique. His muscles flexed with every caress, and though she sensed his need for satisfaction matched her own, Brady seemed in control.

Clara felt anything but control. Her need to climax pulsed through her and she had to remind herself to breathe as she cupped him in her hand.

He tensed and groaned. "Not yet."

Brady muted her protest as his lips found hers again and his touch escalated her yearning to a frenzied pitch. Clara had never been an aggressive lover, but now the need to be assertive overwhelmed her. She placed her hands on Brady's shoulders and kissed him hungrily as she pushed him onto his back. Her lips traveled to the hollow of his neck, his desire salty on her tongue. Now straddling his torso, she stared into his hooded eyes as she applied the condom he'd produced from the nightstand drawer. As Clara lowered herself and made contact, Brady grabbed her hips. She moved with a slow, deliberate rhythm, savoring the moment. When rapture arrived, Brady pulled her to him, his lips stifling her cries of ecstasy.

* * * *

The muted sound of voices woke Clara from a deep sleep. She bolted upright amidst a heap of bedding and her skin burned from head-to-toe as she recalled why she sat naked in an unfamiliar bedroom. Her loins tingled as flashes of a naked Jackson Brady cut through her mind.

A ringing phone refocused Clara's attention and she scrambled from the bed in search of her clothes. She heard Brady say "Calm down, Devyn" as she snatched her sweatshirt from the floor. The bedroom door swung open and Brady smiled at her attempt to cover herself.

"It's for you," he handed her the phone. "Keep it short."

Clara one-handed the sweatshirt as he placed the phone in her other hand, stepped closer and kissed her.

"Clara?" Devyn's voice burst into the room. "Hello!"

Brady's lips hovered near hers and then he headed for the door. "I'll be back in a few minutes."

"Hey," Clara said into the phone.

"What the hell is going on?" Devyn yelled. "The police think you're dead."

"Almost . . . Hang on a minute." Clara crossed the bedroom, found her jeans and stepped into the bathroom. She put the phone on the counter and pressed the speaker button. "You're on speaker." Clara yanked on her sweatshirt.

"So what the hell happened at the Malibu house?"

"Someone tried to kill me—"

"Jesus, Clara!" Panic echoed in Devyn's tone. "Are you hurt? Lisa said the police found blood . . ."

"No. Brady thinks he wounded the man who came to the house." Clara pulled on her jeans.

"Where are you? Are you safe? Are you sure you can trust Brady?"

Devyn's questions bounced off the walls and a knock on the bathroom door halted Clara's response.

"Open the door," Brady said.

"I'll be out in a minute." Clara took the cell phone.

The door opened and Brady extended his hand for the phone.

Clara frowned at him. "We're not done."

"Hey! I deserve some answer," Devyn demanded.

"Agreed. But you need to ditch your phone."

"Why?" Devyn shouted.

"Because I'm sure you're being watched." Brady met Clara's concerned stare. "If I bring you here, I can't have Damian's crew tracking the GPS in your phone."

"Oh," Devyn said.

"Where are you?" Brady opened a cabinet and reached for a bath towel.

"At the Portland Airport, waiting standby for a flight to LA." A garbled PA announcement reverberated in the background.

"What flight?" He placed the towel next to the sink.

A crying child blared across the line, stalling the conversation. Clara caught a glimpse of herself in the mirror and cringed at her disheveled look. Devyn's response brought her gaze back to the phone.

"Alaska, two forty-nine."

Shane appeared behind Brady, handed him an iPad and pointed to the screen.

Brady nodded at Shane, who glanced at Clara before retreating. "Here's what you're going to do. Go to the closest women's bathroom and ditch your phone in the trash."

"What? Why can't I just turn it off?"

Clara heard Devyn's frustration and imagined her rolling her eyes.

Brady's jaw muscle bulged. "Because I want them to think you're still waiting to fly standby."

"Fine. Then what?"

"You're booked on US Airways flight five-zero-nine, which starts boarding in five minutes and is ten gates from where you are now."

"Okay, I'm on the move." Rustling sounds blended with Devyn's voice.

"When you land, a friend of mine will be waiting for you at LAX ground transportation."

Brady still had his attention directed to the phone and Clara stole a glance. He'd shaved and wore a black V-neck shirt with a pair of jeans.

His eyes met hers as he continued. "He'll be holding a sign that says Anaheim Excursions."

"What does he look like?" Devyn's voice quaked with exertion.

"He's six-four, thirty and he'll be wearing a Dodgers hat."

"Got it." Another PA announcement boomed in the background. "Can I talk to Clara in private for a minute?"

Brady smiled at Clara and pulled the bathroom door closed.

"I'm okay, Devyn."

"Yeah, well, that's not going to keep me from worrying."

"I know." The words clogged Clara's throat and she swallowed in an effort to keep her tone even. "Make sure you don't miss your flight. Be careful and I'll see you soon."

"Careful is an understatement." Clara heard the fear she felt in Devyn's words. "I'll see you in a few hours."

The line went dead as a knock on the door accompanied Brady's voice. "Clara, can I come in?"

Clara swung the bathroom door open to find him holding a Target bag. "I had Shane pick up some things I thought you'd need."

"Thanks." Clara smiled and took the sack.

"Shane's fixing a late lunch."

"Okay. I'll be out in a bit." She noticed a softness around his eyes that hadn't been there before.

"Good." He shuffled from one foot to another. "About last night . . ."

A blush crept up Clara's neck. "I'm fine . . . it was fine."

Brady flashed a grin. "I was hoping for great."

Clara laughed. "I'd better shower . . ."

Brady stepped closer. "It's good to hear you laugh."

Clara edged the door close. "Shower."

Lust narrowed his eyes. "You're sure you don't need any help?"

She placed a hand on his chest and gave him a slight push. "Not this time."

"Don't take too long." The closing door stifled the end of his sentence.

A whisper of the cologne Clara remembered from when Brady had visited her in the hospital floated through the air. She set the Target bag on the counter and looked inside. She fished shampoo, conditioner and a toothbrush from the sack, and flushed head to toe at the sight of lacy undergarments lying on top of a couple of T-shirts. Setting aside the toiletries, she pulled the clothing out, finding a pair of jeans and khaki capris concealing a book at the bottom of the bag.

Clara placed the clothing on the counter as she read the title of the book: *Handgun Basics.* She opened the cover and scanned the inscription written in familiar handwriting:

Lesson one: Read this book. Shooting a gun is harder than you think. Trust me.

CHAPTER THIRTY-FIVE

Brady watched Clara, head bent with a phone pressed to her ear, eyes focused on the scuffed wooden floor. She nodded at something Lisa Hibbs said as she raised her gaze to meet his. Brady's heart galloped in his chest, the teenager reaction coloring his cheeks and sending blood pulsing to other parts of his anatomy. A loopy grin parted his lips as Clara blinked, then turned to stare through the window at the undulating Pacific Ocean.

Brady followed her line of sight, taking in the dancing limbs of the wind pummeled trees lining the edge of the bluff. A brewing storm whipped the sea into white caps and he knew if the windows were open, he'd be able to hear the waves crashing on the beach far below.

His gaze traced the outline of Clara's slim figure, barefoot and clad in her new jeans and white T-Shirt, and wondered why she had this effect on him. Why he suddenly felt a need to rush out and buy flowers and chocolate. For so many years, he'd approached liaisons with women as a means to an end. He always treated them with respect, but never allowed an encounter to manifest into any semblance of a relationship. Even Jill, the waitress with benefits, had not managed to penetrate his wall of self-control.

Brady had spent the morning before Shane arrived contemplating his mooniness over a cup of coffee as images of his and Clara's sweaty bodies flitted through his mind. Initially, he'd chalked up his overzealous feelings to the months he'd spent watching Clara as part of his surveillance of Damian. But he knew at some point his feelings had morphed into something much more meaningful. *Maybe even love.*

His phone chirped and he pulled it from his pocket, glancing at a new text message from Pedro Gomez: *Chk in! Need stat on C. Jia Dalh msing.*

Brady read the message twice before being jolted by Clara's conversation.

"I'll be there," she said turning to meet his concerned stare.

Brady shook his head as Clara continued.

"No, I don't need a police escort."

Brady nodded and she cocked an eyebrow.

"Lisa, can I call you back?"

"What?" Brady asked a second before Clara did. "You first," he said as the screen of his phone lit up again with an incoming message from Shane.

"Is that Shane? Does he have Devyn?"

"Yes," Brady said as he read the message: *Hve D. On r way.*

He directed his attention back to Clara. "Why do you need to go to Lisa's office?"

"There's a new development."

"Such as?"

When Clara hesitated, Brady's flinched at the thought that she still didn't trust him.

"I'm going to find out eventually," he prompted.

"An FBI informant has come forward with information that makes Lisa's case against Damian."

"Did she elaborate?"

"No. She said the FBI want to meet with me to explain."

Brady chewed the inside of his cheek. Probably the Feds had been building a RICO case against the Garza family and had found someone willing to testify to the organization's participation in racketeering and corruption. He read the message from Gomez again and the phrase *Jia Dah msing* jumped from the screen.

"What's up?" Clara's voice quavered. "Is it Devyn?"

Brady shook his head. "No." No need to share his speculations about what it might mean that Jia Dahl couldn't be found. "When's your meeting?"

"As soon as I—"

His phone chirped again. Pedro's message was short and full of jumbled letters: *sit Htg fan. Cal ASSP!*

"Call Lisa and tell her you need a police escort to meet you at the Dragonfly Bistro on Palm Boulevard at four."

Clara checked the time on her phone and parted her lips in question.

"That's how long it will take us to get there and for me to make sure no one from Garza's crew is waiting for us."

Clara nodded.

Brady began punching the keys on his phone. "I'll have Shane and Devyn meet us there."

"We're not coming back here?"

He shook his head as he sent Shane's text and then messaged his standard reply to Gomez: *On it.*

Brady pocketed his phone. "Once you meet with the Feds, they're going to take you into protective custody."

"What about Devyn?"

"I'm sure they'll include her."

Clara dropped her gaze and toed a mark on the floor. "And what about you?"

Brady's heart banged against his chest as he crossed the short distance between them. He placed a finger under Clara's chin and lifted her face until her eyes met his. "I've got a few loose ends to take care of; then I'll be in touch."

His lips met hers and she wrapped her arms around his neck. The kiss, the lingering scent of soap and the sweet taste of her lips all seemed designed to obliterate the world. Brady wanted to stay in her arms forever. Wanted to protect her from everything. Wanted to take her far, far away.

Clara pulled back, placed her hands on his chest. "Maybe this should be goodbye?"

"I'm never saying goodbye to you." Brady smiled. "Trust me."

CHAPTER THIRTY-SIX

Clara and Brady arrived at Dragonfly Bistro an hour early. He had her wait at a mini-market down the street while he checked the surrounding area. Shane dropped Devyn off as their police escort arrived and the two women rode in silence to the District Attorney's office. Devyn had been whisked away by Lisa's assistant, Sloan Carter, who had made arrangements for their protective custody.

Clara now sat across from Special Agents Rebecca Owen and Christopher Temple. Lisa placed a glass of water on the conference table in front of Clara and then took the seat next to her. Lisa pulled at the cuffs of her pink blouse and fidgeted with the tablet and pen lying in front of her. When Lisa finally met Clara's questioning stare, nervous energy filled her eyes.

"Clara," Lisa began, "the FBI has a witness who will testify that Damian bribed her to provide him with an alibi at the time of Ally's murder."

Sweat crawled along Clara's hairline as she looked from one agent to the other. The female agent sat erect as if she wore a back brace. Her jet-black hair fell from a perfect center part to her shoulders, curling slightly against her black suit jacket. She'd accented the black ensemble with silver jewelry and a stark white blouse, neither of which softened her hard, angled features.

Lisa continued, "The witness has credible evidence proving the Garza family's involvement in organized crime and bribery of government officials."

Clara opened her lips to speak but found her tongue glued to the top of her dry mouth. She took a sip of water and nodded.

"They would like to offer Damian a deal with regard to the murder charge in exchange for his testimony against his father on RICO charges."

Lisa's words swirled in a cloud of confusion as Clara tried to absorb the information. "What?" She blinked at Lisa and then at the two Feds. "No! You can't offer him a deal."

Lisa placed a hand on Clara's shoulder. "Clara, just listen—"

"If I may . . ." Special Agent Owen interjected, her soothing tone a contrast to her steely-eyed stare. "Clara, we have no intention of setting Damian Garza free." She flipped open the folder lying in front of her, glanced down, and looked back at Clara. "We're prepared to take the death penalty off the table and offer him a life sentence in a federal prison."

Clara shook her head, which throbbed as if her brain would explode.

"Clara," Lisa said, "Damian will still go to prison. He won't get away with what he did."

Clara shoved her chair back and began to pace. She ran her hands through her hair, pressing her temples in an effort to stop the headache blooming behind her eyes.

"This meeting is a courtesy, Clara," Agent Owen said. "We don't need your permission to make a deal with Damian."

Clara spun around and faced the bitch in black. "Of course you don't! As long as you get your man, your job is done. Right?" The tears she'd struggled to contain fell freely down her cheeks.

"We have a responsibility to shut down the Garza organization," Agent Owen countered. "I'm sorry we're not able to accommodate your vision of justice."

"Bullshit." Clara swiped away her tears and then crossed her arms.

Agent Temple had listened to the exchange while reclined in his chair and drew Clara's attention as he shifted and leaned forward. His blond sun-god good looks were quite a contrast to Agent Owen's straightforward appearance.

"Clara," Agent Temple said, his eyes meeting hers, "we are concerned about how this affects you, but as my partner said, we have an obligation to pursue indictments against Ricardo Garza."

"Damian won't testify against his father." Fatigue pulled at Clara as she rested against a wall.

Agent Temple nodded. "If that's the case, we'll have to rely on our other witness."

"If your witness stays alive long enough to testify."

"Clara," Lisa said, "please sit."

Clara shuffled back to her seat. The walls of the conference room seemed to be closing in and the stale air choked her. She longed to be back in the comfort of Brady's cottage, back in his arms with the windows open wide to the fresh ocean breeze.

"The witness has been placed in protective custody," Lisa continued. "She is willing to testify against Damian in our trial, which will most likely result in a plea deal. The FBI plans to use the defense's request for a deal as leverage."

"What's the bottom line?" Clara directed the question at Lisa.

"There are a few points I'd like to sum up first."

Clara nodded and Lisa cleared her throat before continuing, "I spoke to Judge Bailey about the jury tampering you brought to my attention."

Her encounter with Brady on the pier flashed in Clara's mind.

"She called a meeting in her chambers, but before it was held, you went missing." Lisa tapped her pen on the table.

Clara sensed Lisa wanted to ask again who had helped her escape in Malibu, but she pressed on instead.

"While the police looked for you, Agents Owen and Temple contacted me with information about this witness."

"Who is she?" Clara scanned the Feds' faces and then looked to Lisa.

"Jia Dahl," Lisa said. "She's been compiling evidence against Damian in an attempt to save her brother." Lisa opened a manila folder and spread out several documents on the table.

Clara leaned forward and stared at her handwritten notes in the margins. She reached for the closest piece of paper, recognizing the bank statement that had tipped her off to Damian's money laundering. Clara snatched up the rest of the documents. "How did she get these?"

"She broke into your office after you were shot," Lisa said. "She was hoping to find cash or something she could sell so she could buy plane tickets for her and her brother to leave the country." Lisa pointed to the stack of papers in Clara's hand. "Then she decided to blackmail Damian, but when he asked her to provide a false alibi, she decided to come forward."

"In addition to offering Damian a deal," Agent Owen said, "we're hoping to turn his attorney, Alan Sanchez, into another witness by offering him immunity for suborning perjury."

Agent Temple joined the conversation. "As you said, Clara, Damian probably won't testify against his father, but we have to be prepared to offer him a deal."

Clara blew out a breath, laid the papers down and covered her face with her hands. She wanted Damian to pay with his life for killing Ally. Her daughter's voice echoed in her ears: *Take them all down, Mama.*

Clara glared at Agent Owen. "I appreciate you including me in your plans, even though as you said, you don't need my permission."

Agent Owen raised her chin, but didn't blink.

Clara turned her attention back to Lisa. "All I ask is that Damian receives the harshest punishment possible."

"Believe it or not, Clara," Agent Temple said, "if we could lock him in hell for what he's done, we would."

Clara turned to the young agent. "Even hell is too good for Damian Garza."

CHAPTER THIRTY-SEVEN

The guard motioned Damian into a chair and then unlocked the cuffs tethering his hands to his waist. He rubbed his wrists as the guard retreated to a corner of the small conference room. A Sunday morning meeting with his attorneys could only mean one thing and Damian could barely contain his anticipation.

How long would he have to wait? How long until Alan Sanchez, or Alexis Kent, or both appeared to tell him that the prosecution's case had fallen apart? How long before he was back in his penthouse suite, sipping tequila and enjoying the company of some young lovely? Damian smiled at the thought of educating the young woman as to what he liked, bending her to his will. He'd no longer have to tolerate Kandee's useless attempts at pleasing him. She'd been charged with perjury; which Alan had successfully defended by painting a picture of a lovelorn woman trying to help her man. True to form, Kandee played the dumb blonde bimbo to perfection, receiving probation and restitution for her crime.

Ricardo paid Kandee's fine, and after she'd completed her community service hours, he'd paid for her trip back to Portland, Oregon, where her mother lived.

Jia Dahl's round face rose in his mind like a full moon. Damian would have liked one more tryst with the Asian beauty, a thank-you of sorts for providing him with a solid alibi. Despite Alan's objections, Damian knew Jia's love for her brother and the added incentive of an escape plan would motivate her to do as asked.

The door swung open as Alexis Kent, dressed in ritzy Sunday Brunch attire, entered the room ahead of an unfamiliar man and woman. Alexis's stunning beauty seemed to sharpen the harsh features of the other woman and the duo's black suits told Damian they were Feds. His chest tightened as he sat taller in his chair.

While Alexis sat down and popped the locks on her briefcase, the young man stood holding the open door. He poked his blond head through the doorway and then stepped back as Lisa Hibbs hurried into the room. The DDA's cheeks were flushed from exertion and she nervously straightened the collar of her pink cotton blouse as she took the seat next to Alexis and the other woman.

Damian's stomach lurched and twisted as he fought to keep his façade calm. He focused on his attorney, willing her to meet his eyes. When she didn't look up, he spoke in a clipped tone.

"Where is Alan?"

Alexis finally met his eyes and he thought he saw a slight smile cross her lips. "Mr. Sanchez won't be joining us today," Alexis said as she dropped her gaze to the legal pad lying in front of her.

Damian's bowels cramped as his nervous stomach dumped acid into his intestines. He took a deep breath of dank air laced with the combined fragrances of the three females sitting across from him. He exhaled and then asked, "Why are they here?"

Alexis answered without looking up. "Agent Owen and Agent Temple are here to discuss a plea deal based on recent developments regarding Ms. Dahl, your current attempt at an alibi for the date and time of Ally Marsh's murder."

His attorney's voice dripped with malice and he resisted the urge to reach across the table and rip out her tongue.

Alexis looked up and continued, "I'm here to make sure you understand the plea agreement and to . . . ensure your rights are protected." She glared at him.

Damian crossed his arms. "I am not interested in a deal."

"Mr. Garza," Lisa Hibbs said, "Ms. Dahl has agreed to testify against you and your father, Ricardo Garza—"

"Leave my father out of this," Damian growled.

Lisa swallowed audibly and then took a swig from a water bottle. She pushed a few strands of hair behind her ear and pressed on. "As I was saying, testify in regards to your coercing her into providing you with an alibi. In addition, Ms. Dahl also has evidence regarding various criminal activities your father is involved in."

Damian flinched as if he'd been punched in the gut. He took another deep breath. *Stay calm, damn it!*

"I doubt the stripper has any solid proof regarding my father."

Agent Owen finally spoke. "Mr. Garza, I can assure you the agency has been able to corroborate Ms. Dahl's information."

He fixed her with a deadly stare. Her reaction was to match his menacing look with arched eyebrows.

Without breaking eye contact, she continued. "We are prepared to offer you a deal for your cooperation in pursuing criminal charges against your father."

Sweat trickled from Damian's temples to his jawline.

Agent Temple pushed off the wall he'd been leaning against and said, "Mr. Garza, DDA Hibbs has also informed us of your jury tampering endeavor. So the question isn't whether you're going to prison . . ." He stepped closer to the table, his six-foot-plus frame towering over Damian and continued. "The question is, are you willing to testify against your father to avoid the death penalty?"

The question hung in the air like a tight rope suspended between Damian and those who wished to see him and his father punished. Punished for providing a conduit to those interested in the dark side of life.

Damian stared at a spot on the wall as his bowels gurgled and he worked the problem in his mind. Without an alibi, he knew a jury would convict him of Ally's murder. Spending the rest of his life in prison was less than appealing, but a death sentence would bring far too much restriction and eventually death. Damian knew in a less-controlled environment he'd be able to orchestrate his revenge against those who had betrayed him. The real question was, which prison facility provided the best opportunity to reach beyond his confinement?

Damian leaned forward, placing his finger laced hands on the table. The sweet taste of freedom died on his tongue and he swallowed in an attempt to dislodge the bitterness of defeat.

"Agent Temple, is it?" Damian ignored the females in the room. "It is not my father you want." He paused for effect as his intestinal issues began to subside. "I believe the criminal you seek is the bitch who really wears the pants in my family—my mother, Valencia Garza."

CHAPTER THIRTY-EIGHT

Jackson Brady fidgeted with the cup sitting in front of him, adding cream and sugar to his usual black coffee as he ran different scenarios through his mind.

Everything depended on how well he handled Pedro Gomez's meltdown now that Damian's second alibi had gone missing. How well he orchestrated Clara's disappearance after her vile ex-husband's conviction. How well he managed to extricate himself from the Garza organization.

The scent of lavender lingered on his cotton pullover, the fragrance fueling a sense of euphoria as he imagined joining Clara once he'd tied up all the loose ends of this ordeal. He knew he could make her happy . . . if she'd give him the chance.

A string of bells jangled as the café door swung open and a group of young Hispanic women swarmed into Copa Mexicana. He shifted his focus outside the window and surveyed the crowd of tourists taking in the sites along Plaza-Olvera Street. He checked his watch as a server topped off his cup with hot coffee. Gomez didn't usually keep him waiting and Brady guessed he was having difficulty navigating the popular historic area.

Brady's phone vibrated with an incoming text from Shane: *C&D @ sfe hs - DG mtg w/atys & FbI @ Twrs ?*

Brady keyed in a response: *Thx. Yes.*

Shane: *Lt me knw wht PG says*

Brady: *Yep*

He shoved the phone into the pocket of his jeans and took a sip of coffee, his tongue curling against the unfamiliar sweet taste. The gaggle of girls headed for the exit as Pedro Gomez pushed through the door. He bumped into one of the women, causing her paper cup to tilt and spill coffee down the front of her blouse. Her friends shouted something at Gomez as they rallied around their *amiga*. He turned and glared at them, sending the group rushing from the café.

Tension ridged Brady's shoulder muscles as Gomez stepped up to the table, pulled out a chair and sat. The usually impeccable Mexican's clothes were wrinkled and he sported a dark scowl on an unshaven face. He snapped his fingers at a server, who scurried over with a cup of *café de olla* and a plate of *panes dulces*.

Saliva coated Brady's mouth as if anticipating he might eat one of the sweet breads or sip some of the cinnamon-laced coffee. He swallowed and waited for Pedro to speak.

Gomez bit into a small pastry and then washed down the bite with a long sip. He dabbed the corners of his mouth with a napkin, looked at Brady and said, "Where the hell have you been?"

Brady held Gomez's stare for a beat. "Looking for Clara Garza, as you instructed."

Gomez snorted and shook his head. "You can quit looking. She is in protective custody."

The memory of Clara lying in his arms threatened Brady's focus. He gulped cold coffee, cleared his throat. "Haven't had any luck locating Jia Dahl, but I know her brother's left town."

Gomez shoved the last of the roll into his mouth and chewed as he stared at Brady. Minutes passed as the two men made eye contact. Brady knew he needed to keep up the charade of being afraid of Gomez, and he looked away, signaling for more coffee.

"The stripper has gone to the police." Gomez leaned back against his chair. "Which means Damian no longer has an alibi. Again."

As the waitress refilled his cup and brought a fresh cup for Gomez, Brady nodded and wondered if Gomez knew about Damian's meeting with the FBI.

Gomez blew out a heavy sigh. "Ricardo Garza should have rid himself of his mal hijo years ago. Now his son will most likely be Senor Garza's downfall."

His evil kid isn't the only thing Garza has to worry about. "What's next?"

Gomez shook his head. "I have no idea. Alan Sanchez is scrambling to protect his own ass instead of focusing on Senor Garza. No one seems to know what to do next."

Brady waited as Gomez sipped from his cup and then he asked, "Do you have a job for me?"

"Si." Gomez fingered another roll. "Find Flavio Vargas, the hitman Damian hired to kill Clara in Malibu."

Brady's pulse quickened. He was glad to have a name, but had hoped the hitman had died from his wounds. "That's it?"

Gomez pinched off the corner of a cinnamon pastry, held it up and pointed at Brady with the morsel between thumb and forefinger. "I received a tip that Damian also contracted a hit on his mother." He popped the bite into his mouth. "See what you can find out."

Brady reached for his wallet as he said, "I'll be in touch soon."

Gomez waved a hand. "Coffee is on me." He produced a fat envelope from his inside jacket pocket and slid it across the table toward Brady. "This should cover everything, including my current requests."

Brady picked up the envelope, quickly deducing it contained far more than his usual fee. "All right."

Gomez tucked a fifty-dollar bill under his coffee cup. "After your next report, lie low for a while."

Brady cocked an eyebrow and waited for Gomez to continue.

"If Damian cuts a deal with the Feds and his father goes to prison as well, the organization—dios nos ayude—will land in the hands of Valencia Garza."

Brady doubted God had any intentions of helping the Garza Crime family.

CHAPTER THIRTY-NINE

The safe house turned out to be a three-thousand-square-foot mansion tucked away in a West Los Angeles gated community. The home featured four separate suites that formed a square around a beautiful courtyard, complete with swimming pool, sumptuous patio furniture, outdoor bar and an amazing brick fire pit.

Clara and Devyn sat on matching queen beds in one of the suites as Clara recounted her meeting with Lisa Hibbs and the FBI agents. She finished by blowing her nose and gazing through the sliding glass door at the designer courtyard. Late afternoon sunlight had scattered diamonds of light across the surface of the pool.

"I know the death penalty would be a more fitting punishment . . ." Devyn handed Clara another tissue. "But Damian in prison for the rest of his life isn't a bad backup plan. Right?"

Clara nodded in agreement. "I want him to rot in prison."

Devyn crossed to a small wet bar and poured two glasses of red wine. She handed Clara a glass. "Maybe you should consider the Fed's offer to enter witness protection."

Clara shrugged and sipped her wine. "Probably. But I'm going ahead with my plan." Brady's face, etched with betrayal, loomed largely in her mind. Before the police had escorted her to the safe house, Clara had managed to sneak into the women's bathroom and call Shane. She told him about her plan and they spent the next ten minutes debating her sanity and arguing logistics. He'd finally caved to her demands and should arrive any minute to set everything in motion.

"Any chance you're going to tell Brady about your plan?"

Clara rolled the stem of her glass between her fingers and focused on the light dancing through the red wine. A knock at the door catapulted both women to their feet.

"Miss Marsh."

"Yes." Clara crossed the bedroom and opened the door.

"Your financial advisor is here," the FBI agent said. "Would you like to meet with him in the courtyard?"

"Um," Clara hesitated, her eyes darting to the small sitting area next to the wet bar. "No, I think we'll be fine in here."

"All right," the agent said as he turned to go. "I'll send him back."

"Thanks."

Clara waited in the doorway, listening to an agent instructing her guest to follow the hallway, and she smiled when Shane came into view.

He moved toward her, his long strides making short work of the corridor. He stopped in front of Clara and held his arms out in a cross formation, a battered leather briefcase dangling from one hand. "Are you going to frisk me too?"

Clara laughed and said, "Don't be ridiculous." She stepped aside and motioned Shane into the suite.

Devyn stood and extended her hand. "Good to see you again."

Shane gave her hand a quick shake. "You too."

Clara made her way to the sitting area. "Let's sit here."

Shane took the seat opposite Clara, dwarfing the overstuffed chair and placed the briefcase in his lap.

Devyn moved to the wet bar and asked, "Shane, can I get you something to drink?"

"Water would be great." Shane flipped the locks on his briefcase.

Devyn delivered the glass of water and then sat in the chair next to Clara's.

Shane pulled out a stack of papers from the bottom of the briefcase, placed them on the table and then looked up at Clara. He cleared his throat and said, "I did as you asked, but I want to repeat I did so under protest."

Clara nodded. "Does that mean you didn't tell Brady? I know he's your friend—"

"I didn't tell him *because* he's my friend."

"And you have everything?"

"Yes." Shane picked up a clear page protector, withdrew a single page from the middle and then handed it to Clara. "This is the combination to locker two forty-six at 24 Four Hour Fitness on Wilshire Boulevard." He took his wallet from his breast pocket, pulled an ID badge from the center and handed it to Clara. "This will get you past the front desk and into the women's locker room."

Clara glanced at her picture on the badge and noticed the fake name of Abby Roberts.

"The items you asked for are in a duffle bag."

"All right." Clara looked at Devyn and then back at Shane. "And once I'm safely away, Devyn will give you the access information to the account I've set up for you."

Shane gave a slight nod as he pulled two sheets of paper from another page protector. "Okay, let's go over how the two of you will stay in touch once you disappear." He handed each woman a page. "I've set up an email account for you to use as your primary means of communication. All you have to do is sign in, type a message and save it to the draft folder— then sign out. *Do not* send the message." Shane looked from Clara to Devyn. "What did I just say?"

Clara, and then Devyn, said, "Do not send the message."

"Right. All you have to do is sign in and out to read or leave messages. As long as you never send a message, the account can't be traced to either of you. Also, if you don't want me reading your messages, I'd change the password."

"And the phones?" Devyn asked.

"I'll get to them in a sec," Shane said to Devyn. "You're going to need to buy an iPad or laptop specifically for the email account."

"Because?" Clara said.

Shane ignored her and continued his explanation to Devyn. "And you're going to need to keep it locked away somewhere other than your home or office. Understand?"

Devyn nodded as Clara repeated herself. "Because?"

"Because the Garza family is going to be watching Devyn—and probably Brady. If the Garzas find out about the account and aren't able to trace it to you, they'll . . ." he paused.

Devyn completed his thought. "Torture me for information."

"Yes," Shane said. "I would suggest a safe deposit box, although you might have trouble accessing the internet from inside the bank's vault. If you have to leave the bank, go somewhere close and keep your exposure time short."

"Got it," Devyn said.

"Why can't she use the phone you're providing to check email?" Clara asked.

"The phones are prepaid burners and don't have the capabilities to access the internet." He held up a finger. "And they should only be used for emergencies. Clara, your phone will be in the duffle bag, and I'll give Devyn hers when she gives me the bank account information." He pointed at the paper in Clara's hand. "The numbers are listed on your papers, but remember they are only to be used in case—"

"Of an emergency," Clara and Devyn chimed in unison.

"If you have to use your phone, ditch it and buy a new one. Use the email account to share your new phone number."

The room fell silent for a few minutes as they digested Shane's information. The silence pounded in Clara's head as she contemplated her decision for the hundredth time. Once she disappeared, she'd never see Devyn again. Or Jackson Brady.

"Clara," Shane said, "even though you'll be somewhere unknown, you're going to need to take the same precautions as Devyn. I know this goes without saying, but don't disclose your location or talk about anything personal . . . not even the weather."

Shane's eyes bored into hers as if he could read her mind. Clara hadn't decided where she would go when she walked away from this life. Somewhere she'd be safe. A place where maybe she could help others.

Clara met his stare and said, "I understand."

"Okay, the last thing to discuss is the switch at the court house. Abby . . ."

Clara cocked an eyebrow and her lips parted in question.

"Yes, Abby's a real person who's gone to a lot of trouble to look like you." Shane smiled. "She's going to meet you Monday morning in the bathroom down the hall from the courtroom. The two of you will exchange clothing and she'll give you a purse with enough cab fare to get you to 24 Hour Fitness and then the airport."

Clara didn't react to Shane's assumption that she would be headed to the airport. She'd carefully designed her escape from Los Angeles and hadn't even told Devyn of her plans. Of course the quickest way out of LA, not to mention the country, would be on a plane. Clara had bought a ticket for the Long Beach ferry to Catalina Island. By the time anyone looking for her had searched the island, she'd be long gone.

Devyn asked, "How long do you think Abby can pull off her impersonation of Clara?"

Shane shrugged. "At least until after the judge sentences Damian and court is adjourned." He frowned. "After that I'm sure Brady will have figured things out and he's going to be pissed so be prepared."

"I gave Devyn a letter for him, which will hopefully . . ." Clara's voice trailed off.

Shane gave her a slight nod. "I think that covers everything." He closed his briefcase. "I've listed numbers for the burner phones Abby and I will have while we lay low for a couple of weeks before I have to deal with Brady."

"I know he'll be upset, but he won't—won't . . ."

"Beat the shit out of me?" Shane snorted a nervous laugh as they all stood. "I'm guessing he's going to try."

CHAPTER FORTY

Jackson Brady paced the corridor in front of a courtroom teeming with a crowd anxious to hear Damian Garza plead guilty to murdering his step-daughter, Ally Marsh.

Brady scanned the faces of stragglers racing to claim seats, but still no sign of Clara. Squelching a sense of foreboding, he entered the courtroom as the court clerk closed the big double doors.

A quick glance of the empty seats behind the prosecution table confirmed Clara hadn't arrived. Brady checked his silenced cell phone for messages. Nothing. The fact that Shane hadn't returned any of his texts in the last twenty-four hours caused his unease to resurface.

He had his and Clara's "go bags" in the trunk of his car. After their narrow escape from the Malibu house, and the proof he had that Clara was still in danger, Brady assumed she wouldn't hesitate to leave the country with him. His heart stuttered with the thought that she may already be dead.

I would have heard something.

Lisa stood and faced the back of the courtroom as the doors behind Brady creaked open. All heads swiveled and watched as Clara and Devyn made their way to their seats. Brady fought the urge to reach out and grab Clara as she passed by.

Judge Bailey peered over her glasses at the prosecution table. "Are we ready to begin, Ms. Hibbs?"

Lisa nodded. "Yes, Your Honor."

"Very well." Judge Bailey shifted her attention to the defense table. "Ms. Kent, I understand we have a plea agreement."

As Alexis Kent stood, she nudged her client. "Yes, Your Honor."

Judge Bailey waited for Damian to stand. "Mr. Garza, in accordance with the plea agreement, you are pleading guilty to murder in the first degree with special circumstances? Is this correct?"

It seemed to Brady as though the crowd held a collective breath. He wished he had the seat behind Clara, not just for moral support but so he could whisk her away after the hearing. Brady shifted in his seat to get a better look at Clara, who appeared to be staring straight ahead.

Judge Bailey tapped a pen on her desk. "Mr. Garza?"

Damian cleared his throat and Brady thought he detected a slight slump to the bastard's shoulders.

"Counselor . . ." Judge Bailey began.

Alexis held up a finger. "A minute, please."

Judge Bailey nodded and Alexis turned to whisper to her client.

"We're ready to proceed, Your Honor."

"Fine. Mr. Garza, are you plea–"

Damian held up a hand. "Yes." His tone had an edge of disdain.

"Mr. Garza, consider yourself fortunate your sentencing has already been determined, because if it were up to me, you'd be punished to the full extent of the law." Judge Bailey smiled at the jury box and said," Thank you ladies and gentlemen for your service." Then she tapped her gavel. "We're adjourned."

Members of the press bolted from their seats and the remaining crowd began to disperse as a deputy arrived to escort Damian from the courtroom. Brady searched the front row for Clara and caught a glimpse of her being hustled through a side door by Lisa Hibbs.

Brady jumped into the throng filing from the courtroom and pushed his way through the crowd. He rounded the corner and found an empty hallway.

"Shit!" Brady raced toward the bank of elevators he knew led to the parking garage. As he passed the side door to the court room, he heard Lisa Hibbs' quiet voice.

Brady flung the door open and found three startled women. His attention ping-ponged from Lisa to Devyn to a young woman who was dressed like Clara. Brady knew the imposter, but couldn't come up with her name.

He directed a menacing glare at Devyn. "Where is she?"

"She left this for you." Devyn offered Brady an envelope.

He snatched the envelope, tore it open and read the first sentence: *I'm sorry I left without saying goodbye.*

Brady's stomach lurched as his mind fit the pieces together. The young woman in disguise was Abby Roberts, Shane's girlfriend, which explained why Shane hadn't texted him back. Abby and Devyn's delay in arriving for court meant Clara would be long gone by now.

His emotions swung from despair to panic to anger. Brady chose to focus all his energy on the latter and stepped toward Devyn, Clara's note clutched in his hand. "Where. Is. She?" The words felt like bricks on his tongue.

"I honestly don't know."

"She's still in danger and I need to warn her."

"That's why she's gone." Tears welled in Devyn's eyes. "She wanted to protect the rest of us."

"He'll find her. She's going to need help—"

The chime of an incoming text sounded on someone's phone. Brady knew it wasn't his and waited for one of the women to check their phone. No one moved. The tone seemed louder the second time. Brady snatched Abby's phone from her hand before she could read the text from Shane: *CM away. You?*

Brady replied: *Yes. Mt u soon.*

"I'm not meeting him—" Abby began.

"Don't bother lying to me." Brady headed for the door. "Let's go."

The three women stood their ground. Brady reached for Abby's arm, but stopped when his phone rang. The caller ID flashed: *Shane*

Brady answered on the second ring. "Where is she?"

"I don't know."

"Then you better start looking for her."

"Look, I know you're pissed, but she doesn't want to be found . . . by anyone."

"We'll address my anger issues later. We have to find Clara before Damian's hitman does. Because if you think I'm pissed now—"

"I'll meet you at your beach house in an hour."

Brady handed Abby her phone and stormed from the room. He had to find Clara before she had a chance to get farther away from him. Before she made a mistake that revealed her location. Before Damian finally had his revenge.

CHAPTER FORTY-ONE

Scenarios of what could go wrong with Alan's plan ran through Damian's mind like footage from a bad "B" movie. Each failure worse than the one before. In an effort to assuage his doubt, he recalled his father's words from a week earlier: "Damian, for God's sake, you need to trust Alan."

Ricardo, with Alan at his side, had visited Damian after the meeting with the FBI. Father and son argued for nearly an hour over Damian's plea offer. Each insisting they had the other party's best interest at heart, until finally his father snapped.

"Enough!" Ricardo smacked the small table with his palm. "You are not going to be acquitted and I do not want you on death row. You will take this plea and I will go to jail."

"And leave in charge that bitch you forced on me as a mother?" Damian's voice quaked with rage. "Never!"

Ricardo's shoulders slumped. "How long have you known?"

"I found out in my twenties." Damian glared at his father.

Ricardo sighed. "I made the best out of a difficult situation."

"By allowing Valencia to get away with murdering my mother?"

Their silence resonated with unspoken words of a well-intended secret and the wounds it caused. Alan, now the only attorney of record for the soon-to-be-convicted murderer, cleared his throat and then shared his escape plan.

The memory faded as a guard entered the small holding room. Damian moved to rub his face with his hands, the motion halted by the handcuff shackling his right hand to a ring bolted into the concrete wall. He glowered at the manacle. He wanted to rip it from the wall and wrap the chain around the neck of the pompous guard who droned on about what the inmates could expect once they were delivered to Victorville Penitentiary. The guard, a six-foot muscle-bound lunk who probably had a bowl of steroids for breakfast, seemed to relish his role of superiority.

Damian along with three of the other inmates, ignored the guard, whose name tag read Boone, leaving him an attentive audience of one. The young white kid sat next to Damian, trembling in his seat and looking as if he'd burst into tears at any moment. Even though they were headed to a federal prison where violence among inmates was lower than state prisons, Damian didn't think it would be long before someone made the kid their bitch. He almost felt sorry for him, but the kid was on his own.

"All right," Boone said. "Time to go."

Damian stood as a second guard unlocked his handcuff from the wall, cuffed his hands in front of him, and then locked the handcuffs to a chain linking hands and feet together.

The inmates lined up at the door as Boone spoke to someone on the other end of a wall phone. He hung up the receiver and said, "Looks like it's your lucky day, gentlemen. We'll be traveling in air-conditioned comfort today."

As Boone entered a code into the keypad next to the phone, Damian heard locks click and release. The guard pulled the door open and stepped through, followed by the first inmate. Damian's muscles tightened in protest against his shackles. He shuffled forward into a large fenced lot where a van idled twenty feet away. The bright sunshine made his eyes water and the orange jumpsuit stuck to his clammy skin.

Boone stopped the inmates' trek and spoke to the driver. "Where's Johnson?"

"Called in sick," the driver responded.

Boone consulted his clipboard. "What's your name?"

"Raul Reyes."

Boone made a checkmark. "Why this van?"

Raul shrugged. "Beats me. It's what I was assigned."

Damian leaned around the inmate in front of him to get a better look at the driver. He didn't look familiar and Damian's thoughts returned to the likelihood of Alan's plan succeeding.

"We've got five for transport today," Boone said as he stepped aside and motioned the first inmate aboard.

The guy in front of Damian, an elderly Bernie Madoff type, stumbled on the second step and lurched into the van.

Boone chuckled, then said, "Hobble on up, Garza. Hotel Victorville awaits you."

Damian gritted his teeth as he awkwardly navigated the steps and climbed into the van. He hoped he had an opportunity to permanently erase the smile from the smug guard's face.

The van reminded Damian of a small school bus with double seats on both sides of a narrow aisle. He detected a sweet chemical smell, which suggested either the air-conditioning unit's Freon was old or someone had tampered with the system.

The inmates claimed separate seats, and the guards worked each side, cuffing the inmates to a metal bar fastened to the seat back. Damian sat across from the kid who had gone from looking like he would cry to looking like he was going to vomit. Damian's stomach roiled as if in sympathy. Maybe if the kid survived, Damian would cut him loose.

Boone and his partner sat in the front seats as the driver exited the lot. Familiar sights of Los Angeles slipped past the window and Damian said a silent goodbye to the city that had been his playground, his paradise. As the van merged onto the I-10 and headed east, Damian wondered about his new playground. Alan had probably picked an obscure country without an extradition treaty with the United States. But Damian had other plans.

The kid was on his feet, hunched over and sweating profusely. "I'm gonna be sick," he mewled.

Boone turned and barked, "Sit your ass down."

The kid's body contorted with a dry heave.

The inmate seated in front of the kid inched forward. "Jesus, pull over before he pukes all over me."

"Hang on, kid," Boone said as he motioned for the driver to pull off the road.

Gravel crunched under the van tires as it came to a stop and Boone placed a hand on the kid's shoulder. "Okay, let-"

The kid jerked Boone's gun from its holster, shoved the muzzle into the guard's gut and pulled the trigger. Almost in concert, the driver removed a gun from an ankle holster and put two bullets into the other guard, who fell forward, landing next to Boone, who made gurgling sounds.

The driver tossed a set of keys from Boone's belt to the kid, who unlocked his handcuffs, and then stepped up to Damian and smiled. "Mr. Sanchez should be here in a few minutes."

Damian nodded as the kid unlocked his cuffs and leg irons. As Damian rubbed his wrist, the driver worked to unlock the other inmates' restraints.

Damian stood and extended a hand to the kid. "I owe you."

The kid shook his head as he shook Damian's hand. "No. You've already paid me well."

Damian thanked the driver too as a black town car stopped on the opposite side of the highway. With one last glance at the kid, Damian exited the van and marched across the hot asphalt. He opened the passenger door and slid onto the back seat next to Alan Sanchez.

"Well done, Alan," Damian said as he reached for the bottle of Patron chilling in a bar caddy.

Alan smiled. "Your father is in custody awaiting trial, but before he surrendered to the authorities, he sent Valencia away on a long holiday."

"Who did my father place in charge until I am settled?" Damian pulled the stopper free from the bottle and inhaled the woody scent.

"Pedro Gomez and myself."

Damian cut his eyes to Alan and nodded. "Fine." He took a long pull from the Patron bottles. "Now, where the hell is Clara?"

BOOK ONE - THE END

CHAPTER FORTY-TWO

He admired his reflection in the mirror as he dabbed on a touch of *Straight to Heaven* cologne. He'd purchased the spicy masculine fragrance after sampling the scent at Nordstrom's prior to his hasty departure from Los Angeles. The sales girl, who resembled his Juliette, had no idea her pitch claiming women would love the hint of jasmine would place her squarely in his sights.

She knows now. A thread of pleasure coursed through his veins as he recalled seducing her and leaving his mark on the pristine skin of her inner thigh.

Memories of Juliette crept into his thoughts as he made his way to the kitchenette of the well-appointed suite. God, how he had loved her. And though she had declared her love for him, she'd caved under pressure from her father to marry another man. His lips twitched into a sneer as he visualized the wedding present he'd carved into Juliette's thigh the week before her nuptials—a perfect five-point star that trailed into a cross that bled into a heart. Star-crossed lovers indeed.

From a splendid hand-painted pitcher, he poured his margarita concoction into a multicolored glass. Ice clinked and salt flaked from the rim onto the tile floor as he sauntered through the sitting area. The spectacular view from the large sliding glass door stretched out before him. A sandy beach crowded with tourists sloped toward crashing waves rolling in from the vast Pacific Ocean. He raised his drink in a toast to the cloudless blue sky and then took a sip.

The aroma of chicken fajitas drifted from the kitchenette as he finished his drink. A list of things needed to ensure a romantic evening clicked through his mind. He wanted everything perfect for his new Juliette.

He rinsed his glass and placed it on the table set with colorful Mexican dinnerware. The vase of calla lilies needed more water, which he added before removing a couple of wilted flowers. The vanilla candles, a proven aphrodisiac for women, sat strategically throughout the suite waiting to be lit. As far as hotel rooms went, the suite had a lot to offer, but a proper sound system wasn't one of the perks. He ran a hand over the slick surface of a recently purchased Bose SoundDock, ready and waiting for his iPhone playlist.

A soft, disoriented sound emanated from the bedroom. He smiled as he stepped to the open door and gazed at his beautiful guest. A mane of dark hair haloed around her face and her eyes fluttered as she rolled her head from side to side. Two long strides placed him next to the bed as she pulled against the restraints binding her arms and legs to the frame.

Arousal flooded through him, setting his loins on fire. He breathed deeply and focused on what lie ahead. A lot of planning had gone into this evening and he wanted his date with this Juliette to be magical.

The young woman's eyes flew open and she screamed into the duct tape sealing her lips shut.

CHAPTER FORTY-THREE

Voices banged on the door of Clara's subconscious and she squinted at the face swimming before her as she struggled to sit up. "Who the hell are you?"

"Hola, senorita. Por favor, no tengais miedo."

Clara shrank back, her heart bouncing off her rib cage.

"Do not be afraid." The man's smile reached his kind blue eyes. "I believe you had an accident, but nothing appears to be broken."

Accident? Her fuzzy brain tried to connect the dots as she fingered a lump on the back of her head. Clara tried to stand. "I have to—" The room spun and she fell back onto the plush couch.

"Esta bien," The man said. "It is okay. I am Humberto Alvarez and you are in my suite aboard the *Princess of the Sea*."

Clara winced and closed her eyes against the bright light filling the room. Images of last night jerked through her mind like a vacation slideshow, stopping on the image of a margarita. Clara licked her lips, tasting the salty remnants of the drink.

"Are you thirsty?" Humberto asked.

A deep Southern drawl exploded like fireworks in Clara's mind: *You look thirsty.* The memory made her stomach roil. Her eyes snapped open as the man spoke Spanish to a woman who appeared behind him with a glass of water.

"Drink." Humberto handed the glass to Clara. "You will feel better."

The Southern twang echoed in her ears: *You'll feel better and might just grace me with a smile.*

Clara's skin oozed with clammy sweat. A jolt of anger cleared her mind and she remembered refusing the man's offer to buy her another drink. She'd moved to a small table far away from the leering Lothario, where she finished her drink and then headed for her stateroom. When she became dizzy at the top of a flight of stairs, Clara's last conscious thought had been: *Someone drugged me!*

"Senorita?"

Clara's hands shook as she grasped the glass of water. She sipped the water and studied her host, who she guessed to be in his early forties. A smattering of freckles dotted his light complexion and an unruly shock of coppery curls fell across his forehead, his aristocratic features at odds with his Hispanic accent.

He smiled and continued. "As I said, I am Humberto Alvarez, and this is my friend, Lucia Torres." He nodded at the dark-headed Mexican beauty now standing by his side. Humberto loosened the knot of his blue silk tie and unbuttoned the top button of a crisp white shirt. A gray suit jacket hung on the back of the chair he occupied.

She knew they expected her to say her name. Could they be trusted? She glanced around the suite, taking in a room service cart that held a half-empty champagne bottle and two flutes with remnants of the now-flat wine. A door on the other side of the cart probably led to a bedroom and bathroom. Her gaze rested on a cashmere wrap draped on the arm of a small couch, partially obscuring a black beaded clutch.

Clara returned her gaze to Humberto. "Where's my purse?"

He shook his head. "You did not have anything with you when we found you at the bottom of the stairs."

Clara bit her lip. *Shit!* No purse meant no room key. She tried to size up her new acquaintances. She swallowed a sigh of resignation and hoped they'd know how to get into her room. "Elena Cruz." She held out her hand. "Mucho gusto."

Humberto shook her hand. "Nice to meet you also, Elena."

Clara tried to smile, but the face of the stocky American shot through her mind.

"I think I was drugged."

"I am very sorry to hear that." Humberto met her stare and she thought she saw a hint of skepticism in his eyes. "If you were drugged—"

"What do you mean *if*!" Anger warmed her cheeks. "Why would I make up such a story!" She struggled to her feet and took a step toward the door.

"Wait." Lucia touched Clara's arm. "Humberto did not mean to imply you lied."

"Si." Humberto stood as he nodded. "I mean if you were drugged it would make it easier to burglarize your room."

"What?" The ship pitched and Clara's legs wobbled beneath her.

"We have heard of many travelers," Lucia added, "especially American women traveling alone, being drugged and . . ."

Clara's heart skipped a few beats as Lucia and Humberto exchanged a worried look. White noise filled her ears as she sat back down and took a deep breath to keep from fainting.

"I know it is hard to be thankful you were not assaulted," Lucia continued, "but trust me, you were lucky."

Lucky? I don't feel very damn lucky. "I need to get into my room, but my key is in my purse."

Humberto crossed the suite to a desk with a phone. "I will take care of it. What is your room number?"

"Seven-oh-seven."

As Humberto punched the keypad on the phone, Lucia asked, "Is there anything I can get you, Elena?"

Elena. Clara's mind rejected the name. She forced a smile and said, "No. Gracias."

Lucia nodded and began tidying a bureau strewn with a partially empty appetizer platter, plates, napkins and silverware.

Clara tuned into Humberto's conversation when his tone shifted from conciliatory too authoritative.

"Si, bueno." Humberto hung up and turned to Clara. "The purser will meet us at your room in twenty minutes."

"Thank you, Humberto. But you don't have to accompany me."

Humberto picked up his jacket and patted the pockets. "I am afraid you may encounter resistance since you do not have proper identification." He slipped his keycard from a breast pocket. "I will vouch for you."

A film of sweat coated Clara's upper lip and she said a silent prayer that her new passport remained locked in the safe.

"Lucia," Humberto said, "please order lunch for us and add Elena to our dinner reservations."

"That's not necessary," Clara said. "I think I'd like to catch up on my sleep and just stay in tonight."

Humberto shook his head. "Nonsense. It is our last night at sea before we stop in Mazatlan, which is our final destination, and we would love for you to join us."

Clara weighed the offer and decided she'd be safer with this reserved couple, than risking running into whoever had drugged her. "Gracias." She nodded. "Dinner would be nice."

"Bueno." Humberto smiled. "We should go." He kissed Lucia on the cheek and then opened the door for Clara.

She stepped past him into the corridor, recognizing the concierge level of the ship. Clara knew her stateroom would be two levels down, and recalled the bar she'd visited last night had been on the lido deck, which was one level up. Humberto stopped at a bank of elevators and Clara pushed the DOWN button. The doors whooshed open and they stepped inside. In her distracted state, Clara hadn't noticed the masculine scent emanating from her new friend, a pleasant combination of pine, rosemary and a hint of freesia. The cologne seemed fitting given his sophisticated demeanor. Clara cast a sideways glance at Humberto as the elevator arrived at her floor. Humberto smiled and held back the door, allowing her to exit first.

The purser stood in the hallway in front of Clara's room. "Mr. Alvarez?" he asked, extending his hand.

Humberto shook his hand. "Si. And this is Elena Cruz."

Clara also shook the man's hand, relieved to see compassion reflected in his eyes.

"Senior Purser Adams, Ms. Cruz. I'm so sorry you were attacked last night. I've filed a report regarding your stolen purse with our security chief and he would like you to visit his office at your first opportunity."

Clara gritted her teeth at the mention of a filed report. Shane had been adamant she avoid the authorities so she wouldn't show up on any news wires. She hoped her grimace represented some semblance of a smile as she thanked him.

He turned and swiped his keycard. "Now, let's check your room." He swung the door open and stepped into her stateroom.

Clara gasped and the floor seemed to buck and roll beneath her feet as she took in the devastation before her. Humberto gripped her elbow and placed a supportive hand on the small of her back.

"Oh my God . . ." She took a tentative step forward.

The mattress had been pulled from the bed frame and lay halfway on the floor. All the drawers in the small dresser were open and bare. And hangers devoid of clothing littered the carpet in front of the small closet.

Clara rushed into the closet and stared at the empty open safe. Despite Humberto's efforts to hold her up, she crumpled into a sobbing heap.

Purser Adams knelt down next to her, "Ms. Cruz, I'm afraid you'll be unable to stay here."

"What the hell," she said between sobs, "am I going to do now?"

"You will stay with us." Humberto helped her to her feet.

"Do you think you can make me a list of what's been stolen?" Purser Adams asked as Humberto guided Clara toward the door.

She stared at the purser as if he'd grown two heads. How could he not know? Her new life had been stolen before it had begun!

"Si," Humberto answered. "We will get you a list this afternoon."

Clara let Humberto escort her from the room, retracing their steps back to his suite. What choice did she have now but to let this kind man come to her rescue?

Without her burner phone she couldn't call Devyn. Or Shane. Or . . . Brady. She doubted Brady would be pleased to hear from her after her disappearing act from Los Angeles. Clara shuddered at the thought of the thief calling Devyn. She'd be worried about Clara. And what if the bandit worked for Damian? Not only would Damian know where Clara was headed, a call to Devyn would put her in harm's way.

Clara would have to find a way to contact Devyn. To make sure she was safe. To tell her that fate had re-charted Elena Cruz's course and landed her in Mazatlán, Mexico.

CHAPTER FORTY-FOUR

A knock thudded on the door. "Hola, Elena."

"Wrong room, buddy," she mumbled and buried her face in the pillow.

"Elena, are you awake?"

Elena? Who the hell— Clara's eyes flew open. "Shit! That's me." She jumped out of bed and hurried to the casita door. Hand on the knob, she glanced down at her thin tank top and snug- fitting boy shorts. As she pondered greeting her host, a sheet of paper glided under the door and rested at her bare feet.

Clara scooped the note from the tile floor and padded back to the bed. Perched on the edge of the mattress, she read Humberto's short message.

Buenos días, Elena,

She paused. "Elena. Elena Cruz. I need to start thinking of myself as Elena." She continued reading.

I will be gone until late afternoon. Please make yourself at home and let Maria know if you need anything. Lucia and I would like for you to join us for dinner tonight at six. It is not a formal affair and Lucia has left some clothes for you with Maria.

Hasta pronto, Humberto

Clara looked again at the sleeping attire Lucia had given her, wrinkling her nose at the skimpy outfit. She'd be more comfortable borrowing clothes from Maria. The housekeeper's practical albeit colorful ensembles leaned more toward Clara's modest style.

"Elena Cruz really needs to buy some clothes." Clara placed the note on the nightstand, pushed up from the oversized twin bed, and pulled the sheet and cream colored comforter up over the pillow.

A rush of anger colored her cheeks as she recalled her misfortune three days ago on the *Princess of the Sea.* Her plan had been perfect and all she'd had to do was arrive safely in Cabo San Lucas. Instead, Clara found herself stranded in Mazatlán, with nothing to rely on but the kindness of strangers.

When Humberto had offered her the casita, he'd describe it as a glorified spare bedroom, but Clara found she had all she needed, specifically privacy. The space shared a wall with the main house but had its own entrance. The five-hundred-square-foot dwelling felt larger thanks to a vaulted ceiling and picture window. A bistro table and chairs sat below a smaller window and completed the kitchenette. Humberto had given Lucia credit for decorating the interior and Clara thought the warm earth tones reflected Lucia's welcoming demeanor.

Clara headed for the kitchenette. "Elena Cruz needs coffee," she said, prepping the machine and setting it to brew. Three short steps placed her in the bathroom, where she turned on the shower and brushed her teeth while the water heated. Steam rolled across the mirror, blurring her reflection as she frowned at her now dark brown hair. Physically she no longer looked like Clara Marsh, but she hadn't mentally made the leap to her knew identity. A surge of tears welled in her eyes as she stepped into the shower and let the hot water cascade over her.

"How the hell do people who enter witness protection adjust to completely different lives?" she asked as the steam enveloped her.

Of course, she knew the answer; they were driven by fear and the instinct to survive. Even though Damian would die in prison, dread that he would seek revenge from behind bars had been motivation enough for Clara to change her name and disappear.

She heaved a sigh into the steam and tilted her head back to wash her hair. As she finished her shower, her mind replayed the events that placed her in the kind hands of

Humberto Alvarez. The cruise ship company had eventually located her purse, which still contained her booking confirmation but nothing else. Humberto had pulled some strings and used the booking document to request a replacement passport for Clara's alter ego. She had no idea what magic lay behind the phrase "pull some strings", but doubted Humberto had employed any shady tactics to help her. Still, she'd feel better once she no longer needed anyone's help. A tear slid down her cheek, merging with the shower spray. "Buck up, Elena! No one said starting over would be easy."

The delicious aroma of strong Mexican coffee tantalized her as she dried off and wrapped herself in the towel. She poured a cup and then pulled open the bifold closet doors. She sipped the delicious brew and contemplated which white T-shirt she would wear today with one of the two pairs of shorts that made up her borrowed wardrobe.

Maria's voice floated through the casita door. "Senorita Elena?"

"Un momento." Clara pulled a shirt over her head, stepped into a pair of khaki shorts and then hurried to open the door.

A smiling Maria greeted her. "Buenos dias."

"Buenos dias."

"I fix breakfast. You come to eat." Maria motioned for Clara to follow her.

"Oh, gracias." She pointed to her feet. "Let me grab some shoes."

The diminutive housekeeper smiled and nodded before returning to her tasks. Clara hurried to add undergarments to her ensemble, then stepped into a pair of flip-flops and headed for the main house. The heavenly scent of chorizo and eggs led her to the kitchen, where Maria had set to the task of loading the dishwasher. Clara estimated she and the maid were close in age, but years of physical labor had bowed Maria's frame. She wore her long hair in a bun and had a pleasant round face with fine wrinkles fanning out from her eyes when she smiled.

A dinette table with a place setting for one, sat in a bay window, providing a spectacular view of the marina. Clara sat down, her stomach growling as she picked up a fork and dug into the perfectly formed omelet.

Halfway through her savory breakfast, Maria refilled her coffee cup. "More?" She pointed to the half-empty plate.

Clara shook her head. "No, gracias."

"Senorita Lucia left clothes for you." Maria pointed to several hangers adorned with an assortment of garments hanging from sturdy wall hooks just inside the laundry room.

Clara hoped her trepidation didn't show on her face as she nodded at Maria, who cocked an eyebrow, but said nothing as Clara followed her with the breakfast dishes and placed them next to the sink.

"Breakfast was delicious, Maria. Gracias."

Maria eyed the half-eaten contents and shook her head. In the short time Clara had been Humberto's guest, she'd learned that Maria expected her meals to be devoured. Clara wanted to explain about her nervous stomach but simply smiled instead. She made a beeline for the laundry room, grabbed Lucia's clothes and disappeared down the hallway toward the powder room.

As Clara passed Humberto's study, she noticed a laptop sitting on his desk. She backtracked, stepped into the masculine room and closed the door. She tossed the bundle of clothes onto a leather chair in front of the desk and took in her surroundings. Floor-to-ceiling bookcases lined one wall and a fireplace with an ornate mantle occupied the other side. The two walls bookended a bank of windows that looked across the mouth of the marina. Humberto's desk sat centered on the wall opposite the large windows.

Clara lifted the laptop screen and pushed the power button. She held her breath as the computer hummed to life. "Shit!" she hissed when the sign-on screen opened and asked for a password. She plopped down into the desk chair and glared at the password prompt, then snatched up the receiver of the desk phone and listened to the dial tone buzz in her ear. Should she call Devyn from a traceable landline? What if she didn't answer? Should she leave a message . . . and say what? *All's well except I was drugged and robbed on the way to my new life.*

Clara dialed the number of Devyn's burner phone only to be greeted by an automated voice telling her something in Spanish. She banged the receiver back into its cradle, crossed her arms and leaned back in Humberto's chair.

Her searing gaze bounced from the laptop to the phone. "Elena Cruz needs a damn job so she can buy a damn laptop and a damn cell phone," she said as she lowered the laptop screen.

The phone rang, causing Clara to jump to her feet, knocking a pile of papers from the corner of the desk onto the floor. As she scooped up the loose documents, a business card floated down to her feet. She set the papers onto the desk and then bent over to retrieve the card. JUAN VEGA, PROCURADOR was set in bold black type in the middle of the card, with another line Clara couldn't translate: TENGO LO QUE NECESITAS! An address and phone number were printed below the message.

"Elena Cruz needs to learn Spanish!" she said as she flipped the card over, hoping for an English translation, but instead she found handwritten note in Spanish scribbled on the back: Tiene armas. Again she couldn't translate the whole

282

message, but Clara recognized one word. *Armas* was Spanish
for guns. She found a notepad and pen and jotted down
Juan's information. Shane had told her not to try and buy a
gun in Mexico; still this Juan might come in handy.

Clara clipped the pen to the notepad, gathered up the
clothes and then headed for the casita. Once inside, she
closed the door and tossed Lucia's loaned outfits onto the
bed.

A purple garment caught her eye and she pulled a
beautiful plum-colored blouse, embroidered with small gold
dragonflies, free from the pile. She traced a shimmering wing
with a fingertip and her mind filled with memories of her
daughter. Ally had fallen in love with the gossamer-winged
insect after writing a school report in the sixth grade. Doodles
of dragonflies had become part of her signature. Clara
thumbed tears from her eyes and held the hanger up to her
shoulders. The rayon top appeared to be a perfect fit. She
returned her attention to the heap and noticed a note taped to
the next hanger.

> *Elena,*
>
> *I noticed your beautiful dragonfly necklace and
> thought of you when I saw this outfit. Please accept
> this gift as a welcome to Mazatlán. Even though
> I have only known you a few days, I believe we will
> become great friends. Bienvenidos, amiga ~ Lucia*

A flowy black skirt hung on the next hanger, which also had a small silk bag tied to the neck. Clara lifted the bag free, gently emptied the contents onto the bed and smiled at the gold-colored dragonfly earrings. Strappy dark purple sandals also hung around the neck of the hanger.

She closed the blinds and changed into her new outfit. The sleeveless blouse fit perfectly and flared slightly over the top of the knee-length skirt. As she studied herself in the mirror, she frowned at her stringy hair.

"How the hell am I going to style this mop without any products?" She opened the cabinet beneath the bathroom sink and found what she needed: a stack of old rags.

An hour later, Clara admired her handiwork. She didn't have thick hair, but it would still take a few hours for her rag-rolled curls to dry. Well she might as well take advantage of the hot Mexican sun. Once again dressed in her T-shirt and shorts, she fixed a glass of ice water, took her borrowed notepad and headed outside to the small brick patio between the casita and the main house.

Clara settled into one of the lounge chairs and tapped the pen against her lips. "Step one," she said as she contemplated what she needed to get back on track. Originally, Shane had given her three aliases to choose from along with five destinations so that not even he would know who or where she was. "Okay, I need a job so I can buy a phone and a laptop so I can contact Devyn," she said as she bullet-pointed each item and then added clothes to the end of her list.

"Senorita?" The man's voice catapulted her to her feet and she spun around to face the intruder.

"Hola, senorita." A warm smiled graced his handsome face. "I am Captain Torres." He extended his hand, and when she didn't respond, he continued. "Lucia's brother, Marco."

"Pleased to meet you." Clara grasped his hand. "I'm Cl–" She cleared her throat. "Elena Cruz."

"Ah . . . I have been invited to dinner to meet Humberto's beautiful house guest." Captain Torres's warm smile had morphed into an amusing grin. "I came early to discuss a police matter with him."

"Oh, I don't think Humberto's back from town."

"Esta bien. I will wait in his study." He gave a slight bow and crossed the patio to the main house. He turned to face her again, his stare bringing color to her cheeks. "Pleasure meeting you, Elena Cruz."

She did a finger wave, gathered her things and headed for the casita. Sitting in the hot sun had raised a film of sweat on her skin and she decided to rinse off. Her new outfit hung on the partially open closet door and she smiled as she passed by, stepping into the bathroom.

"Oh . . . my . . . God!" She stared in disbelief at her ragged tied hair, which made her look like a crazy cartoon character, explaining Captain Torres's amusement.

"Well, Elena," she snarked at the mirror, "hopefully you can transform this frightful creature into the beautiful house guest Captain Torres is expecting to see at dinner."

CHAPTER FORTY-FIVE

Humberto's note had said dinner wasn't a formal affair, but as Clara took in the massive Spanish colonial table set for twelve, she wondered if he had invited more than just Captain Torres to dinner.

Pleased with how well her new clothes fit, not to mention her hair had behaved and now flowed in soft curls down her back, Clara had decided to be early. Though she'd made the choice to trust Humberto, her recent setback kept her on high alert and she wanted to take in her surroundings and be ready for whatever, or whoever, the night had in store. She'd also spent the afternoon coaching herself on embracing her new identity . . . after all, her new friends knew her as Elena Cruz.

Elena strolled around the dark table, recounting the place settings. Twelve seats would mean eight new people to meet. She fingered Ally's locket and whispered, "I hope the new people wear name tags."

The elegant room had the same high ceilings as the rest of the house, which allowed several large paintings to adorn the walls and one in particular captured Elena's interest. From across the room, she admired a spectacular ocean scene, complete with a blue sky over a catamaran sailing an azure sea. She moved closer and could almost feel the ocean spray as white sails reached for the sky and the vessel navigated a small rock island while multicolored passengers pointed and snapped photos of sea lions lounging in the sun. The caption at the bottom of the canvas read *Sail Bula* and Elena smiled at the artist's name: Lucia Torres.

"Buenos noches," Maria said behind her.

Elena turned and smiled at the housekeeper, who had already busied herself collecting some of the place settings and stacking them at the end of the table. "Buenos noches, Maria." She joined the housekeeper. "How many are coming to dinner?"

She held up six fingers. "Seis."

Elena nodded, but failed to mask her surprise, which elicited further information.

"Senoritas Rosa and Lupe from Casa del Angel." Maria folded a cloth napkin in half and then reached for another.

"Angel House," Elena translated.

Maria nodded. "Si." She placed the pile of napkins on the top plate and carried the stack to a large hutch at the end of the dining room. Elena scooped up the extra silverware and followed Maria who placed the dishes in the cabinet. "Oh, gracias, Elena," Maria said, patting the top of the hutch, "por favor, aqui."

Lucia glided into the room. "Elena, bonita!" she gushed as she took Elena's hands in hers.

"Well, I have you to thank." Color rose in Elena's cheeks. "The clothes are lovely. Gracias."

"It is my pleasure." Lucia pulled out two chairs and motioned to one as she sat.

Elena gathered up her skirt and sat opposite the Mexican beauty, who looked radiant in a lacy cream-colored top paired with a tight caramel-colored skirt. A bright orange fire opal rested against her dark skin in the hollow of her throat.

Lucia smiled at Maria and said, "Dos sangrias, por favor."

Maria nodded and hurried from the dining room.

"Elena, since you are new in town . . ." Lucia paused "I thought you might like to meet my sobrina and her amiga who work with me in helping women who have been . . . abused."

Elena's pulse quickened, but she managed a weak smile. Like an echo from the past, the word *abused* bashed against her brain. She breathed deeply, hoping to stem the flood of Clara's memories waiting to be unleashed.

Lucia pressed on. "What happened to you on the ship was unfortunate—but perhaps timely. We need a woman who speaks English to assist us with American tourists who find themselves victims of violence."

Maria appeared with their drinks, giving Elena a moment to process Lucia's proposal. How should she respond to a matter so close to her heart? Humberto's voice reached them before he entered the dining room, followed by Marco Torres. Elena thought she detected tension in Humberto's tone, but he flashed his usual welcoming smile before planting a kiss on Lucia's cheek.

"Elena," Humberto began. "Allow me to introduce you to my dear friend, and Lucia's brother, Captain Marco Torres."

A knowing smile played on Captain Torres lips as he gave a slight bow. "Your—" he made a small circle in the air near his head "—hair is lovely."

Humberto looked from Elena to Torres. "You two have met already?"

Elena resisted the urge to pat her hair. "Yes, this afternoon."

"Bueno!" Humberto clapped Torres on the back, then headed for a crystal decanter and glasses sitting on a buffet.

Marco winked at the women and trailed after Humberto. Elena sipped her sangria and couldn't help but notice how well Marco's backside filled out his dark dress slacks. Both men wore white short-sleeved linen shirts, but Humberto sported a pair of Levi's instead of trousers.

When the men returned, Elena could smell the tequila in their tumblers. Her stomach lurched at the familiar scent, and for a second, she had to fight the urge to bolt from the room.

Maria appeared again, carrying a tray of appetizers, which she placed on the buffet. "La cena estara lista en veinte minutos," she said to Humberto before leaving.

Elena knew *cena* translated to *dinner*, but despite the savory aroma filling the room, she wasn't sure her nervous stomach would calm enough to eat anything.

Lucia addressed her brother. "Marco, yesterday, I invited Rosa and Lupe to join us so that Elena can meet them." She checked her watch. "They are late. Do you know if something has delayed them?"

He shook his head. "I spoke with Lupe earlier and she was looking forward to coming tonight." His phone vibrated simultaneously with Humberto's ringing phone. The two men exchanged a glance before taking their calls.

"Bueno," Captain Torres's tone all business. "Cuando?" He nodded as Humberto's spoke to his caller in a calming voice.

Torres said, "Han identificado el cuerpo?"

Lucia was on her feet, pacing between the dueling conversations. "Marco, tell me." Her eyes pleaded with him. "Tell me who is dead?" He held up a finger and then headed for the other end of the room.

"Estoy seguro de que ella esta bien, Lupe." Humberto touched Lucia's arm.

"Rosa?" Her face contorted with worry. "Humberto, let me talk to Lupe."

The blend of English and Spanish made Elena's head spin, and though she couldn't translate most of conversations, she understood something terrible had happened.

"Le dire, Lupe. Nos vemos pronto." Humberto disconnected. "Lucia, please sit."

"No!" She stomped her foot. "Not until you tell me what the hell is going on."

Marco Torres came to his sister and wrapped her in his arms. "Lo siento."

Lucia remained rigid in her brother's embrace. "Quien, Marco?"

Clara's heart hammered in her chest, stripping her of her new identity as she caught a glimpse of Maria standing in the doorway, tears streaming down her cheeks. Humberto took the housekeeper's hand in his and guided her to a chair.

Lucia whispered to her brother, "Who, Marco?"

His voice broke before he answered, "Rosa."

Lucia's grief reverberated in the wail that bounced off the dining room walls.

CHAPTER FORTY-SIX

The waitress delivered his second margarita with a smile that encouraged a big tip. While attractive enough, her age showed in fine lines at the corner of her eyes. His tastes ran a little younger.

He'd selected a lounge chair strategically positioned between the women's restroom and the stairs, watching as each long-legged lovely climbed to exit the pool. Of course, he had to endure the occasional soccer mom stuffed into a bikini with a kid hanging from her hip as she labored out of the pool like a pack mule.

He licked salt from the rim of his plastic cup and took a long sip of the tart margarita as he watched a group of young Canadian women bump glasses in a toast. Their uproarious "Cheers!" cut through the eighties soundtrack blaring from the bar speakers.

He met and held the eyes with one of the beauties. She winked at him. He smiled and raised his glass. *Maybe.* She looked nothing like Juliette, even with her deep dark tan and long honey-colored hair, but her wink felt like a challenge.

The band of beauties splashed away from the swim-up bar and held court in the shallow end of the pool. His winking cutie maneuvered herself into a spot with a direct view of his chair. *Persistence.* A trait he admired. If she only knew what reward awaited her.

The face of his second Juliette flashed in his mind. It had been a week since their date, which had ended badly. He'd changed hotels and kept a low profile, even though he was confident he'd left no trace of himself behind.

He sighed remembering how perfect she'd been. Long, jet-black hair. Innocent dark eyes. Luscious red lips. An unspoiled young virgin. He hadn't planned to hurt her and found her attempt to fight off his romantic advances amusing at first. He'd enjoyed toying with her, slowly stripping off her clothes, licking and sucking her exposed flesh as he went. When she kneed him in the groin, he exploded with anger and took her viciously. Usually a violent attack took the fight out of his dates, but not this one. When he leaned in to kiss her, she slapped him and he flew into a rage. The next thing he knew, he'd choked the life out of her.

I should've kept her restrained.

He definitely needed to find a balance between drugging and restraining his Juliette's, as he had his first date, and killing his second beloved. Both approaches had made branding their inner thigh with his signature mark easy, but he knew a string of bodies could end his fun sooner than later.

The Canadians had begun their ascent up the pool steps. He appraised each creature as they strutted past him, his winking lovely the last to emerge. Her skin glistened and he could now see she had stunning brown eyes flecked with gold. She graced him with a sparkling smile and winked again as she passed by his chair, leaving a telltale scent of coconut trailing behind her.

Definitely.

CHAPTER FORTY-SEVEN

Elena arrived early at Casa del Ángel, grateful to have the office to herself and free access to a computer. In the week since Rosa's death, she had provided support wherever needed. Humberto gave her the keys to a battered, baby blue VW Bug, and a cell phone, so she could cover Angel House for Lucia.

Which is how she now sat staring dumbfounded at the first message Devyn had posted to their fake email account two days after Clara fled Los Angeles:

Damian escaped! Contact me ASAP!

She shivered and her blood ran cold as the words 'Damian escaped' jumped off the screen at her. She fumbled with the laptop's cursor and clicked on the next message:

Clara, Jesus! Where are you? Scared out of my mind! Call me when you get this!

Devyn's terrified voice echoed in Clara's mind as she read the third email:

Clara, I'm so worried. Please call so I know you're okay . . . Love you.

Tears blurred her vision. She picked up her cell phone to call Devyn, but she didn't remember the burner phone's number and calling Devyn's personal phone would be a mistake. The draft folder showed one more item. She swiped at her eyes and opened the last email. Heat flooded her cheeks as she read the cryptic paragraph:

I hope you're sitting somewhere enjoying the sun instead of lying somewhere dead because I'm looking forward to kicking your ass for disappearing so efficiently. Brady

Clara placed trembling fingers on the laptop keys. Should she tell Devyn, and subsequently, Brady, about the incident on the cruise ship? Could Damian have been behind the attack? Should she reveal her location? Should she beg to be rescued? Her fingers moved across the keyboard, a plan formulating in her mind as she began typing a message to Devyn.

D ~ I'm safe. Incident on my trip south left me with no cash or ability to communicate. Need funds wired and will send bank info soon. Do you know where the hell Damian is? Thinking I need to hit the road . . . C ~

She reread her words to make sure she hadn't been too specific. If Brady could figure out where she was, then so could Damian. *Shit, unless Damian already knows I'm in Mazatlan!*

The phone rang and she snatched up the receiver. "Hello," her voice quaked. "I mean . . ."

Lucia's voice filled her ear. "Hola, Elena. Is everything okay?"

Clara felt like a ping pong ball. Devyn's emails had resurrected Clara and now Lucia was calling her Elena.

"Her response tumbled out. "I'm fine. Yes. Everything's fine."

"Bueno . . ." Lucia hesitated. "Inez is on her way to relieve you for lunch."

"Okay." She knew she'd need more than a lunch hour to set her plan in motion. "Actually, Lucia, I'm not feeling well. Do you think Inez can cover the rest of the day?"

"Si, si." Concern echoed in Lucia's tone. "I will call her now and she should be there shortly."

"Gracias, Lucia. I'm sorry to—"

"No, no," Lucia cut her off. "You have been so supportive. Por favor, go home and feel better."

"I will. Talk tomorrow." Mentally, Clara had already begun sorting through the list of actions she needed to take, each seeming more important than the other, as she retrieved her passport from her hiding place in the floor. Then she set pen to paper to organize her thoughts.

1. Open bank account
2. Email bank info to Devyn
3. Pick destination and map route
4. Buy a gun
5. Pack belongings
6. Retrieve hidden cash
7. Write thank you notes to Humberto and Lucia

Shane had been adamant Clara not buy a gun. Not only is it difficult to purchase a gun in most countries, and is illegal in Mexico, Shane feared she'd end up on someone's radar. But with the news of Damian's escape, Clara decided buying a gun was the lessor of two evils. She fumbled in her purse for Juan's number, dialed and waited for the call to ring through.

"Bueno," a voice barked into her ear.

"Is this Juan?" She hoped she sounded calm.

"Si. Who is this?" Juan's baritone voice sent a tremor down her spine.

She hesitated. "Elena Cruz."

"What do you want?"

"A friend gave me your name and said you can help me with a specific purchase."

"You know Tequila's?" He didn't wait for a response. "Meet me there in an hour."

Dial tone filled her ear and she disconnected on her end. She signed back into the fake email account again to check to see if Devyn had replied. As she waited for the program to open, Inez pushed through the door. Clara glanced quickly at the draft folder, which showed no new messages. She signed off and lowered the laptop screen.

"I brought chicken tortilla soup from Gus Gus," Inez said, placing a white paper bag on the desk. "Now go home." She motioned toward the door. "Eat soup and rest."

"Gracias, Inez," Clara said as she gathered her purse, phone and the white paper bag. The spicy aroma of the soup made her stomach growl. "Buenas tardes." She gave Inez a small wave and stepped outside into the baking afternoon heat.

Clara unlocked the VW, climbed behind the wheel and headed for the Golden Zone. Clara had been to the Golden Zone once to pick up pastries for Humberto and thought she recalled seeing Tequila's on her way to Panama's. The tall bakery sign came into view and she angled into a parking spot at the curb. The other thing she remembered was a bank two blocks up from Panama's. She locked her car and headed for HSBC Bank. Half an hour later, she'd opened a new account with the fifty dollars Humberto had given her for incidentals, and had the incoming wire instructions for

Devyn. Back on the sidewalk, Clara headed in the direction of Tequila's.

A car backfired and Clara gasped as her heart beat wildly against her ribs. A crowd of young tourists pushed past her and she stumbled into step behind them.

By the time she arrived at Tequila's, sweat ran in rivulets between her breasts. She stepped into the dark, cool interior and scanned the place for a man sitting alone. She was fifteen minutes early and the only men sitting at the bar, bent of their beers, didn't appear to be Hispanic. The bartender smiled and motioned for her to sit wherever she liked. She chose a table toward the back and sat in a chair facing the door.

A waiter delivered chips, salsa and water to her table, and then asked, "Something to drink?"

"Corona, por favor." She smiled.

He nodded. "Bueno."

Clara pulled her list from her purse, unfolded it and marked off the first item. She looked out the window and wondered how far the old VW would make it?

"Your cerveza, senorita."

Clara whipped her head around at the familiar voice and came face-to-face with Jackson Brady.

CHAPTER FORTY-EIGHT

Brady placed a Corona in front of her and sat down. His intense gaze holding hers, the stare down uprooting long-buried desire in Clara. After Ally's death, Brady had provided a thread of sanity in the unraveling horror of her life.

He looked like he hadn't slept in days, even though his clothes, an olive-colored shirt over a pair of tan chinos, had that slept-in look. The waiter delivered a Tecate to Brady, who clinked the long neck of her Corona and raised his beer in a toast.

"Congratulations on staying alive." He took a long swallow and then pointed his bottle at her. "Its bad luck if you don't take at least a sip after a toast."

Clara crossed her arms. "How do you know Juan?"

"He's Shane's guy."

It struck Clara that, like Damian, there seemed no end to the ties and connections Brady and Shane seemed to possess.

"How did you know I landed in Mazatlan?"

"We didn't. After Damian's great escape, Shane and Devyn spilled the beans about your plan, which led us to the cruise to Cabo. Shane and Devyn went to Cabo and I came here. I suspected once you heard about Damian, you'd try to buy a gun."

The fact that he didn't know about her ordeal on the cruise ship must have shown on her face, because he cocked his head to one side.

"What?" Brady asked.

"I . . . Nothing." She cleared her throat. "Does Devyn know I'm okay?"

He nodded. "Why did you get off the ship in Mazatlan?"

Elena tipped up her Corona and took a couple of sips. The tang of the lime she'd squeezed into the beer a tad too sour on her tongue. "Four days into the cruise, someone drugged me, ransacked my room and took everything." She swirled the Corona to mix the lime and beer better.

"Where have you been staying?"

"With the people who rescued me on the ship."

Brady pulled a phone from his pocket. "Names?"

"Why? They've been nothing but kind."

Brady sighed. "Clara, I don't . . ."

"Shhh," she hissed, scanning the bar and leaning close. "My name is Elena," she whispered.

"Fine." He leaned toward her and she caught her breath as his familiar scent wafted over her. "Elena . . . Damian's coming after you. He probably had someone follow you onto the ship."

Her hands began to shake, and Brady reached across the table, taking them in his. His touch felt warm but did nothing to settle her churning gut.

"Cla—Elena," he said in a calm voice, "I want to have Shane checkout your new friends. Tell me their names."

"Humberto Alvarez and Lucia and Marco Torres." She placed her hands in her lap when he let go and began typing the names into his phone. *Just breath . . .*

Brady drained his beer. "Drink up. We're leaving."

She shook her head. "I can't just leave without telling them goodbye."

Brady's eyes grew a shade darker, a sign she remembered meant he hadn't told her everything. It was her turn to ask, "What?"

"Valencia Garza is dead."

Clara blinked at the news about her former mother-in-law. She'd never liked the woman, but for Damian to kill his mother . . .

Brady broke into her thoughts. "I think Damian hired the same hit man he sent after you in Malibu."

"And you think that's who drugged me on the ship?"

"No." Brady reached for her Corona and took a drink. "I think Damian has someone following you. I think he has plans for you . . . before he—"

"Kills me."

He nodded as she finished his sentence.

Brady's phone buzzed with an incoming text. "Your friend Alvarez is well connected and wealthy." He looked up at her and she thought she saw question in his eyes. "Marco Torres and his sister, Lucia . . ." Brady raised his gaze again as he pronounced the word "sister" in two distinct syllables. "Are the children of Antonio Torres, deceased, and former mayor of Mazatlán."

As if she'd been summoned, Clara's phone rang with an incoming call from Lucia Torres.

"Good," Brady said. "Now you can tell your wealthy, well connected friends goodbye over the phone."

She narrowed her eyes at his bossy tone and answered on the third ring. "Hi, Lucia."

"Elena, can you come to the hospital?" Lucia sounded desperate. "Another young woman has been assaulted. I have tried to question her, but she won't talk to me. Can you come?"

"Yes." Clara stood. "I'll be right there."

Brady gripped her arm as she dropped her phone into her purse. "Where are you going?"

"To the hospital." She knew she should pull her arm away, but didn't.

He loosened his grip without letting go. "All right, but we're leaving as soon as we can.

"You don't need to come with me."

Brady chuckled and drew her closer. "I'm not letting you out of my sight."

"And how do you suggest I explain" —she looked him up and down— "you?"

"Tell them I'm your friend Clara's fiancé, that she's gone missing and I'm here looking for her."

CHAPTER FORTY-NINE

As Clara navigated the busy streets of Mazatlan en route to the clinic, Brady replayed their reunion at Tequila's. His knees had almost buckled when he crossed from the bar to Clara's table. His emotions roller-coastered from being relieved she was alive, to pissed she'd disappeared, to wanting to hold her in this arms. As he'd placed the Corona in front of her, Brady took in long dark hair that framed a thinner face. It had only been ten days, but her transformation from Clara Marsh to Elena Cruz looked complete.

Clara honked and swerved the VW around a slow-moving *pulmonia*. The taxi driver honked at her and gave a one finger salute as she sped by.

When she slammed on the brakes at a red light, Brady palmed the dashboard.

"Nervous being alone with me?" she asked.

"Hardly."

She snorted a half laugh. "Just keeping up with the crazy Mexican drivers."

"Well, I'd like to arrive in one piece."

Clara smiled, popped the clutch and shot forward.

Brady adjusted his seatbelt. "Explain to me again why you need to go to the hospital?"

She jerked the steering wheel hard to the left and shot around a delivery truck. "Because Lucia Torres runs Angel House, which helps women of domestic violence and—"

"She knows about Ally?" he cut in.

Clara shook her head as she short-shifted into third and blew through a yellow light. "All they know is that I'm from LA and had planned to relocate in Cabo."

"Shane said he told you to keep your back story simple, but—"

"To be broad and general." Her turn to cut him off. "I used my mom's initials to create Elena Cruz, my unwitting knowledge of Mexico in deciding my destination and . . ."

The Volkswagen's brakes screeched as she slammed to a stop to avoid hitting two children crossing against the green. The school girls squealed and hurried off the road.

Brady wiped sweat from his brow. "And?"

"And had planned to volunteer at a hospital in Cabo because my mom was a candy striper back in the day."

They rode in silence for a block before Clara turned into the parking lot of Hospital Balboa. Brady unfolded himself from the battered baby blue death trap and followed Clara through the emergency room doors. Cool antiseptic air blasted him as she rushed toward a stunning woman conversing with a doctor.

Clara touched the woman's arm and they embraced.

"Oh, Elena, muchas gracias por venir."

"Lucia, where are Humberto and Marco?" Clara asked.

"They have gone to the Inn at Mazatlán to check the victim's room for evidence."

Clara smiled at the doctor standing next to Lucia.

"This is Doctor Morales; he is caring for the young woman who was attack . . ." Lucia's dark eyes bored into his as Brady attempted a charming smile. "Who is this?"

"Oh," Clara gave Brady a quick glance. "This is Brad Jones." She turned her attention back to Lucia and continued. "He called Angel House earlier looking for his girlfriend, so I called and told him about the victim."

Brady's muscles tightened at her lie, even though inwardly he admired her swift background shift.

"Senor, is your girlfriend Canadian?"

Brady cut his eyes to Clara, who gave a slight head shake. "No, she's an American." Knowing she'd be pissed, he added. "Her name is Clara." Clara's nostrils flared as Lucia touched his arm.

"This young woman is Canadian." She hesitated. "Be glad she is not your girlfriend because she has been brutally abused and . . . and . . ."

Doctor Morales stepped forward. "Maybe Elena should speak with her now."

Lucia nodded, and then they followed the doctor a short distance down a corridor, stopping in front of a closed door.

The doctor placed a hand on the door knob but hesitated. "She is muy emotive . . . um . . ."

"Very emotional," Lucia translated.

Doctor Morales nodded. "Emotional." He lightly wrapped on the door as he pushed it open. "Senorita, you have visitors."

The young woman shrank into the bed as if she wanted to disappear.

"Esta bien," the doctor assured. "They are here to help."

Brady leaned against the back wall as Clara stepped forward and stood next to Dr. Morales. She smiled and said, "Hi, I'm Elena. What's your name?"

"Chlo–Chloe."

Clara inched closer to the bed. "I'm very sorry this happened to you."

Chloe began to sob.

Clara held the young woman's hand in hers. "Chloe, can you tell me about your attacker?"

"He's American." She twisted the tissue in her hand. "Not tall but thin . . . boyish."

Clara nodded. "Do you think he's a teenager?"

Chloe shook her head. "No, maybe mid-twenties."

"Can you remember the color of his hair or eyes? Anything that stood out?"

A head bob was followed by swipe at her nose with the tissue. "Blond hair, sort of dirty looking, and brown eyes."

"You're doing great, Chloe." Clara squeezed her hand. "I know this will be difficult, but can you tell me what happened?"

"H–he . . ." Sobs shook her shoulders. "R–raped me and then . . ." She moved aside the bedcovers. "Look what he did! He branded me!"

Clara gasped and stumbled back into Brady as he came forward, then the two of them crept slowly toward the gruesome artwork running the length of Chloe's inner thigh. The angry red wound seemed to shout at them. A crown of stars arched over a cross that bled into a heart.

"No!" Escaped Clara's lips before she could contain the outburst. Brady instinctively wrapped his arms around her, providing support as she began to crumble to the floor.

"Elena?" Lucia looked searchingly from her friend to Brady. "Is she okay?"

"It's just the shock of seeing such a horrific wound," he said. "I think she needs to sit down."

"Si, in the waiting area." Lucia led the way from Chloe's room as the doctor quietly explained to the injured girl that he'd prescribed a sedative to help her sleep.

Brady guided Clara to the nearest chair. "I think she could use some water too."

"Si," Lucia called over her shoulder as she headed in the direction of the nurses' station. "I will be right back."

"He found me," Clara whispered. "He's here to kill me . . . I-I . . ." She looked up at Brady and the fear in her eyes almost stopped his heart.

CHAPTER-FIFTY

He paced the dingy room like an animal looking to escape his cage. In a terse text message, he'd been instructed to pack his things and leave the luxurious Inn at Mazatlán immediately:

Be sure not to leave anything behind. Be sure not to attract any attention. Be sure to be at the flea bag hotel before high noon.

The Master was mad. But everything that had gone wrong could be explained. He just needed a few minutes of the Master's time to clarify how the hysterical Hispanic girl had created a situation that required him to silence her forever. And surely the Master would understand why he had to abandon the Canadian bitch and disappear before she regained consciousness.

His eye began to twitch and he pressed on the corner to control the nervous tick. After another lap around the threadbare carpet, he dropped into a sagging arm chair, leaned his head back and closed his eyes.

It's true what they say about Canadians—they can hold their liquor. A vision of the blonde beauty tossing down her third shot of tequila appeared behind his eye lids. He could almost smell the fiery liquid as she blew out a breath. When she licked her lips the memory of his arousal warmed his loins.

He jumped to his feet and resumed his pacing. "Fucking bitch!"

Her light complexion had provided a perfect canvas for his tribute to Juliette. He didn't know why, but his victim woke up as he put the finishing touches to the heart tailing from his perfect cross. He covered his ears, but even in the pathetic hotel room, he couldn't block out her haunting thick accent.

"What the hell!" She'd struggled against her arm restraints. "Where are my clothes?"

He'd tried to reassure her. "It's okay, Juliette. Be still, my love—"

"My name's Chloe, you freak." She tried to kick out at him and screamed, "What did you do to my leg?"

He hadn't hesitated. He'd wrapped his hands around her throat and squeezed. He released his grip after her eyes rolled back and she'd stopped struggling. Then he gave her another shot of Ketamine, swept the room for any remnants of himself, and made a hasty exit.

He should have killed Chloe because she did not go 'quietly into that goodnight.' She didn't retreat to her hotel room afraid, injured and degraded. She didn't do what all those before her had done. No, the bitch had called for help.

His phone vibrated and he thumbed away the locked screen to see an incoming text from the Master: *Arrived. Be at your hotel in ten.*

The flicker of fear he'd felt when instructed to report to this seedy hotel now sent waves of dread coursing through him. His first instinct had been to run, but the lure of his final payment for his role in the Master's end game, kept him in check. He sucked in a calming breath and released it slowly. If the Master had wanted him dead, he would have just ordered someone to do the deed. Coming to Mazatlan surely meant he planned to make good on his original promise.

After all, the Master had already spent thousands of dollars to assure his protégé got off on a technicality and was released from jail. If the Master hadn't intervened, Billy Boyd knew he'd be rotting in some prison. Knew he'd be claimed by some brute who liked thin, blond southern boys. Knew he'd wish he were dead every time his "boyfriend" said, "Squeal for me, Billy." The horror of what could've been raised bile in the back of his throat.

"I've done everything I've been asked to do!" Billy shouted at the grimy beige walls. "I know all about Clara and her new life. Her new name. Her new friends."

Billy had begun their plan of terrorizing women, and though there had been a couple of missteps along the way, his latest masterpiece would send Clara a clear message. But what if the Master's reason for coming was to send a clear message to those who displeased him?

"Dead men can't spend ill-gotten gains, you fool," he muttered under his breath. He should be thankful to be alive and run. He should run now!

He hooked his duffle bag over his shoulder and hustled to the door. A knock thudded as he reached for the doorknob and he stumbled back a step. The handle jiggled, followed by a fist bump against the thin panel separating him from the Master.

He dropped his bag, flipped the deadbolt and opened the door.

Damian Garza's sneer told him pleading his case would be futile. And the large Hispanic man behind Damian, who stared at him with cold dead eyes, fanned his fire of dread and consumed him.

CHAPTER FIFTY-ONE

Clara shook her head. "It's not him." Her trembling limbs belied her confident statement.

"It's him."

Clara looked up at Brady. "But she described a blond kid with a southern accent." The hair bristling at the back of her neck knew the truth.

"You saw the markings on her leg."

Clara nodded. "Star-crossed lovers." Her thudding heart drummed a beat of dread.

"It's him. He just didn't do the deed."

Brady's hand on her shoulder felt reassuring, but she couldn't relax, adrenaline burned through her veins, fanning her desire to run. "But why someone else?"

Brady shrugged as he pulled his phone from his pocket. "I'll have Shane look into Damian's jail time. Maybe someone owed him a favor."

Lucia, a cup in each hand, smiled at Brady as they passed in the hallway. She shrugged as she stood in front of Clara. "I could not decide between coffee or water." Concern reflected in her eyes.

Clara reached for the coffee, the strong aroma assaulting her senses. "Gracias, Lucia."

Lucia managed a smile. "You are okay?"

"Si." She sipped the coffee. "Her wounds are just so horrifying."

"My niece . . ." Lucia touched her fingers to her lips, "Rosa had the same wounds."

The emergency room doors swooshed open before Clara could ask about Rosa's wound. No one had mentioned the young girl having a cross carved into her thigh. Had it been the man who tattooed Chloe? Or had it been Damian? Humberto met Clara's worried gaze as Marco rushed to her side. She shot a warning look in Brady's direction as Marco knelt on one knee next to her chair.

"Elena," he took her hand in his. "You are very pale and your hand is so cold."

"The young girl's wounds upset her, upset us both," Lucia said as she melted into Humberto's embrace.

"We should get you ladies home," Humberto said. "There is nothing more we can do tonight."

Clara noticed Brady had inched his way closer to the small group, his head cocked toward them as she asked, "You didn't find anything at the hotel?"

Marco shook his head as he came to his feet. "Not at first glance. I will have a forensic team process the room tomorrow. Hopefully, they will discover something useful."

"Come," Humberto took Lucia's hand. "We will start fresh in the morning."

Clara met Brady's stare as he stood behind Humberto who instinctively turned to face the newcomer.

"Oh, Senor Jones," Lucia said. "Please let me introduce you to my brother, Captain Marco Torres and my . . ." She hesitated. "Our dear friend, Humberto Alvarez."

Brady offered a tight smile and shook hands with both men.

"You are related to the victim?" Humberto sounded skeptical.

"No, I . . ." Brady began, but Clara chimed in.

"No he's . . ."

Lucia tried to finish the sentence. "He is looking for . . ."

Her lips were moving, but Clara heard nothing over the clanging of a metal tray as it hit the floor. Over the shriek of a nurse. Over the distinct familiar voice offering an apology.

The buzzing in her ears grew louder. Clara shook her head and the echo of a vase shattering on the floor cut through the maddening noise. Perspiration engulfed her as if the waiting room had become a sauna. She tried to control her thoughts, but the sound of Ally's scream filled her mind. Clara white-

knuckled the arms of the waiting room chair as her memory catapulted around a corner and she came face-to-face with Damian in her mind. His sneer burned through her memories and her skin felt scorched.

She heard Brady's voice calling to her, but the horrifying video of cradling her daughter's limp body in her arms played on just for her. If only she'd arrived in time to save her daughter. To offer herself as sacrifice. To stop Damian.

"Clara!" Urgency filled Brady's tone. "Look at me!"

The buzzing had become so loud she could no longer hear her heartbeat. She could no longer discern between the past and the present. She could not stop the gunshot from another time and it now seemed to pierce her heart as the buzzing became overbearing.

Clara sprang from her chair and bolted from the waiting room. Damian's evil laugh chased her through the hospital doors onto the tourist-filled street, hot on her heels as she ran for her life.

CHAPTER FIFTY-TWO

Damian had to see the kid's handiwork for himself. The sleeping girl looked small in the hospital bed, her rising and falling chest the only indication she was still alive. He slid the sheet carefully from her leg. She stirred as he lifted the gauze from her wound. It emitted a fetid antiseptic odor and seemed to ooze with anger. The kid did good work. The stars arching over the top of the cross seemed to twinkle at his admiration. Distinct lines defined the cross and the added flare of tailing off into a heart completed the imagery.

Damian smiled as he traced a finger over the angry red cross. The girl's leg twitched and she whimpered. He tensed when a metal tray clanged to the floor. He forced a dazzling smile as he turned to face a nurse backing down the hallway. "Lo siento." He extended a hand and placed the other on his chest. "I am so sorry to have startled you."

The nurse continued to backpedal, wariness tightening her aged skin. Damian held his hand up in mock surrender. "Esta bien," he said. "I am her surgeon." The nurse looked less skeptical, but the young girl had become hysterical, her high-pitched keening filling the room.

Damian gave a quick bow and turned on a heel to retrace his steps back to the fire exit door he'd used to gain entry into the hospital. He stopped in his tracks as her name, oh so familiar, echoed down the hallway.

"Clara!" A male voice shouted again, drawing Damian back toward the nurse who now cowered against the wall. As he rounded the corner and stood at the edge of the waiting room, he saw a slim woman crashing through the emergency room doors, her long hair swirling behind her.

She turned and looked through the plate glass window and Damian relished the terror he saw in his ex-wife's eyes.

CHAPTER FIFTY-THREE

Brady watched as Clara bounced off the emergency room doors when she cut the corner too close. He called after her and tried to hold her manic gaze, but she stared past him as if hell itself lurked in the hospital corridors.

Brady rushed into a crush of tourists exiting a tour bus. He could see Clara ahead of the crowd and called to her, "Clara! Wait!"

Behind him, Brady heard Captain Torres shout, "Elena! Espere!" Followed by, "Policia! Reciben nuestra del camino!" Brady reached the edge of the swarm, who were now chattering among themselves and pointing as Clara climbed into a pulmonia.

"Damn it, Clara! Stop!" His words swallowed by a cacophony of noise orchestrated by heavy traffic, tourists, hawkers, and the occasional rift of music drifting from the open-air restaurants. When he reached the curb, the pulmonia had melted into obscurity among the hundreds of cars jamming the busy boulevard.

Captain Torres stopped next to him, bent at the waist, hands on knees as he caught his breath. Brady sucked in air too then coughed as the exhaust-filled air burned his lungs. After a minute, Torres straightened and said, "I believe you have some explaining to do, Senor Jones." Torres directed his gaze to taillights glowing red in the distance. "Who the hell is Clara?"

Brady stiffened at the captain's authoritative tone, but he knew he'd need his help to find Clara before Damian did. Brady nodded and said, "It's a long story, and I'll tell you everything, but right now Clara's in danger. Do you have any idea where she would go?"

"Come." Torres turned and headed back toward the hospital. "We will need Humberto's assistance."

Brady glanced once more at the teaming boulevard. "Damn it, Clara." He heaved a sigh, then turned and followed Torres.

Humberto Alvarez met them at the entrance, his girlfriend glued to his side, her face drained of color. "Torres, what the hell is going on?"

Brady's eyes darted around the hospital waiting room as he marched toward the hallway where the nurse had dropped her tray. He paused before turning the corner, wishing he had a weapon. The foul odor of vomit from the injured girls room greeted him as he rounded the corner and continued down the hallway where he found a door opened into an alley. As Brady closed the door, he caught a whiff of cigar smoke. Cuban, Damian's preference. He pushed back through the door and swept the dark alley with a discerning gaze. Empty.

Brady took a step toward the next street, but stopped when the door banged opened behind him. He tensed, ready for battle, and turned to find Alvarez standing in the doorway. He should have been relieved, but his chest tightened knowing that Damian had a head start in finding Clara.

Humberto beckoned. "We need you to come with us."

Brady nodded and followed Humberto back to the waiting room, where Captain Torres stood talking to six uniformed policemen. Brady couldn't keep up with his rapid Spanish, but knew Torres was instructing them to find Clara, since the Captain used both of her names.

Torres dispatched his men and then crossed the room to where Humberto and Brady waited. Brady's phone vibrated with an incoming call. He connected and said, "Clara?"

"It's Shane," his friend responded. "I thought you were with Clara?"

"She's in the wind." Brady turned his back to Torres and Alvarez. "I think Damian's here and Clara saw him and ran. Can you track her phone?"

"Devyn and I are boarding a plane for Mazatlan, so not until we land."

"Why are you coming here?"

"Because I think you're right. I'm pretty sure Damian's there."

Brady heard someone in the background say "I'll take your bags sir."

Captain Torres tapped Brady on the shoulder as Shane continued. "We have another problem."

Brady said, "Explain."

"Damian has a half-sister, Sarita Garcia, and I think she's in Mazatlan too."

"And?"

"She's also looking for Damian."

"Do we need to be worried about her?"

"Maybe. She's jefe of a large cartel." A voice told Shane he needed to turnoff his phone. "Gotta go. Torres knows her. Text you when we land."

Brady pocketed his phone as he turned to face his companions. "Gentlemen, what can you tell me about Sarita Garcia?"

Lucia sucked in air as the two men exchanged an anxious look, before Torres countered with, "Why do you ask?"

"Because her half-brother, Damian Garza, is here to kill Clara; I need to know if his sister is someone to concerned about."

"Si," Torres replied.

"Then we need to find Clara. Now!" Brady looked at each of them. "Where would she go?"

"She has not returned to my home," Humberto said. "And I do not believe she has the means to leave Mazatlan."

"She is not answering her phone," Lucia offered. "Maybe she will find a hotel for the night."

"I have my men searching all the hotels," Torres said. "Senor . . ."

"Brady."

"Brady," Torres continued. "Why did Elen—*Clara* run from you?"

Brady's jaw muscle jumped as he gritted his teeth. He forced himself to relax as he said, "She's not running from me. She's scared, so she's just running." Before he realized what he was saying, he added, "I wouldn't hurt her . . . I-I'm in love with her."

CHAPTER FIFTY-FOUR

Clara heard Brady and Torres calling after her, shouting for her to wait, to stop. But fear propelled her through the crowd, her heart clawing at her chest, trying to escape. Her fight-or-flight instinct, caving to the overwhelming need to flee.

Damian had found her, and she knew he'd come to kill her. How he'd found her was irrelevant. The more pressing question was how would she disappear this time?

The pulmonia driver swore as he slammed to a stop behind a delivery truck double-parked in front of Panama's. Clara tossed a hundred pesos onto the seat next to the driver and shouted, "Gracias, senor!" She sprang from the converted Volkswagen and headed for Joe's Oyster Bar.

Joe's sat on the beach between a Ramada Inn and the Hotel Playa. Clara walked through the open-air lobby of The Hotel Playa as if she were a guest and proceeded through the *palapa* restaurant down onto the beach. The latest hip-hop tunes blasted from Joe's massive stereo system, drowning out the voices of the teeming crowd. Clara climbed concrete stairs from the sand, pausing at the top to scan the early evening drinkers before making her way to the back wall. Joe's had two walls that formed a *V* connected to a twelve-foot seawall overlooking the ocean. Clara sat at the very end of the seawall, which gave her a view of both entrances into the bar. As the sea breeze blew through the bar, Clara realized sweat had drenched her cotton tank. A waiter appeared and said, "Cerveza?" He held up two fingers. "Two for one happy hour."

Clara needed to keep her wits about her, but didn't want to draw attention by sitting alone, not drinking, and probably looking out of her mind. "Si. Corona and agua."

The waiter nodded as he disappeared into the growing crowd.

Clara had only been to Joe's a few times and found the idyllic place mesmerizing. One could sit on the seawall for hours with a bucket of beers in ice, breathing in the salty sea air and enjoying the vast Pacific.

As she always did, she glanced at the horizon. The place where she imagined her daughter waited for her. *I miss you, dear Ally.*

The waiter set a bucket and bowl of sliced limes on the table in front of her. Clara dug in her purse for pesos, noticing a missed call as she handed him a hundred pesos. She waved off his offer to bring her change as she tapped her phone alive. Recent calls showed Lucia's number and one voice mail. Clara wanted to listen to the message but knew better. Damian might have found a way to track her phone. And she assumed Brady had already asked Shane to trace it.

Clara powered off her phone. "Well they can't if it's not on." She took a bottle of water from the bucket, chugged it down and then replaced it with a Corona. She nursed her beer and contemplated her next moves. Leaving Mazatlán by plane or boat would be a challenge because Marco Torres would have already alerted the airport and harbors to look for her. Returning to Humberto's would put everyone at risk. She would not let Damian harm anyone else because of her. Images of Lucia's niece suffering at the hands of the monster Damian must've sent crept into her mind. Damian probably had him following her as soon as she left Los Angeles. Clara shuddered at the thought that it could've been her instead of Rosa.

She took another slug of Corona and rehashed her escape. Her decrepit Volkswagen wouldn't make it very far, but should make it to Durango. From there, she would be able to fly out of the country and she'd have five-plus hours in the car to decide where.

First she'd need to retrieve her hidden cash. Good thing she'd finally agreed to accept a small salary for covering Angel House. Once she relocated, she'd reach out to Shane for a new identity and access to her bank account. Clara knew doing so would put Brady on her trail, but hopefully she'd be onto another destination before he could find her. Clara's pulse quickened as the memory of Brady's lips on hers came flooding back. A pang of guilt tugged at her heart and tears burned her eyes. Brady had done nothing but try to help her and probably would give his life to protect her.

She blinked away tears to bring the ocean's horizon back into focus. "I can't," she whispered to herself. "I can't let myself be in love with him."

Clara palmed away her tears, heaved a sigh and took in the standing-room only crowd that had amassed over the last thirty minutes. She looked over the side of the seawall and decided she should be able to climb down to the beach using the fabricated rock outcropping that hugged the wall. *Safer than blindly navigating the horde of partiers.*

She pulled her phone from her purse, turned it on and checked her voice mail list. Another message from Lucia and a new one from Humberto. She also had a text from an unknown number: *Don't run.* The text had to be from Brady, but she'd already made up her mind. Clara stuffed the unopened bottle of water into her purse, then dropped her phone into the bucket of melting ice, watching as it settled on the bottom next to the unopened Corona.

She slung her purse across her body and scanned the crowd one last time. She didn't spot anyone paying undo attention to her. Clara dropped her gaze for a few seconds, then looked up. Still nothing suspicious, which gave her the courage to turn her back on the rowdy crowd and shimmy over the wall. Three big foot-holes later, she hit the deep sand and headed north.

A blood-orange sun descended behind a dark cloudy horizon and frigate birds' road the increasing wind like kites. Waiters closed up beach umbrellas in anticipation of the thunderstorm crawling toward land.

The unusual stormy weather summed up how Clara felt about her life right now. She needed to close up her time in Mazatlan and move on before the coming storm engulfed her. She looked across the steel-gray ocean as the sun slipped from the clouds and lit up the horizon in a burst of fiery colors.

Clara Garza said a mental goodbye to Elena Cruz. Blew a kiss to her daughter Ally. Then blended in with the crush of hotel guests hustling into the Hotel Costa de Oro ahead of the brewing tempest.

CHAPTER FIFTY-FIVE

Damian Garza set his coffee cup on the table and responded, "Entrar," to a knock on the sitting room door.

A male servant stepped into the room. "Senor, you have a visitor."

"I am not expecting anyone."

The servant shrugged. "She says she is your sister."

The word *sister* caused Damian to pause a beat before he said, "Bien. Show her in."

The servant nodded and retreated.

Damian poured himself more coffee and popped a hunk of sweet concha into his mouth. He shook his head at the idea of a sister. He could not imagine where this woman would get such an idea—although he could see his father cheating on Valencia, the cold, calculating bitch who had claimed to be his real mother. *She is not anyone's mother now.*

He stood and walked to a picture window that provided a view of the marina. He found it interesting that this woman would think she was related to him given he had traveled to

Mexico using a false passport. Alan had assured him that his new name had come from an infant who had died fifty years ago. Obviously, this female was deluded and should be easy to dispense with. *I have other pressing matters.*

After he had dispensed with Billy Boyd, Damian rented the villa in the harbor where the kid thought Clara was living. Damian had his men patrolling the streets of Mazatlan and scouring the various restaurants and shops of the marina. One remained at the hospital, trying to get the names of Clara's companions.

It was only a matter of time before Damian finally made his ex-wife pay for meddling in his affairs. Anger pricked his scalp as he recalled being arrested and locked up. If the bitch had died after he shot her, his escape from Los Angeles would have been much simpler.

"Soon," he said to the panoramic view, "and then I will be able to get on with my life." A twinge of excitement accelerated his pulse as he imagined all the young innocents waiting to be defiled, their soft pristine flesh begging to bare his mark.

A rap on the door brought Damian back to the matter at hand. "Entrar."

The door swung open and Damian's knees weakened as a beautiful woman marched into the room. She carried herself with an air of sophistication and authority. But what made the color drain from his face was that she looked exactly like pictures of his mother.

The woman smiled and extended her hand. "Sarita Garcia."

An unfamiliar sultry scent washed over him as he instinctively shook her hand. He focused on keeping surprise from his voice and asked, "What can I do for you, Miss Garcia?"

Sarita's smile widened, showing dazzling white teeth. "Such formality for family." She sat in one of the two armless chairs situated across from a caramel-colored leather couch. Damian chose the middle of the couch. He leaned back, spread his arms across the cushions and smiled, hoping to convey he wasn't intimidated by her penetrating gaze.

"You have our mother's eyes," she touched the end of her nose, "and nose."

"Miss . . ." Damian vacillated between wanting to dispatch with this intruder and the burning curiosity as to what she could possibly want.

"Sarita," she cut in, her large, dark eyes assessing him.

"Sarita, I believe you are mistaken." Damian refused to look away. "I am an only child and my mother died soon after my birth."

His guest's lips curved slightly and he saw a small resemblance of himself in her face. "You are mistaken, my dear brother." Sarita crossed her legs and continued, "Your father, Ricardo Garza, had an affair with my mother, Estrella Garcia, when I was two."

Damian gritted his teeth at the mention of his parents' names.

"Our mother was desperate to hide the affair, and you, from my father." Sarita looked down briefly, then back at Damian as she resumed her story. "So Ricardo took you away and my father was told the baby was still born."

A flood of emotions roiled in Damian's gut but he wore a mask of indifference for his guest. Who the hell did this *puta* think she was spewing fiction about his childhood? He doubted she would be so careless if she knew what he had planned for her once his father debunked her story.

A hint of sadness flickered across Sarita's face before she finished, "Our mother and my father died in a car crash when I was a teenager. I only recently learned of you when I found a box of old letters and photos sent from Ricardo to Estrella."

She cocked her head slightly and he knew the shock of hearing his mother had been alive for most of his life showed on his face. *What if she is telling the truth?* And, if she was telling the truth, then he'd been wrong about Valencia killing Estrella. No matter. Valencia had done plenty to him over the years to warrant him having her killed.

"I have brought the letters and photos for you and, of course, you will want to speak to your father." Sarita smoothed her tight skirt and asked, "How is Ricardo doing in prison?"

Damian was done playing defense. "He is well. Thank you for asking." He forced a smile and said, "May I offer you something to drink?"

"Si, tequila."

Damian crossed to the bar and poured two shots from a colorful glass decanter into matching tumblers. He delivered a glass to Sarita and returned to the couch.

She took a dainty sip and said, "Muy bien."

Damian lifted his shot in toast and then gulped down the smoky liquid.

"Salud," Sarita said, following suit. "Damian, I would also like to talk about combining our separate business ventures into a joint family effort."

Damian didn't respond but held her intent gaze.

"I believe your knowledge of exotic dancers would be a good compliment to my various endeavors."

Jesus! Does she know everything about me? Damian smiled and said, "Thank you for your generous offer, but once I have concluded my business here, I will be leaving Mazatlan."

Sarita stood and reached for his empty glass. "Uno mas?"

337

Damian nodded. "Si."

"You should come visit me in Durango," she said as she poured two hefty shots. "So we can get to know each other better." She handed Damian his drink, clinked his glass and returned to her chair.

"It seems you already know quite a lot about me." Damian took a sip.

Sarita held her tumbler in both hands and smiled at him. "Si." She swirled the amber alcohol. "I know you are searching for your ex-wife, Clara." She paused as if waiting for a drumroll. Sarita tossed back her shot and smiled. "And I know where she is."

CHAPTER FIFTY-SIX

After an awkward silence following Brady's declaration of
love for Clara, Humberto suggested they return to his house
to regroup.

During the half-hour drive, Brady explained the
horrendous history Clara shared with Damian, ending with
Ally's murder, his attempt to kill Clara and his obsession
with finishing the job. They listened quietly and Lucia wiped
away tears.

Upon their arrival, Humberto and Torres began making
calls, and Lucia let Brady into the casita where Clara had
been staying.

"The housekeeper says Clara has not been here since this
morning," Lucia said. "I will leave you to your search."

Brady managed a smile. "Gracias, Lucia."

"De nada." She returned his smile, then took a step toward
the open door.

Brady had his back to her, studying the small tidy, space
when she asked, "Does she know you love her?"

Brady turned and shrugged. "I don't think so."

"Then you will tell her as soon as you see her. Si?"

Brady nodded. "Yes."

"Bueno," Lucia said and then left him alone in the casita.

Brady heaved a sigh. "Sure, I'll tell her, but I'm pretty sure she doesn't want to hear it."

He studied the minimal furnishings and tried to shake off thoughts that had haunted him since Clara's disappearing act. *Why didn't she stick to the original plan? Why did she disappear on her own? Why did she leave me hanging?*

No matter how many times he'd asked Shane for an explanation, the answer was always the same, "She wants to protect us from Damian."

Brady banged the bathroom vanity doors closed and moved to the closet, which yielded nothing except a lingering scent of lavender, which conjured up memories of their one night together. *Maybe she felt the same way about him and that's why she ran.*

The kitchen cupboards held a few dishes, coffee and a package of chocolate cookies. His stomach growled as he helped himself to a cookie and took a bite.

"Okay, Clara . . ." Brady turned in a circle as he munched his snack. "Where's your perfect hiding spot?"

Brady continued his search, pulling up area rugs, tossing the bed and shuffling through the nightstand drawers. Nothing.

"Shit!" Brady reached for the casita door and noticed an air-conditioning vent between the door and high ceiling. He doubted five-foot, five-inch Clara had managed to tuck anything into the opening, but knew he had to check.

He lugged over a chair from the eating area, climbed up and peered into the dark duct. He couldn't see anything and felt around to be sure he hadn't missed something. On his second pass he felt an envelope. "Finally!"

He seized his prize and jumped down from the chair. The packet contained a copy of her passport, directions to a place called Casa de Angel, and Juan's name next to his cell number. Brady carried the chair back to the small table and went in search of the others.

He found Clara's search and rescue team in the library. Humberto waived him in and Brady tossed the envelope onto the desktop. "Which of you knows Juan Vega—and where is Angel House?"

Alvarez and Torres exchanged questioning looks as Lucia said, "Of course that is where Elena would hide!" Her cheeks colored. "Sorry, I mean Clara."

"Si," Humberto agreed. "She is probably at Angel House."

Brady nodded. "Which must be where she hid her passport, because it's not in the casita."

"And you think she might reach out to Juan for a new passport?"

Brady nodded again. "I found her because she asked him for a gun."

Humberto shook his head. "Juan will not sell her a gun."

"Agreed." Torres said. "But he would help her with a new passport."

"I need to get to Angel House." Brady held his hand out. "I'll need a car and a gun."

Humberto looked at Torres who nodded and then Humberto pulled a key chain from his pocket. He removed a key and handed it to Brady. "You can use the Jeep sitting out back." He headed for his gun case, unlocked the bottom drawer, and removed a well-used Glock and clip. "Do not get caught with this."

Brady nodded as he shoved the piece into the back of his jeans and headed for the door. Torres was on the phone with Juan and Lucia was on his heels as he left the library.

"I will come with you," she said, "and let you into Angel House."

"No." Brady said a little too sternly. "It may not be safe." He smiled in an attempt to apologize. "Would you do me a favor and text my friends Humberto's address?" He pulled

342

his phone from a pocket. "They're flying in on one of Juan's jets and land in an hour."

"Si." Lucia returned his smile and thumbed her phone alive. "Give me the number."

Brady rattled off Shane's number as Humberto came to Lucia's side and said, "Torres is speaking with his men, but so far no one has seen Clara."

Brady extended his hand. "Thanks for everything you did for Clara."

"I will accept your thanks when you bring her back safely," Humberto replied.

Brady nodded in acknowledgement and then headed for the Jeep. *I just need to get to Clara before Damian does.*

CHAPTER FIFTY-SEVEN

Clara crept into Angel House through the back door and stood in the kitchen listening for a beat. The only thing she heard was the never-ending traffic on Cameron Sabalo Avenue.

The air-conditioning chilled her and she wished she had a change of clothes. "Hopefully, something from the donation closet will fit," she whispered as she moved from the kitchen to the front of the building where the receptionist desk sat. She wheeled away the chair and knelt down. The tile she'd removed earlier looked as if it had never been disturbed. She took a letter opener from the middle desk drawer and lifted the tile away, revealing a plastic bag. She clutched the bag and came to her feet.

Clara peeked inside to verify her cash was inside and went in search of a new outfit. She opened the closet door and scanned the items of clothing stacked in neat piles on the shelves. A skirt with a tropical print lying on top of a golden-colored top caught her eye.

She took the clothes, ducked into the bathroom, and stripped to her underwear. She felt his presence before he stood in the bathroom door way and the blood in her veins turned to ice as she met the cold dark eyes of her ex-husband.

"Hello, darling," Damian said as looked her up and down. "Still beautiful as ever."

Clara cringed as he moved behind her and brushed her hair from her neck. She frantically scanned the countertop for a weapon as he trailed his lips from earlobe to shoulder.

"Relax." He smiled at her reflection in the mirror. "There is nothing you can do now but surrender to me and accept that the end is near."

Damian turned her toward him and traced a finger over the scar left from his last attempt to kill her. He ran his hand under her bra and thumbed her nipple.

Clara glared at him. When he leaned in to kiss her, bile burned the back of her throat. *He's not going to torture me before he kills me.* She slapped his face and rage burned in his eyes. She took a step back, and as Damian lunged for her, she saw Brady standing in the doorway with a gun pointed at Damian.

"Leave her alone, Garza," Brady commanded.

An evil sneer spread across Damian's face before he turned toward Brady. "My lucky day."

He took a step toward Brady. "You get to watch me torture Clara, before I kill you both."

Damian hurled himself at Brady as a gunshot echoed off the bathroom walls. The two men hit the floor with a thud and the gun bounced from Brady's hand. Damian landed a solid blow to Brady's jaw as Clara scrambled for the gun.

Damian grabbed her hair and pulled her backwards into the hallway. He encircled her throat with a massive hand, strangling her as he stood. Blood stained the sleeve of his linen shirt. Clara heard a thump and felt Damian's arm jerk as he was struck several times. Pinpoints of bright light pricked her eyes as her lungs screamed for air.

She clawed at Damian's hand as Brady landed another body blow. Damian flung Clara aside like a ragdoll and she crashed into a bookcase. Brady had Damian in a choke hold from behind and Damian was trying to elbow him in the ribs.

"Shoot him, Clara!" Brady shouted. "The gun's at your feet."

She scooped up the gun, aimed it at Damian and pulled the trigger. Brady lost his grip as the bullet tore through first Damian, then him. Damian lurched forward, arms outstretched for Clara, before crumpling to his knees and crashing to the floor.

Clara raced to Brady's side. Crimson red bloomed on his shirt and his eyes were closed. "Brady!" Gun still clutched in her hand, she shook him. "Open your eyes, damn it!" Clara ran to the receptionist desk, fumbled with the phone and dialed Lucia.

"Clara?" Lucia asked. "Are you—"

"Send an ambulance to Angel House!" Clara looked over at Brady. "I sh-shot Brady!"

"Si, si. We are on our way too!" The line went dead before Clara could respond.

She shook off the tears threatening to overcome her and leaned over Brady. He lay motionless but was still breathing. A small pool of blood had formed under his head, the coppery smell nauseating her. She gulped some air and glanced at Damian's prone body.

As much as Clara hated the idea of going near him, she needed to make sure he was dead. Blood seeped from underneath him as she circled his body before toeing him in the ribs. No reaction. She stepped on his wounded shoulder and pressed down. Nothing.

A siren wailed in the distance and a sense of relief washed over Clara. She extended her leg once more to kick Damian's side and gasped when he seized her ankle and yanked her off her feet.

Clara landed hard on her ass, but managed to hold onto the gun and held it in a two-handed grip, as Damian staggered toward her. She pulled the trigger and he flashed a maniacal grin when the bullet went wide.

"Aim for center mass," Brady croaked behind her.

Damian trained his crazy stare on Brady as Clara closed her left eye and focused on Damian's massive chest. He turned his deranged gaze back to Clara and a sinister grin curved his lips as she squeezed the trigger, firing three shots into his heart.

Shock contorted Damian's face as life quickly pumped from his body. He took a last step and Clara rolled out of the way before he hit the floor.

She sat with her back to the wall, the gun trained on Damian. Her whole body shook and she struggled to keep his lifeless body in her sights.

"I think he's dead," Brady said as he crawled toward her.

Clara glanced quickly at Brady. "Not until the coroner s-says so."

Brady reached her, pulled himself into a sitting position and rested his head in her shoulder. "You're cold." His breath was warm on her skin. "Go get dressed. I'll watch him."

Clara shook her head. "I'm fine." His closeness calmed her. "Where the hell is the ambulance?"

Brady's head lolled forward. "Jackson!" She elbowed him. "Don't die, damn it . . . I-I . . ."

Why can't I tell him?

The front door burst open and Marco Torres rushed in with his gun drawn. He knelt next to Damian and checked for a pulse and then he reached for Clara's gun.

"He is dead, Elen—Clara." He turned his hand palm side up. "Give me the gun."

Clara glanced at Torres, then back at Damian. "You're sure?"

He nodded. "Si."

Clara handed him the gun and shifted her attention to Brady. "Where's the damn ambulance?"

"They are here, along with Humberto and Lucia." Torres stood. "I can let them in now."

Humberto was first through the door, followed by two paramedics and then Lucia. Torres handed the gun to Humberto as the medics rolled Brady away from Clara and onto his back.

"Is he alive?" she asked as she watched Humberto wipe down the gun.

The younger paramedic looked up at Torres who repeated Clara's question. The medic shrugged his shoulders and went back to work on Brady.

"He will be fine," Torres said with a less-than-reassuring smile.

"Come." Lucia took Clara gently by the arm and helped her to her feet. "You should get dressed."

As the two women shuffled toward the bathroom, Clara looked over her shoulder at Damian's body, then at Brady.

She should've thanked Brady for coming to save her. She should've held him in her arms. She should've told him she loved him.

CHAPTER FIFTY-EIGHT

Clara wished the muted voices would shut up and let her sleep. When she heard his name, her eyes flew open and she jerked upright in the uncomfortable chair.

"Senor Brady, you are very lucky." The speaker wore a white lab coat and stood with his back to Clara. "The bullet managed to miss the right subclavian artery and exit your shoulder without doing any major damage."

Clara relaxed slightly, relieved her poor aim hadn't resulted in serious harm to Brady.

"I am more concerned," the doctor continued, "about your concussion."

Clara watched as Brady gingerly touched the back of his head. She could see Shane standing on the opposite side of the room and Captain Torres standing at the foot of the bed.

"I'm fine, Doc," Brady rasped, holding up two fingers. "There's only two now, not four."

"Still," the doctor said, "I would like to keep you overnight for observation."

"I'd really like—" Brady tried to protest, but Shane intervened.

"Doc says you need to stay, so you're staying."

"Bueno," the doctor said as he made a note in the chart he'd been holding. "I will be back to check on you this evening."

The doctor had blocked Clara's view of Devyn, who yelled Clara's name as soon as he stepped away. Clara rushed into her friend's arms and hugged her. Devyn mewled something about being glad Clara was alive and Damian was dead.

As they parted, Devyn wiped tears from her cheeks. "I've missed you so much."

"Me too," Clara said around the lump in her throat.

Shane hugged her next. "Way to survive." He smiled down at her. "I think you could teach me a thing or two."

"May I have a moment alone with Clara and Senor Brady?" Captain Torres asked.

"You got it," Shane said as he shook Torres's hand. "I'll be back in the morning," he said to Brady as he held the door open for Devyn.

"We're your ride back to Senor Alvarez's." Devyn hugged Clara again. "We'll wait for you in the hall."

Clara nodded as they left the room, then she met Brady's intense stare and struggled to keep herself from jumping into his hospital bed. From submitting to the passion his stare held. From finally admitting she loved him deeply.

Captain Torres cleared his throat and said, "Clara, I am glad you were not hurt."

She smiled at him, "Gracias, Marco."

Torres looked at Brady who nodded, then he said, "Senor Brady and I have agreed on the following account of events."

Clara glanced back at Brady, who had managed to sit taller.

"Senor Brady stated he arrived at Angel House and found Damian Garza . . ." he paused and Clara could tell lying made him uncomfortable. "Found him holding you hostage with a gun."

Clara cocked an eyebrow and stepped up to the bed.

Torres held up a finger and continued, "The two men struggled over the gun and Garza shot Brady."

Clara looked at Brady as Torres finished.

"When Garza turned his attack on you, Brady fought with him again, managing to obtain the gun and shoot Garza before falling and hitting his head."

Clara parted her lips, but Brady silenced her with a slight headshake.

"Clara," Torres touched her arm so she'd look at him. "It is very important the police report states that the gun belonged to Senor Garza."

Clara nodded. "But—"

"And," Brady interjected, "it's equally important your real name is kept out of Captain Torres's report."

Torres agreed. "Si, there is a dead body and an illegally obtained gun. It is better this way."

"Marco," Brady croaked. "Can I have a few minutes with Clara?"

Torres nodded. "I must wrap this up before dinner at Humberto's." He kissed Clara on the cheek and then left her alone with Brady.

"Come closer," Brady said, his voice almost a whisper.

Clara moved to the head of the bed and smiled down at him. "I'm glad you're going to be okay."

He offered a weak smile. "I'm glad you're a good shot."

"Lucky." She shook her head. "I was aiming for his head."

Brady's burst of laughter morphed into a groan as pain contorted his face.

Clara placed a hand on his shoulder. "Are you okay?"

He nodded. "It only hurts when I laugh." He reached up and touched her cheek. "It's over, Clara." He searched her face as if looking for agreement. "We can get on with our lives."

The word *we* sent her pulse into overdrive. "I'm glad it's over too." She took his hand in hers. "We have lots to talk about when you get out of here."

She moved to step away, but Brady held her hand tight. "I-I . . ." He looked down at their entwined fingers. "I'm in love with you."

When he raised his eyes to meet hers, Clara leaned in and kissed him. His familiar scent mingling with an antiseptic aroma. She'd only intended to brush his lips, but found herself relaxing in the comfort of his embrace. Clara slowed the kiss down, eventually pushing back from Brady. His lips curved in a delirious grin and she instantly regretted the words coming out of her mouth, "I should let you get some rest."

Brady's eyes narrowed. "Not exactly the response I expected."

Tears sprang to Clara's eyes and she fought to keep her voice from breaking. "I just need some time to . . . to sort things out."

Before Brady could respond, a knock thudded against the hospital room door. Still holding her gaze, Brady barked, "What?"

The door pushed opened and a tall young man stepped into the room. He smiled at Clara and said, "It's good to see you again, Ms. Marsh."

He'd used her maiden name, so obviously she knew him, but Clara couldn't place him. He pulled a slim wallet from his board shorts, flipped it open and said, "Special Agent Christopher Temple."

Clara made the connection and asked, "Did you follow Damian here?"

"Not exactly." Temple pocketed his ID. "The FBI is investigating a drug cartel in Durango that is moving product through Mazatlan into the US." He looked in the direction of the door as Shane and Devyn slipped in and leaned against the back wall. "My target led me here, and when I learned of Damian's demise, I reached out to Captain Torres."

Brady joined the conversation. "So Torres has given you the specifics?"

Temple nodded. "Yes, I just spoke with him on the phone."

Brady still held Clara's hand, which was now slick with sweat. "Then you shouldn't have any questions for us."

"Correct." Temple pushed a lock of blond hair off his forehead. "Torres asked me to share information I recently obtained regarding Damian's half-sister."

Clara's heart jumped in her chest and the familiar sensation of flight flooded her body. Brady tightened his grip and placed his other hand at the base of her spine as if he sensed he needed to hold her in place.

"We're listening," Brady said in a calm voice.

"Her name is Sarita Garcia." Temple pulled a small black notebook from another pocket. "She lives at her parents' villa in Durango."

"Sister?" Clara shook her head. "Damian doesn't have a sister."

Clara could see Shane punching the keys of his phone as he left the room, Devyn close on his heels, as Agent Temple continued.

"I followed her here last week and yesterday to a villa in the marina, where she met with Damian."

The need to run crashed through Clara like a boulder and she tried to pull her hand free of Brady's. If he noticed, it didn't show as he asked, "Does she know Damian's dead?"

Temple nodded. "Yes. I managed to get a table close to hers last night at Diego's and overheard one of her men give her the news."

Clara's knees shook and she gripped the bed rail with her free hand for support. Brady pressed his hand into her waist and said, "And?"

"And . . ." Temple looked at Clara, then back at Brady. "She told her man she wants Clara delivered to her alive."

CHAPTER FIFTY-NINE

"I have to go." Clara wrenched her hand from Brady's.

"Damn it, Clara!" Brady exclaimed, climbing out of the hospital bed. "You can't run?"

"The hell I can't!" Clara headed for the door, which opened as Shane and Devyn filed into the room.

"Stop her!" Brady yelled, fumbling with the IV still connected to his arm.

Agent Temple grasped her arm and Shane blocked her exit.

"Clara, let's work this out together this time," Shane said.

"Ms. Marsh," Temple added, "I can arrange for you to be escorted back to the United States by tomorrow and check into getting you into WITSEC."

Clara continued to shake her head. Didn't they understand? If Damian's sister hunted her, that would put everyone at risk . . . again. She turned a wild-eyed stare toward Agent Temple and said, "Make it happen!"

He nodded, pulled a phone from yet another pocket and left the room. Devyn had encircled an arm around Clara's waist and Clara leaned into her.

Brady, his ass hanging out of the backless hospital gown, banged hangers in the closet as he grabbed his clothes. "You're not fucking going anywhere without me!" He bent to pull on his khakis and lost his balance. "Shit!"

Shane raced to Brady's side and guided him back to the bed. "Hey man, I don't think you should be up and moving."

Brady shoved at his friend's chest; to no avail. Shane held onto Brady's shoulders until he calmed down. "Shane, don't let her run."

Clara came back to the bed and placed a hand on Brady's chest. "Okay, I won't run." Tears slipped down her cheeks. "We'll come up with a plan that's best of all of us."

Brady nodded and then upchucked all over Shane's Nikes.

Agent Temple returned and said, "Ms. Marsh, I've put in the request with my supervisor and he will call as soon as a plan is in place." He looked at a message on his phone. "I have to go."

"Thanks, Agent Temple," Clara forced a smile.

"Where will you stay tonight?" Temple asked her as he read another text message. "Torres is stationing men here at the hospital, so this might be the safest place."

A quick scan of the room told Clara everyone, especially Brady, would sleep better if she stayed. "Okay, then I'll stay here."

Temple headed out the door, saying, "I'll be in touch."

The room seemed eerily quiet, as if her acquiescing to remain at the hospital had lured her friends into a false sense of security. Shane helped Brady back into bed as Devyn pressed the nurses call button. Clara watched, a helpless feeling filling her gut. Despite what she'd said, she wouldn't put them all in danger again. But disappearing this time wasn't going to be easy. Shane would refuse to help her. Devyn would beg her not to go. And Brady . . . well he would never let her run by herself.

CHAPTER-SIXTY

An orderly had cleaned up Brady's vomit and a nurse gave him a sedative. Clara watched the man who loved her, the man she knew she loved, struggle to stay awake. She pulled up a chair, took his hand in hers and held his gaze until his eyes finally closed in sleep. His chest rose and fell in an easy rhythm and she relaxed for the first time in hours.

Torres's men stood watch outside of Brady's room and Devyn had gone to fetch coffee for the three of them. Clara already knew Shane wouldn't try to talk her out of running and turned toward him when he spoke.

"I can't help you run."

"I know," Clara responded. "But you understand I can't put everyone at risk—again?"

"Brady's in love with you in case he didn't tell you."

"He did." Tears welled in the corners of Clara's eyes.

"Well, then you know he'll never stop looking for you." Shane looked at Brady. "Let him help you figure things out this time."

"I'm in love with him too." Clara swiped at her tears. "And if I disappear alone, maybe he won't end up on Sarita Garcia's hit list."

Shane shook his head. "Jesus, you're stubborn."

Clara nodded. "I know."

Shane rubbed the stubble on his chin. "Do you have a plan?"

Clara sighed. "No."

"I talked to Alvarez and he said he'd help you."

Clara shot Shane a questioning look as he handed her a slip of paper from his pocket. "Here's the information you'll need to access your money."

Clara took the note. "I thought you couldn't help me."

"You've got about . . ." Shane looked at his watch, "twelve hours before Brady's discharged." He attempted a smile. "Then I'll have to tell him you've disappeared again."

Clara glanced at Brady. "Understood."

"I told Humberto you'll need a phone and a laptop, which he said he can provide."

Clara nodded as Shane continued, "Devyn's new number is on the back of the paper, along with a new email address for the two of you to use."

Clara flipped the note over. "You know Brady's going to demand this information."

"Yes," Shane agreed. "And Devyn and I are going to tell him the two of you are using the same numbers and email address as before."

Brady stirred in the hospital bed and mumbled Clara's name. The two coconspirators froze as Brady lolled his head from side-to-side before settling down.

Shane heaved a sigh and said, "Humberto already has a destination in mind for you and is looking at flights." He held his hand out to her, which she took, and he brought her to her feet. "Clara, I truly wish you'd wait for Brady, but also understand why you feel a need to protect him. Us."

Clara's tongue suddenly felt too big for her mouth, so she nodded.

"Go. Now—before I change my mind." Clara heard an echo of regret in Shane's voice.

"Torres's officers know to let you leave the hospital and a police car is waiting to take you to Alvarez's." Clara shook Shane's hand as he continued. "Get your plan in place before morning. And take care of yourself."

"What about Devyn?" Clara's voice broke.

"This was her idea." Shane kissed Clara's cheek. "She mumbled something about not being able to say goodbye again and went for coffee."

Clara bent and kissed Brady, which he slept through. "Goodbye," she whispered as tears streamed down her cheeks. "Tell them both I love them," she said to Shane.

Shane cocked an eyebrow. "Sure, leave the dirty work to me."

Clara cast one last glance at Brady, mentally promised him she'd be okay. Then left the hospital quietly and quickly, like a thief in the night.

CHAPTER SIXTY-ONE

The young officer escorted Clara to Humberto's massive front door and announced their arrival with a knuckle rap. Lucia opened the door, motioned Clara in and thanked the policeman. He gave her a nod and returned to his car.

Humberto's and Marco's raised voices echoed down the hallway from the study. Clara couldn't understand most of their conversation, but did recognize the name of Humberto's friend Kaitlan Graham, who'd been arrested.

"Come." Lucia took her hand. "You can shower while I finish packing for you."

Clara trailed after Lucia as Marco shouted an expletive. His angry voice followed them as they continued down the hallway. "I cannot release Ms. Graham," Marco yelled, "until I know if she is involved with the dead man!"

"Maldicion, Marco! Kaitlan is not involved," Humberto countered. "The stupid turista probably messed with the wrong people."

Lucia pushed through the back door, pulling Clara onto the patio.

"What's going on?" Clara asked as they stepped into the casita.

"A body was found this morning on the beach in front of the Hotel Playa." Lucia said. "Humberto's friend Kaitlan was found in the dead man's hotel room."

Clara raised an eyebrow. "I see."

Lucia folded a pair of tan capris. "You should shower." She placed the capris in a small suitcase and picked up a silky cream-colored blouse. "We need to get you to the hotel."

"Hotel?" Clara asked.

"Si." Lucia reached for a pair of black sandals. "Humberto will explain." She handed the sandals to Clara. "Vaminos!"

Clara carried the shoes to the small bathroom and turned on the shower. When she closed the door, she found black Bermuda shorts sharing a hanger with a sleeveless dark blue top. Lucia's graciousness brought tears to Clara's eyes. She wished she could repay her new friends for their kindness, but fate, once again, had dictated a different plan. Clara stepped into the shower and sobbed into the steaming spray. She finally had justice. Revenge for Ally. Damian Garza would never hurt another person! His death should have brought Clara peace, but instead she'd incurred the wrath of his sister. *Of course he has a crazy fucking sister.* A fresh wave of tears tasted salty on her lips. Once again, Clara would have to disappear. Leave behind her friends. Flee the man she loved.

Brady's text flashed in her mind: *Don't run.*

Dressed and ready to go, Clara took one last look around the casita and then went in search of the others. She found Humberto, Lucia and Marco waiting for her in the study. Humberto sat at his desk, cell phone to his ear. Lucia busied herself at the massive bookcase, rearranging books. Marco stood in front of the large picture windows, his back to the room.

Marco turned and smiled at Clara as she entered. He crossed the room to meet her, taking her hands in his. Clara returned his smile. "Thank you so much for all your help, Marco."

"It has been my pleasure." Marco squeezed her hands. "I am very sorry you have to leave us. Is there no chance I can convince you to stay?"

Clara shook her head. "No, it's better if I leave."

"Bien," Marco said. "I must leave you in Humberto's capable hands. Two of my men will also be watching over you until you board your flight tomorrow."

Clara nodded, the lump in her throat blocking a response.

Marco kissed her cheek. "Estar a salvo mi amiga." His eyes searched hers once more before he made his exit.

"I believe under different circumstances," Lucia said as she left the disarray of books to join Clara, "my brother would try to claim your heart for himself."

The glob of emotion in Clara's throat now threatened her ability to breathe as Lucia wrapped her in a hug. Lucia handed her a tissue and held up Ally's dragonfly necklace.

"I found this on the floor next to the nightstand."

Clara held out her palm. "I-I can't believe I almost left this behind."

"Here." Lucia spun her around. "Let me."

Clara fingered the dragonfly locket, then turned and hugged her friend. The two women abruptly separated when Humberto slammed down the phone.

"Humberto," Lucia said. "Clara is ready."

"Si." Humberto ran fingers through his hair as he moved to the couch. "Please, sit."

Lucia joined Humberto on the couch and Clara perched on the edge of a matching leather chair, her attention focused on her host.

"You still insist on leaving?" Resignation laced Humberto's tone.

Clara bobbed her head. "Shane said you have a destination in mind."

Humberto unlatched a briefcase resting on top of the coffee table. "Belize," he said, as he placed a stack of cash on the tabletop.

Clara fingered the Mexican money. "Humberto, I don't know how I'll ever repay the two of you for all of your generosity and kindness."

Humberto lifted a laptop and cell phone from the case and placed them next to the cash. "It has been our pleasure to assist you and welcome you into our family." He waved a hand over the items on the table and continued, "It is Shane you have to thank for these items."

Tears pricked Clara's eyes as he handed her a passport. "Lucia and I always have extra passports on hand in case we need to vanish at a moment's notice."

Clara ran a fingertip over Elena's passport photo as Humberto explained. "Juan was able to exchange Lucia's picture with yours."

"I hope you like your new name," Lucia said. "It is my grandmother's name; God bless her soul."

Clara smiled at Lucia. "It's perfect."

"Unfortunately, Juan's pilot had a charter to Cabo this morning and will not be back until tomorrow afternoon." Humberto said as he stood. "I wish you could stay here until your flight, but Marco's certain Sarita Garcia is scouring the marina for you."

Clara and Lucia both came to their feet. Lucia gathered the items from the coffee table and placed them back in the briefcase.

"He feels you will be safer at a hotel with his men standing guard," Humberto said as he closed up his briefcase case. "So we need to deliver Sofia Salazar to Hotel Pueblo Bonito Pronto!"

CHAPTER SIXTY-TWO

Clara had slept fitfully at the Hotel Pueblo Bonito, her recent goodbyes keeping the sandman from carrying her off to slumber land. She now occupied a hard plastic chair on the small patio overlooking the softly lit courtyard, pool and dark ocean. She sipped coffee and watched the gray Pacific slowly morph into a brilliant blue as the sun rose behind the hotel.

A cleaning crew scrubbed the pool walls, while hotel staff swept worn tiles and wiped down lounge chairs. Clara longed to don a swimsuit, grab a trashy novel and stake a claim poolside. But reality dictated she shower and dress, eat something and review the key points of her new identity. She had plenty of time to accomplish these tasks since her flight to Belize didn't leave until 4:10 p.m. The clock on the swim-up pool bar was barely visible, but she thought it read 7:10.

"I'd better hurry," she said to the dove roosting on the patio railing. "Only nine hours until I leave."

Tears trailed down her cheeks, before coming in waves . . . After all, she had time for a good cry.

371

Clara now nibbled at the chicken quesadilla she'd ordered for lunch. It didn't taste any better than the pastry she'd washed down with coffee earlier. When one of Marco's men had delivered her lunch, he'd told her they would be leaving for Juan's airstrip at two. She'd already packed her meager wardrobe and secured her laptop, phone and cash in the briefcase. When she reached for her new passport, Clara noticed a thick book lying beneath the biography Humberto had sketched for Sofia Salazar. She smiled when she pulled the yellow-and-black *Spanish for Dummies* from the case. She put the book into the sleek, leather handbag Lucia had given her. The book bumped on something and Clara fished a black leather wallet from the bottom of the purse. She flipped it open and discovered more cash, including some coins, along with an *IMSS* medical card in her new name. She smiled at Humberto's thoroughness as she re-read her new bio.

Sofia, a wealthy widow, relocating to Belize from Guadalajara after her late husband, a successful rancher, died of a heart attack. Sofia loved doing charity work for her church and was also interested in learning English as a second language.

The bio was thin, which would make expanding her background easier as she settled into her new life. Clara's phone pinged with an incoming text and her eyes misted as

372

she read Devyn's goodbye message: *Brady's better today. He's been asking for you. Thought you'd want to know. I'll miss you tons. Stay safe! Love, D ~*

Lucia had said almost the same thing when she'd called earlier to say goodbye, apologizing for Humberto and Marco, who were still trying to clear Kaitlan Graham of murder.

Clara pushed aside the cold quesadilla, tossed the bio into the briefcase and walked out onto the patio. She gazed at the vast ocean, now a deep blue mirror image of the cloudless sky. She just wanted to get on with it. Start her new life. Let Brady get on with his life . . .

"Sofia Salazar is ready to run!"

CHAPTER SIXTY-THREE

Clara Marsh stepped from the unmarked police car and took the briefcase offered by the young officer holding the door. Her knees shook and the hot afternoon sun raised a film of sweat on her skin. She hitched the leather purse high on her shoulder and inhaled and exhaled a deep breath as she marched toward the jet waiting to take Sofia Salazar to Belize.

Juan stood at the bottom of the ramp. "Senora Salazar," he said, offering his hand to assist her in taking the first step, "glad you made your flight."

Clara smiled at him and climbed the stairs to the open doorway. The captain welcomed her with a slight bow. "We are on schedule." He motioned toward the cabin. "So please take your seat."

Clara nodded, stepped past him and found Jackson Brady lounging in an oversized passenger chair. A broad grin lit up his face and he came to his feet as she stood slack-jawed, gawking at him.

374

"Thank you, Captain," Brady said. "I'll take it from here."

"Bueno." The captain bowed slightly. "We will take off shortly."

Clara heard the captain's retreat to the cockpit as she met Brady's twinkling eyes.

"Wh-why aren't you still in the hospital?"

"Doc gave me a clean bill of health." Brady focused on uncorking a bottle of champagne. "Shane took a little more convincing." He poured the bubbly liquid into two flutes and turned to face her.

"Jackson." She never used his first name and his eyes narrowed as she continued. "I can't let you come with me. I can't let you risk your life for me again. I don't want you on Sarita Garcia's radar."

"It turns out Senorita Garcia has her hands full with your young FBI friend." Brady handed her a glass. "Evidently she's involved with the dead guy found on the beach."

"The one Humberto's friend is accused of killing?

Brady nodded and raised his glass. "To Agent Temple!" Brady sipped from his glass. "Remember it's—"

"Bad luck if you don't drink after a toast." Clara tipped her glass and swallowed half the contents. She resisted the urge to lick the sweet residue from her lips. "Explain."

"It's all very complicated—money laundering, drug trafficking, murder." He still wore a broad smile, but she noticed a tinge of pain around his eyes. "Sarita Garcia is going to be very busy with trouble here in Mazatlan."

Clara polished off her champagne and waggled her glass for more. "Still . . ." Brady poured more bubbly into her flute, his proximity as heady as the fizzing liquid she wanted to inhale to keep from snaking her arms around his neck and pulling him to her.

"Clara," His gaze seemed intent on igniting the desire slowly awakening deep within her. "The threat is over for now." He tucked a lock of hair behind her ear.

She took a small sip of champagne. "What if she comes after us?"

"Shane's going to keep track of her and alert me if anything comes up."

Clara couldn't take her eyes off his lips as he kept talking and took a bigger sip.

"The sooner we put some distance between us and Damian's whacked sister, the better."

Brady moved away from her to pour himself another glass and Clara directed her gaze out the small plane window. Could she actually put her tragic past behind her and move on? Allow herself to be happy? Embrace Brady's love for her?

Clara trusted Shane, who would most likely be in touch with Humberto, Marco and Lucia. She smiled at the thought of her old and new friends watching their backs.

The captain stepped into the cabin, drawing her back to the issue at hand. "Senor Salazar," he said, "if you and your wife would please take your seats, we are ready to depart."

Clara held Brady's amused stare. "Wife?"

"Well, we'll need to make it official when we get to Belize . . ." A whisper of doubt clouded his eyes. "Devyn insisted on playing wedding planner and has gone ahead of us to make the necessary plans."

Clara crossed the short space separating them and kissed him as if he were the oxygen she needed to breathe. The Captain announced over the speaker to buckle their seatbelts as Brady sat and used his good arm to pull her onto his lap. As the plane hurtled down the runway, Clara wrapped her arms around his neck and kissed him deeper.

As they climbed into the sky, Sofia Salazar pushed back from Roman Salazar and said, "Yes, I'll marry you!"

THE END

ABOUT THE AUTHOR

Kimila Kay lives in Donald, Oregon along with her husband, Randy, her adorable Boston Terrier Maggie and feisty back cat named Halle.

Her professional accomplishments include three anthologized essays in the CUP OF COMFORT series, and in three separate contests, two first place awards and a third place award in the romantic suspense category for PERIL IN PARADISE. Kimila is currently a member of a writing critique group and Willamette Writers.

PERIL IN PARADISE is the first novel in a planned cross-cultural series, which will include Malice in Mazatlan, Chaos in Cabo, Vanished in Vallarta and Lost in Loreto.

MALICE IN MAZATLAN

CHAPTER ONE

White foamy water lapped at the inert figure as the next incoming wave lifted the limp form and carried it up the beach. The body then rolled languidly toward the sea as if tethered to the outgoing surf.

Humming a tune, he'd heard last night at Joe's, the maintenance worker raked the sand in front of the Hotel Playa; preparing the beach for the swell of *turistas* who had come to Mazatlan to bask under the warm March sun.

He loved this time of the morning. Just him, the ocean, and the salty sea air. Occasionally, a beach hawker or early rising tourist threatened to disrupt his tranquility. Usually, though, he managed to maintain his fantasy. Imagining he strolled his private beach below his beautiful villa that overlooked the spectacular Pacific Ocean.

"Mierda," he swore as he marched toward the tourist lying in the sand. When would they learn? The waiter had seen it before, tourists enjoying too many *cervezas* in the sun, followed by a night of tequila shots at Joe's. The ritual usually morphing one or two vacationers a week into sloppy drunks.

The taste of the shots he'd had last night lingered on his tongue as he approached the young man muttering, "They should know their limits." A glint caught his eye and he shook his head as he plucked a broken margarita glass from the wet sand, the jagged edge slicing his thumb. The worker huffed an expletive as the surf washed over the man, enhancing a dark stain ruining the back of a cream colored shirt. He wrinkled his nose at the lingering smell of vomit wafting off the tourist and watched as pink rivulets followed the retreating water. A pounding wave rolled the tourist onto his back and the worker crossed himself. As if the *turista's* lifeless eyes pleaded for help, the maintenance worker reached for his walkie-talkie and whispered a prayer, "Vaya con Dios, senor."